CHARMED BY THE WOLF

KRISTAL HOLLIS

First Published in Great Britain 2017
By Mills & Boon, an imprint of HarperCollins*Publishers*
1 London Bridge Street, London, SE1 9GF

© 2017 Kristal Hollis

ISBN: 978-0-263-93018-4

89-0917

Our policy is to use papers that are natural, renewable and recyclable products and made from wood grown in sustainable forests. The logging and manufacturing processes conform to the legal environmental regulations of the country of origin.

Printed and bound in Spain
by CPI, Barcelona

"Here  **you up."** Nel held out a coffee cup to **Tristan.**

"I'm not cold." He accepted it anyway, his eyes tracking her every movement as she sat on the couch. He sat next to her, closer than she expected. His posture was rigid, his breathing tight and controlled. Nothing like the easygoing, self-assured guy she'd danced with all evening.

Nel cleared her throat. "Was everything okay on patrol tonight?"

"Penelope, what are you doing?" He placed his mug down on the table next to them.

"Trying to distract myself from the storm by having a conversation with you…except you're not cooperating."

Thunder broke overhead and Nel jumped. Tristan took the coffee cup from her hands and put it down next to his.

"Storms bother you?"

She nodded. "My dad used to read me stories as a distraction."

Tristan leaned forward, grazing his cheek along her jaw.

"What kind of distraction are you looking for tonight?"

Southern born and bred, **Kristal Hollis** holds a psychology degree and has spent her adulthood helping people and animals. When a family medical situation resulted in a work sabbatical, she began penning deliciously dark paranormal romances as an escape from the real-life drama. But when the crisis passed, her passion for writing love stories continued. A 2015 Golden Heart® Award finalist, Kristal lives with her husband and two rescued dogs at the edge of the enchanted forest that inspires her stories.

For Keith.

Through all the ups and downs,
you remain my constant.

Chapter 1

How dare the sun show its bright, bold face today?

And the serene, clear blue sky was simply all wrong.

The beauty and tranquility belittled the horrific tragedy that took place here, seven years ago to the day.

In his wolfan form, Tristan Durrance padded across the isolated forest cove. It had taken a long time, but the pack was finally healing. The violent loss of Mason Walker, the eldest Alpha son, had struck all the Wahyas in Walker's Run hard, but particularly Tristan. Mason had saved his life, become his mentor and his closest friend. His senseless death was a deep wound that hadn't quite closed.

Tristan wished he had been with Mason and his younger brother, Brice, on that fateful day. His presence wouldn't have prevented the rogues' attack, but he could've evened the odds. Maybe Mason wouldn't have died and Brice wouldn't have nearly lost his leg, if Tristan had only listened to his instincts.

Something had felt off that morning. The sensation had wormed its way beneath his skin and inched into his muscles, making him restless and irritable.

Much like today.

He blamed the feeling on working too hard, too little sleep and the anniversary of his best friend's brutal murder.

Tristan never found peace when he came to the cove, but usually the dark, dank, somber woods nursed his misery. Today, however, all signs of the violent past were obliterated by fresh green moss, tiny blades of grass and delicate flowers with colorful petals stretching toward the barrage of morning sunbeams breaking through the tall, skinny pines. Even the gentle breeze carried the fresh, fragrant scent of summer.

He scratched at the ground, his paw slicing through the gossamery green disguising the greedy soil that had soaked up Mason's blood. Life had sprung from death, yet Tristan found no solace that it had. Everything and everyone had moved on.

Why couldn't he?

Stuck in a rut, he didn't quite know how to get out of it or if he wanted to. Most wolfans his age were mated and had a wolfing or two in tow. He wished them the best, all the while resigning himself to a life of bachelorhood. Coming from a long line of wolfans mated unhappily-ever-after, he preferred to be alone than to spend his life stuck in a doomed relationship he could never be free of.

Life is what you make of it, so make the choice to be a better man.

Mason's voice whispered through Tristan's mind. A memory rather than comfort from beyond the grave. In life, Mason had spoken those words to Tristan on more than one occasion and he found the sentiment both inspiring and irritating, depending on mood and circumstance.

Right now, Mason's words of wisdom deepened Tristan's restlessness. After all, he had made the choice to be a better man. He gave one hundred and ten percent to pack, family and community.

His efforts were never enough. Never good enough. People always wanted more.

Tristan stretched out over the freshly unearthed dirt and rested his chin on his paws.

"Brice has a daughter now. Brenna—she's a real cutie." Just as if Mason were next to him, Tristan used the telepathic communication Wahyas employed when in their wolf form. *"She has the Walker coloring, with a touch of red that she got from her mama. And her eyes... I swear, sometimes I see you looking at me through her eyes."*

Silence answered, as always.

Still, Tristan shared everything that had happened with the pack since his last visit, a year ago. When there was nothing left to tell, he pushed up on all four paws.

"Gotta go," his thoughts whispered, because there was no sense in expressing how much he missed his friend. If Mason's spirit could hear or sense Tristan, he would already know.

Head down and with a slow pace, Tristan left the cove. With the day off from the sheriff's department, the longer he stayed away from his cell phone, the better. Everyone in the pack and at least half of the human residents in Maico had his number on speed dial. No one ever called to say hello or ask how he was doing. Not even his family. If his phone rang, someone, somewhere, had a problem they wanted him to fix.

The nearly two-mile trek back to his truck was uneventful, except for the occasional curious deer who watched him pass. The forest animals within the Walker's Run territory had grown to trust Wahyas, who never hunted to kill.

Cautiously, he approached the clearing where a dirt road dead-ended. A forest green truck was parked so that the front end pointed away from the woods. Tristan gave a quick look around. Merely a habit. No one—more particularly, no humans—ever came out here.

He trotted to the truck and sat on his haunches. A tingling sensation sparked at the base of his neck, spiraled down his spine and spread along his nerves as he shifted. An instant later, he stood as a man and yanked open the driver's-side door. The ringtone he'd set for the Alpha's calls greeted him. Leaning across the crumpled clothes on the seat, he reached into the glove box and grabbed his phone.

"Where have you been?" Gavin Walker's irritable growl added to Tristan's foul mood.

He shoved aside his true feelings and responded respectfully. "Same place I always am on this particular day. Things are beginning to grow again." Tristan kept the strain out his voice. "By next summer it might be a nice place for a picnic."

Concern threaded through Gavin's long sigh. "When you leave, come by my office. And I expect to see you sooner rather than later." He ended the call, saving Tristan from the chipper lie that he was on his way.

He tossed his phone on the dashboard and reached for his knee-length shorts.

"Excuse me." A soft, sweet feminine voice froze his movements.

Damn!

Not expecting anyone to be in the area, he'd forgotten to guard his blind side.

Stiffly, Tristan made a quarter turn left. In front of the vehicle stood a woman wearing a thin-strapped summer dress with an unusual hem that was higher on the sides so that if she turned he'd get a glimpse of her thigh. And her hair, tied back with a blue ribbon, was the color of honey. He loved honey. Especially on biscuits.

He felt a smile bud on his lips despite his mood and the unfortunate circumstance of being caught bare assed by a human female.

"Sorry to bother you," she continued, hesitantly, "but are you a sheriff's deputy?"

"I am," he said politely, though it should've been obvious. His double-cab F-150 had red-and-blue emergency lights embedded in the grill. And the doors, one of which currently shielded the woman from the extent of his nudity, were detailed with the Maico Sheriff's Department logo.

"Great." Relief lightened her worried expression. "I was down at the abandoned plantation house when you drove past, earlier."

"What were you doing there?" The dilapidated structure had been condemned for the better part of twenty years. Such a shame. The architectural design was amazing. Under different circumstances, Tristan would love to buy the old place and restore it, but the huge house was much too big for a single man.

"Taking pictures and making some sketches. I thought it would be fun to paint." Her gaze slowly traveled from his face all the way down to his bare feet. Thankfully, the open truck door shielded him midchest to the knees. Still, her whiskey-colored eyes rounded. "Oh!"

The bottom of her dress flared and swirled as she quickly turned away, giving him the glimpse of the shapely thighs he'd so hoped to see.

"Why are you naked?"

A warning streaked through Tristan's mind. When two of his friends had been caught naked by human females, they'd kept their natures secret and a whole lot of trouble followed. Now they were mated to those women.

Tristan didn't want to add to his troubles, nor did he want a mate. Truth was his best course of action. She wouldn't believe him anyway.

"I'm a wolfan. I was in the woods as a wolf and came back to the truck to turn human, but you interrupted me before I could get dressed."

"Ha, ha." Her head shook with an indignant bob. "I walked all the way up here because I need help, not sarcasm."

"What kind of help?" Tristan pulled on his shorts and T-shirt.

"My car won't start and I can't get cell service." Without looking behind her, she waved her phone at him.

He shoved his feet into his sneakers. "Get in."

She peeked over her shoulder before scurrying toward the passenger side of the truck. Tristan waited for her to climb inside and buckle her seat belt before he slid behind the wheel. In seconds, the truck cab filled with her scent. It was soft, feminine, with a touch of vanilla-like sweetness; she smelled utterly delicious.

"What's your name?"

"Penelope Buchanan."

"Tristan Durrance, at your service." Since she sat to his right, Tristan didn't need to look directly at her to notice the nervous clench of her laced fingers resting on her lap. "Relax before you break your fingers. I promise, I don't bite."

No sooner had the words left his lips than his tongue glided over his teeth, testing the sharpness of his canines.

He forcibly relaxed his jaw. Never could he ever bite a female, especially during sex.

If ever seriously tempted, he'd have all his teeth pulled

immediately. He'd rather be a toothless wolfan than make the soul-crushing mistake of claiming a mate.

"It's not you." Flattening her moist palms against her thighs, Penelope looked straight ahead rather than at the man seated next to her. Tall, broad shouldered and blond. If that wasn't striking enough, he had the sculptured face of a Greek god. Adonis incarnate. Just her luck.

Incredibly shy, Penelope had a hard time initiating conversation with an average-looking guy. The one next to her would've left her speechless if she hadn't made a promise to herself to break out of her comfort zone.

"I don't want an expensive car repair bill." Not particularly clever conversation starter, but at least her voice didn't squeak.

"No one ever does." Tristan cranked the engine and drove carefully along the pothole-riddled dirt road. "What brings you to Maico?"

"There's a new children's program at the Walker's Run Resort. I'll be assisting with the arts-and-crafts workshops." She gave Tristan a furtive glance. Though his gaze seemed focused on driving, she had the impression he knew every breath she took and when. "I've never done anything like this before."

A few months ago, on her birthday, Penelope had realized that she was now the same age as her mother had been when she died. Not only did Penelope's heart ache for the years lost between mother and daughter, but a new ache had sprung. Because of her untimely death, Penelope's mother's hopes and dreams were now unfulfilled.

Unless she made changes, Penelope's life would be no less tragic. After all, the only thing worse than a life ending too soon was a long life never lived.

"The Walkers are good people. You'll do fine working for them."

Amicable silence filled the space.

"Can I ask you something?" Penelope studied his profile and silently sighed. He'd be a perfect model to sketch and paint.

"Ask away."

"Why were you naked?" So very, very naked, though the open truck door kept her from seeing too much.

"Checking for ticks. The woods are full of them."

"Oh, no!" Penelope inched her skirt up, turning her legs to look for possible hitchhikers.

"I can check you." Tristan flashed a daring smile along with a wink. "If it will make you feel better."

She wouldn't say the thought of Tristan stripping her down and running his hands all over her body made her feel better about ticks or car repairs, but it certainly made her feel hot and incredibly turned-on.

She adjusted the air vent toward her face.

"What happened to your arm?" Tristan's voice held no disdain, no disgust. Merely curiosity.

Still, Penelope quickly folded her undamaged arm over the scarred one. "Car accident." Oh, but it had been so much more, and the scars ran far deeper than the jagged, five-inch reminder along her wrist and forearm.

Tristan turned into the overgrown driveway and parked next to her white Corolla. Penelope unbuckled, shoved open the door and slid out of the passenger seat before he'd pulled the keys out of the ignition.

She unlocked her car to pull the hood latch. His footsteps crunched the dry grass behind her.

"Hey. I didn't mean to upset you." Strong, gentle fingers molded around her shoulder and leisurely slid down her arm to cradle her wrist. Tristan's thumb lightly caressed the hideous scar. Usually she had no feeling in the damaged skin, except for the needle-stabbing sensation that accompanied terrible storms. But Tristan's touch was feather soft and tickled.

Penelope turned around. Breathless, she stared into warm, decadent eyes the exact color of Hershey's dark chocolate.

Oh, she loved chocolate. Faithful and true, it never failed to bring up her spirits, which was why she indulged in eating a piece, or three, more often than she should considering every bite she swallowed ended up padding her backside.

Something flickered in his gaze, something predatorial. Something primal.

In a blink, it was gone.

"Let's check out what's under your hood."

"Excuse me?"

Already headed to the front of the car, Tristan walked with a loose-limbed swagger that resonated confidence, strength and sex.

Blatant desire flooded her, head to toe, and she grew damp in places not already glistening in the morning humidity.

Penelope didn't usually have this reaction to strangers. Usually not to the men she dated, either—at least, not this overwhelmingly. And certainly not on the first meeting.

Thankfully, Tristan was bent over the engine and didn't see her jelly-kneed walk.

"When is the last time you had the car serviced?"

"A few months ago, maybe." Penelope avoided driving in downtown Atlanta traffic as much as possible, riding the MARTA to work and taking the bus for errands.

"A few as in three? Six?" He glanced sidelong at her. "A year?"

"Definitely less than a year." She nodded confidently. Tristan *hmmphed*. "The battery posts are corroded."

"Is that bad?"

"Definitely not good, but it's something I can take care of for you." Tristan went to his truck and came back with a toolbox, a can of Coke and a bottle of water.

After using a wrench to remove the battery cable connectors, he popped the tab on the cola. Instead of drinking it, he poured the contents over the corrosive buildup.

"How's that going to help?"

"Trust me, it works." While the soda worked its magic, Tristan checked the oil. "Looks clean, but it's a little low. You should take the car in for service. Soon." He fished a business card from the toolbox and handed it to her. "Ask for Rafe. He's the owner. Tell him Tristan sent you and he'll take care of you."

"Thanks."

Tristan set to work, scrubbing the connectors and posts with an old toothbrush. "Why the name Penelope? Was your mom into Greek literature or something?"

"Yeah," Penelope answered, stunned. "She loved *The Odyssey* by Homer. How did you know?"

"My mom did the same to me. Ever heard of Tristan and Isolde? It's not a Greek legend, but—" He flashed her a quick smile that sent her heart racing.

"At least your name is easier to pronounce. Kids used to call me Penny-lope." Antelope and cantaloupe were also among their taunts.

"Ever go by Penny?" He poured water over the battery, rinsing away the gunk.

"No. My mother never allowed anyone to call me that. She said I wasn't a piece of currency shoved in a piggy bank." Penelope dabbed the back of her hand along her moist brow.

"I see her point." Tristan wiped the battery down with a blue shop towel. "Penelope was a queen. Your mother wants no less for her daughter."

Penelope's heart tweaked that a stranger had made a connection she had never seen herself. "Something simpler, less formal, would've been nice, though. Especially growing up. Penelope is quite a mouthful."

Tristan reconnected the cables. "That should do it." He cleaned his hands and dropped the towel and wrench into the toolbox. "Crank her up and let's see if she purrs."

Penelope slipped into the driver's seat and turned the key. The engine roared to life. No expensive car repair in the immediate future. Relief and gratitude nearly brought tears to her eyes.

Tristan closed the hood and strolled to her, toolbox in hand. "Do you know your way?"

"I have GPS."

He squinted against the bright sun shining in his face. "Reception can be quirky. Why don't you follow me? I'm headed to the resort anyway."

"Great!"

He gave her a quick nod and turned toward his truck.

"Tristan."

He swung around.

"Thanks. For everything."

"My pleasure, sweet cheeks."

Sweet cheeks?

Penelope wasn't sure if she should be flattered or appalled.

But he did just fix her car, so she'd let it slide this time.

Tristan stowed his toolbox behind the second seat and climbed into the truck. He backed out of the driveway and waited for her to follow.

They drove about thirty minutes before arriving in the

picturesque town of Maico. He turned down Sorghum Avenue. Tooting his horn, he stuck his arm out the window, pointing at Wyatt's Automotive Services.

Yeah, yeah. She got the hint.

Across the street was the town square—a quaint little park with huge canopy trees. Surrounding the square were a dozen or so mom-and-pop stores, including a market. The crowning jewel, though, was the large, Colonial-style courthouse.

"I have to paint that," she said. Getting her car serviced didn't seem like such a chore if she could sit in the park with her sketchbook.

Another ten minutes and they pulled into the entrance to the Walker's Run Resort. Unlike the posh, contemporary-style resorts in the city, this one looked like a huge log cabin, with its giant wood pillars and rafters, and natural stone accents. Penelope loved it immediately.

Tristan waved her toward the valet service, while he parked a little farther away, in a spot designated for resort security.

When she stopped, her door opened and a handsome twentysomething's face ducked inside. "Welcome to Walker's Run." He offered her hand to help Penelope out of the vehicle. "Are you checking in?"

"Sort of. I have a meeting with Cassie Walker. I'm supposed to start working here."

"Penelope Buchanan?"

"Yes."

"Thanks, Jimmy. I'll take her in." Tristan waved toward the doors. "After you," he said to Penelope.

"My car?"

"Jimmy will take care of it." Tristan's hand rested against her lower back.

Oh, boy.

Hopefully the bones in her legs wouldn't melt before she reached Cassie Walker's office. Penelope would hate to meet her new boss while imitating a puddle at Tristan's feet.

He held open the heavy wooden doors for Penelope to enter. The lobby was just as charming as the outside, with polished wood floors, richly colored rugs and tapestries, and dark leather couches and chairs in the seating areas. And, her instant favorite, an indoor totem pole with the faces of three wolves carved into it, so lifelike they appeared to be jumping out of the wood, and topped with a fierce-looking bird—its wings spread as if to protect them.

I love it. I love it. I love it.

Tristan chuckled softly.

"Oops. Did I say that out loud?"

"No. Your face is very expressive. Makes it easy to read your thoughts." He winked. "Every last one of them."

The waggle of his dark gold eyebrows did not bode well for her.

They stopped in front of a windowed office, the blinds partially closed. Tristan rapped his knuckles against the wooden frame of the open door before stepping inside the office, Penelope in tow. "Hey, Cassie."

A petite woman with striking red curls pinned back with a silver clip looked up from her computer. "Tristan, hi. What are you doing here? Don't you have a meeting with Gavin?"

"I do, but I wanted to introduce you to Penelope first."

"Penelope Buchanan?"

Penelope nodded.

"Oh, I've been expecting you." Cassie stood.

Tristan's phone buzzed. He quickly answered, "On my way," then shoved it back into his pocket. "Gotta go." He clasped Penelope's hand and kissed her knuckles. "It's been a pleasure, Nel."

"Nel?" First sweet cheeks, now Nel. Had he really forgotten her name already?

Smiling, he leaned close, his lips brushing against her ear. "Like you said, Penelope is a mouthful—and a bit formal, considering you've seen me naked."

Chapter 2

"Penelope?" Cassie stared at her curiously. "Are you all right?"

"Um, yeah."

Tristan was no longer in the office, but Penelope's body still registered his heat next to her.

"Sorry, I'm a bit distracted."

"Tristan has that effect on women." Cassie laughed softly. "Not on you?"

"I'm very happily married and Tristan, well, he's family." Cassie waved to a chair in front of a simple but solid wooden desk.

Penelope took her seat, swallowing her question as to Tristan's marital status. She hadn't seen a ring, but these days lack of one didn't necessarily indicate the man was unattached, and asking her new boss personal questions about a stranger seemed unwise.

Casually, Penelope glanced out the glass interior window of Cassie's office and glimpsed Tristan nearing a side corridor. He turned, his gaze locking on hers. A current passed through her body, warm and exhilarating. He tipped his head and disappeared down the hall.

Several seconds passed before she breathed again.

"Please don't get your hopes up."

Penelope snapped her attention back to Cassie. "Excuse me?"

"Tristan is a great guy but a huge flirt. I don't want you to be hurt or misled."

"I assure you, my heart is quite safe from his charms." She wasn't foolish enough to invest serious hope in a man out of her league.

"Good." Cassie withdrew several forms from her desk drawer and fastened them to a clipboard. "As we discussed on the phone, the resort is experimenting with new programs this summer. Originally, we planned to hire you as an assistant to the children's arts-and-craft teacher. However—" An apprehensive grimace replaced Cassie's smile.

"You've decided not to hire me?" Penelope swallowed her disappointment.

"Oh, we want you to work for us." A loose curl bounced free from the silver clip in Cassie's hair. "But we do have a slight change. The instructor you were going to assist left unexpectedly. Instead of assisting, you're now in charge of the program."

Excitement and fear wrestled in the pit of Penelope's stomach. "Um, what do you mean by *in charge*?"

"You will plan the daily activities and teach the workshops."

"I'm not an art teacher, per se."

"According to your résumé, you are an elementary school teacher, and in our phone interview you mentioned that you are an artist."

"I said I like to paint." Having never shown her work to anyone, Penelope wasn't sure she could claim to be an *artist.* "I may not have the right skill set, since I've never taught an art class."

"I have faith in you," Cassie said. "We aren't asking you to turn these kids into prodigies. Simply help them have fun creating handmade souvenirs."

"Is there a curriculum?"

"Here's what Linda had planned." Cassie handed Penelope a three-ring binder.

She flipped through the pages of activities, supplies needed and the link information to online how-to videos.

"The hours are the same, seven-thirty to noon, Monday through Friday. And, instead of a suite inside the resort, we can offer you a cabin on the property. I thought you might like the extra space and solitude to paint in your spare time."

"I like how you think."

"Is that a yes?" Cassie rested her folded hands on her desk.

"Yes."

"Fantastic!" Cassie picked up the clipboard. "I need your signature on these forms, then I'll show you the activities room."

Penelope reviewed the documents and signed in the appropriate places. Handing the clipboard back, she knocked over the silver frame on Cassie's desk. "Oh, I'm sorry." She picked up the picture of a striking black wolf. "This is a great picture. Do you know the photographer who took it?"

"I did." Cassie reached for the framed photo and smiled lovingly at the picture before placing it back on her desk. "The Walker's Run Cooperative, of which the resort is a subsidiary, runs a wolf sanctuary. That's my husband's wolf in the picture."

"Your husband owns a wolf?"

"No one owns the wolves. Brice is his wolf's handler. Co-op members are tasked with safeguarding the health and well-being of individual wolves."

"Is his wolf tame or did you use a telephoto lens?"

"The Co-op wolves aren't tame, but they aren't dangerous, either. Unless you threaten their families."

"Could I go into the sanctuary to take some pictures? I'd love to expand my portfolio to include wildlife." So what if she didn't exactly have a *professional* portfolio. Never even considered one, since showing her work to anyone had been something she hadn't dared.

Only learning to paint after her parents' deaths, Penelope had received art therapy as part of her own recovery. She fell in love with turning swipes of color into pictures and dreamed of being a professional artist. But Penelope's aunt and uncle had convinced her of the impossibility of such a foolish notion when she was without a modicum of talent.

"For the safety of the wolf pack, only Co-op members are allowed access."

"How does someone become a member?"

"One is either born into the Co-op or marries into it."

"That exclusive, huh?"

Cassie offered a sympathetic smile. "There are great scenic views in the area and your cabin is up the mountain near a river. I'm sure you'll find plenty of inspiration." She flipped through the signed papers. "Everything looks good, but I'll need a copy of your identification."

As Cassie turned away to scan Penelope's driver's license and social security card on the printer behind her desk, Penelope used her phone to capture a snapshot of the wolf photo. If she couldn't get into the sanctuary to photograph the animals herself, at least she could use the one in Cassie's picture for inspiration.

"I heard Tristan call you Nel. Would you prefer that on your name tag?"

"Sure." Why not? It would be easier for the kids to say and remember.

"Welcome to the Walker's Run Resort family, Nel." Cassie returned the identification cards to Penelope. "I hope your time with us will be memorable."

Considering that, in her first few hours in the area, she'd met a naked man with the face and body of a Greek god, Walker's Run already had the memorable part down pat.

"I wanted to be the first to tell you." Behind the large mahogany desk, Gavin Walker leaned back in his leather chair and stroked the short-cropped white beard framing the unhappy curl of his mouth. His dark brows, a contrast to his snow-white hair, frowned.

Tristan's stomach instinctively clenched and the feel-good high the encounter with Nel had given him plummeted.

"Jaxen's release from Woelfesguarde is being finalized this week. I'm granting your father's petition for Jaxen's reinstatement into the pack." Gavin paused, as if expecting Tristan to respond.

At the moment, it wasn't possible. Tristan's brain was emulating a train wreck. With the jumble of thoughts and emotions crashing and exploding in his head, coherent words weren't possible.

Jaxen Pyke was a criminally minded, narcissistic bully. He was also Tristan's blood-kin. A cousin. The only one on his father's side. Both Tristan and the majority of the Walker's Run pack had heaved a good-riddance sigh when Jaxen was eventually booted from the pack. The time on his own apparently hadn't fostered any remorse or a need for reconciliation, because Jax eventually took up with a rogue pack and continued his merry criminal path. Until three years ago when an assault charge landed him in Woelfesguarde, a wolfan-owned-and-operated penitentiary.

"Do you understand?" Gavin continued. "Jaxen is coming home."

"When?" The single word sounded clipped and tight and full of hostility to Tristan's ears. No doubt the Alpha heard it, as well.

"Saturday." Gavin's calculating gaze seemed to target every twitch Tristan's jaw made as he ground his teeth. "I am allowing him to reenter the territory, but he'll need to earn back his place in the pack."

"Does Aunt Ruby know?" Tristan rubbed the furrow between brows. Of course she didn't know. Ruby's first call would've been to Tristan. His ears would still be ringing from the tongue-lashing she served every time something happened concerning Jaxen.

Gavin affirmed with a shake of his head. "I wanted to tell you before Cooter and I pay her a visit this afternoon. I've asked your father meet us there."

The Alpha and the pack's chief sentinel delivering the news would leave Tristan with one less worry on his mind. He eased into his next breath, thankful he'd have time to psych himself up before dealing with Jaxen's arrival.

"If that's all." Tristan stood.

"There's something else." Gavin leaned forward, rested his arms on the desk and steepled his fingers.

There always is.

Tristan remained standing. "Yes?"

"Considering Jaxen's history, he'll need someone to help keep him out of trouble."

"I agree." Wholeheartedly and without reservation.

"Notify me immediately if he inches one paw out of line."

"Wait—" Tristan stepped forward. "You're putting me in charge of Jaxen?"

"You're the most logical choice."

"Like hell I am."

"You're a sentinel and his blood-kin." Gavin's stony expression usually meant the matter was settled.

"If Jaxen screws up, it's on him. I don't want to be in the same position I was last time."

Fifteen years ago, Jaxen's fate with the Walker's Run had rested on Tristan's shoulders. The truth led to banishment, a lie to freedom.

Tristan had chosen the truth over family. Neither his father nor his aunt had forgiven him.

"I'm hoping your influence will keep him from backsliding."

"You have no idea what you're asking of me," Tristan forced out.

"For god's sake, Tristan. You're both adults now. You need to let go of that grudge."

A searing-white flash momentarily blanked Tristan's vision. What he harbored was a hell of a lot more than a little grudge.

"Everyone makes mistakes, especially young people." Gavin walked around the desk and laid a hand on Tristan's shoulder. "Be the better man. Help Jaxen because it's the right thing to do."

"For whom?"

"For you and your family."

Family?

Disgust slithered into the pit of Tristan's stomach.

His family was the epitome of dysfunction. His parents could barely stand to be in the same room with each other and they had little or no regard for him—the product of an accidental mate-claiming. Ruby only barely tolerated him and Jaxen, whom Tristan had once hero-worshipped, had left him to die.

"I'm not asking you to police him." Gavin leaned against his desk, his hands folded against the silver buckle on the belt fastened around the waist of his jeans. "Be his friend again. Let him know he can count on you."

Good ole dependable Tristan.

How that character trait had come to him was beyond his understanding. No one else in his family had been plagued with it.

The alarm on his watch beeped. "Gotta go."

Wearing an expression indicative of an Alpha who expects his orders to be carried out, Gavin tipped his head.

Tristan walked out of the office, quietly closing the door with a greater appreciation for the Alpha's son's door-slamming habit. Instead of externalizing his anger or frustration like Brice, Tristan always internalized. Mostly he tried to ignore those feelings. His family was too loose with their tempers. He hated their arguments and outright fights. As soon as he was old enough to live on his own, he'd moved out.

Over the years, he'd learned the only way to deal with his family was individually and briefly. Jaxen's homecoming would definitely upset the rhythm Tristan had established.

Walking down the long corridor from Gavin's office toward the lobby, Tristan's steps grew heavier. His current schedule barely allowed time for sleep. How would he manage squeezing in "befriending" his long-lost cousin, whom Tristan would rather have stayed lost?

A wolfan could only handle so much and Tristan had been stretched beyond his maximum limits for far too long.

God, I need some fresh air.

His fingers closed around the cold brass handle to yank open the large, heavy wooden door to exit the resort. A newly familiar feminine scent rushed his senses.

"Hey, Tristan!"

He turned to his left.

"I'm officially a resort staff member now." Penelope's lightly tinted lips parted with a soft smile. "And Cassie arranged for me to stay in a cabin up the road. I'll have plenty of room to paint."

"That's great, Nel." He stepped into her, his hand resting against her hip as he moved them away from the entry doors opening toward them.

A genuine smile broadened his mouth. Genuine because he could feel it all the way to his gut, tingling with a warm, fuzzy, effervescent sensation that dispelled the heavy shroud that had cloaked him a few minutes ago.

"Umm." Her voice was a mere puff of soft breath. Her curious gaze caressed every angle of his face, her pupils growing larger with every beat of his heart.

The wolf in him sighed. There was no other way to describe the rush of contentment that raced up his spine and down his chest, then settled in his groin.

Tristan had the sudden, uncharacteristic urge to spend the day with her, learning her laugh, her mannerisms, her likes and dislikes.

Damn! He'd been working too many long hours and sleeping too few for those unbalanced thoughts to surface.

"It was nice meeting you, Nel."

He dashed outside, sucking in lungfuls of fresh air before her scent imprinted on and permanently rewired his brain.

Chapter 3

"You're not on duty today." Carl Locke sucked his teeth, his hard gaze fastened on Tristan.

"There's something I want to discuss with you." Tense, Tristan sat in one of the two wooden chairs positioned in front of the sheriff's paper-laden desk and waited.

Elected sheriff less than two years ago, Locke was a hard man to work for. Mostly because he held a grudge against the Co-op's influence on the town. An outsider and new to the area, Locke viewed everything the Co-op did with suspicion. He felt the previous sheriff, who had known the truth about the Co-op, had been too lax in his duties. Gavin's stubbornness and refusal to clue in the new sheriff to the Co-op's purpose only compounded the problem.

Since Tristan was a member, Locke scrutinized his every action, his every decision, and the constant conflict had turned a job Tristan loved into a nauseating chore.

Last year, after a fiasco involving his friend Rafe Wyatt and Sheriff Locke, Tristan had quit the department. Gavin had been furious. Tristan's position as a deputy afforded him some flexibility in running interference between the pack and human law enforcement. Gavin didn't want to lose that advantage.

Locke, surprisingly, neither accepted nor rejected the resignation. Instead, he placed Tristan on leave for two weeks. A vacation, of sorts, to give him time to decompress and carefully consider his decision.

With nowhere to go and no one to go with him if he did, Tristan had stayed with his mother at her condo in Atlanta. The visit didn't suddenly forge a mother–son bond, but it had provided the chance for Tristan to reassess… everything.

Including Gavin. His decision to cage Rafe in wolfan form, to display him like a circus animal in front of the sheriff to prove that the Walker's Run wolves were docile had almost cost Rafe his life and came damn close to exposing the pack and the existence of Wahyas, worldwide.

Gavin had never apologized, never admitted he'd made a bad choice. He stuck by the affirmation that he'd done what was necessary to protect the pack.

So what the hell was he thinking now?

Didn't he realize that allowing Jaxen to waltz right back into the territory was a disaster waiting to happen?

"Spit it out," Locke barked.

"Sir?"

"You look like you're chewing your words, trying to find the right ones. Is this about the Co-op?" Irritation flickered in Locke's squinted gaze. He shoved aside the paperwork in front of him. "Whatever you got to say, just spit it out. I ain't got all day."

"Jaxen Pyke," Tristan began, as if giving an ordinary report. "He's got a long list of minor offenses as a juvenile. He left Maico about fifteen years ago." Actually, Gavin had banished Jaxen because of his involvement in a liquor store robbery where a human was severely injured. "Hooked up with less than desirable associates who helped him graduate to more serious violations. Including assault, for which he spent the last three years in Woelfesguarde."

"Isn't that the fancy private facility in the Northwest?"

Tristan nodded. Human law enforcement believed the compound to be an elite, but highly effective rehabilitation center. In truth, it was a state-of-the-art wolfan correctional facility, situated in the harshest undeveloped region of Montana. With only the barest necessities provided, Woelfesguarde was no country-club prison. One either survived it or didn't. "Pyke's release is being processed. He's coming home. I expect him to be here sometime Saturday night."

Locke leaned back and crossed his arms over his stomach. "Is he Co-op?"

Technically, no. According to Gavin, Jaxen had to *earn* his way back into the pack.

Whatever the hell that means.

"Jaxen is family." Tristan tasted the bile creeping into his mouth.

"When it comes to enforcing the law, I don't give special considerations to anyone. Not to the Co-op, not to my deputies' families."

"Good!" Tristan leaned forward, resting his elbows on his knees. "Someone besides myself needs to understand how dangerous he is."

"An assault conviction is enough to convince me."

"Maybe not. When you get his records—" as Tristan knew Locke would "—you'll find most of his convictions are nonviolent misdemeanors. The only violent charge, the assault, stems from a bar fight. He claimed self-defense, but took a plea rather than face a trial."

The Woelfesenat, a secret, international wolf council and the ultimate ruling authority on wolfan matters, would've never allowed Jaxen's case to go to court. If convicted, he would've been incarcerated in a human prison. Long-term confinement for a Wahya, especially during a full moon without access to a sex partner, posed an unacceptable risk of the wolfan eventually losing control of his Wahyarian, the primitive beast that lurked within every Wahya.

The Woelfesenat would've had Jaxen put down if Adam Foster, Alpha of the Peachtree pack and an internationally renowned lawyer, had failed to negotiate an alternative. Instead of a trial and subsequent conviction, Jaxen was sentenced to serve thirty-six months at Woelfesguarde.

"What do you know that isn't in the official record?"

Bitterness coated Tristan's tongue and he fought the urge to hurl. "Remember our first meeting after you were sworn in? You asked if I had any impediments that could affect my job performance, and I told you it wouldn't affect my duties, but that I have a blind side."

"Yeah. When you were a kid, you slipped off a rock outcropping and cracked open your head." Locke tapped his pen on his desk. "What's that got to do with Pyke?"

"I didn't slip, Sheriff. I was pushed."

Fingers cramped and achy, Penelope returned her pencils to the holder and shook out her hands.

After settling into the cabin yesterday, she'd planned out about two weeks' worth of activities for the children's workshops, which left her wide-open for a three-day weekend before starting her new job.

This morning, she'd taken a leisurely drive around Maico to orient herself with the town and bought a few groceries from the market. She'd also stopped by the au-

tomotive shop Tristan had recommended. Short-handed
due to a virus going around, the owner had scheduled her
car service for next week. If Nel had dropped Tristan's
name, she might've gotten the oil change and battery
check today, but would've had to wait all day. Since the
car seemed to be running fine, she opted to come back
next week.

This afternoon, she'd immersed herself in art. Usually,
she made quick sketches of a scene she wanted to paint.

This one had taken several hours, but she was incor-
porating several disconnected elements. Before picking
up a paintbrush, she wanted to make sure the image in
her mind would actually make sense on canvas. To check
the accuracy of the two focal subjects, she picked up her
phone and swiped between the snapshot of the black wolf
she'd taken in Cassie's office yesterday and the photo
she'd taken today of Cassie sitting on the floor in a small
nook off the main lobby, playing with her daughter.

Precocious and quite verbal for child a few weeks
shy of her first birthday, Brenna had noticed Penelope
watching them and immediately determined that Penelope would be her new best friend. At the toddler's insistence and Cassie's invitation, Penelope had joined them
in the dining hall rather than eating lunch alone.

Old habits were difficult to change, and putting herself out there to meet new people was harder than she'd
imagined. Cassie tried to help, introducing her to staff
members and the townsfolk who stopped by the resort
restaurant.

Left to her own devices, Penelope preferred to hole
up in the cabin to paint, curl up with a book or sit on the
back porch drinking hot coffee and wishing for a dough-
nut like the one Tristan had devoured as he rushed into
the resort while she was there with Cassie and Brenna.

Dressed in slouchy black shorts, a black T-shirt and a dark gray skullcap despite summer temperatures, he'd flashed her a quick smile and a wink before disappearing down the corridor to Gavin Walker's office. The high from his attention had lingered all day.

Penelope uncurled her legs and touched her bare feet to the floor, curling her toes in the plush rug before padding into the kitchen. It was after midnight, and supper was little more than a memory to her stomach.

She slipped on her sneakers, grabbed an apple from the basket on the counter and strolled out the back door. Sitting on the porch swing, she munched her snack.

The moon, not quite full, beamed in the sky, big and bright, bathing everything in a soft, silvery glow.

She stepped off the porch and her skin warmed as if sunshine had disguised itself in moonbeams. As long as the thin strip of dark clouds remained in the distance, there would be enough light to follow the walking trail without use of the flashlight.

Quiet in Atlanta where she'd lived was definitely different than the quiet here. She could actually hear her thoughts, with no interference from the static of urban living.

Even in the utter stillness, she didn't feel frightened or alone. Cassie and her husband and daughter lived a mile up the mountain. Gavin Walker and his wife, Abby, lived in private quarters adjacent to the resort. And security officers routinely patrolled the property, although she hadn't caught sight of them.

Her ears tuned to the chorus of crickets and the soft gurgling of the river. Tiny lights blinked among the dark trees in a hypnotic dance. Watching fireflies wasn't on her mental list of the new experiences she wanted to explore, but it should've been because they were simply mesmerizing.

A loud rustling echoed in the woods. The possibility of an unintentional wildlife encounter hadn't crossed her mind when she left the cabin.

A rustle of commotion erupted ahead. There was an ear-shattering squeal, followed by low animalistic growls.

Wolves!

Cassie had said the Co-op wolves weren't dangerous. They had handlers and were confined to the sanctuary miles away, which meant the ones in the woods had come from somewhere else.

A flurry of movement divided in two directions, one headed straight for Penelope. She turned to run, tripped over a tree root and hit the ground with a startled cry.

Run! Her mind screamed; however, her body had other ideas. Her feet seemed stuck in quicksand and neither of her legs would move.

"Security?" she cried out, hoping one of the patrols would hear.

The bulk of the commotion moved away from where Nel had fallen, except for a loud thumping that steadily came closer until a large wolf emerged from the shadows.

Her chest locked in the last pant of air. Her shoulders rose and dropped with the effort to breathe, but nothing entered her lungs. Unable to scream, unable to run, she pulled herself into a turtle-shell posture, covering her head and neck with her arms.

Getting eaten by a wolf was definitely not on her list of things to try before she died. And she certainly was about to die, a horrible, painful death.

A caustic tear burned a trail down her cheek. She didn't dare wipe it away, fearing the animal now hovering over her would chomp into her if she moved.

Warm puffs of breath grazed her hands, which were clasped over the back of her neck. Despite her arms helmeting her head, the animal nudged past Penelope's defensive pose and found her ear. A cold, damp nose pressed against the shell.

Come on, sweet cheeks. Sit up and show me your pretty face.

"Tristan?" She peeked beneath her arms.

The wolf gently touched his paw to her shoulder. If the animal was going to eat her, he was taking his time sizing her up.

"Tristan," she called again.

The woods remained silent. In her panic, she must've imagined his voice.

The wolf plopped his rump next to her. Head cocked to the side, his gaze mapped every inch of her body.

Back aching, knees throbbing and toes going numb, she needed to move and stretch before she lost all feeling in her limbs. Slowly, she unfurled from the defensive huddle and sat up.

The wolf didn't move, growl or otherwise display any aggression.

He was nearly double the size she expected for a wolf, and his coat was a beautiful blend of light to dark golds and soft browns. In contrast, his pointed ears were richly dark except for the outer rims tipped in white.

"How unusual." Without thinking, she reached to feel if his ears were as velvety as they looked.

The wolf didn't shy away; in fact, he seemed not to notice until she actually touched him.

A spark of static electricity zapped her palm and the charge spread throughout her body. The wolf yelped and backed away.

"I didn't mean to shock you." She held up her hands. "I just wanted to rub your ears."

The wolf gave her a funny look.

"Yeah, weird. Right?" Idiotic, actually. That animal was a wolf, not a Labrador. "All righty." Penelope stood slowly to avoid startling him. "I'm going back to the cabin." She hiked her thumb over her shoulder.

The wolf simply stared.

Mindful of her movements, she turned and plodded purposefully along the worn path. A quick look behind her confirmed the wolf followed. She stopped, he stopped. She started, so did he.

She climbed the porch steps; he sat at the edge of the trail.

Safe and locked inside the cabin, she grabbed her phone and took a picture from the kitchen door of the wolf watching her. A howl sounded in the distance. Her wolf cocked his ears, then threw back his head and answered the call. He needed to return to his pack and she needed to get to bed.

She gave a little finger wave, her nails tapping against the glass plane of the kitchen door. The wolf acknowledged with a nod, then bolted into the woods.

"Best decision ever." Penelope congratulated herself on answering the ad that brought her here.

A gloriously naked man, a friendly wolf…her life was already more exciting than it had ever been. And she'd only been at Walker's Run for two days.

Whatever else the summer held, she was ready.

Chapter 4

The incessant tick of the large clock on Ruby's living room wall thumped inside Tristan's achy head. After spending the day volunteering at Youth Outreach, he would've rather crashed in his large plush bed for a few hours before going to work tonight. Not that he would've gotten much sleep. Whenever his mind quieted, Penelope filled his thoughts.

In spite of their unconventional introduction, he hadn't expected to see Nel again. Bumping into her so soon after their first meeting had made it difficult for him to forget her. Excitement sparkled in her eyes and the sweetest smile plumped her cheeks, and the most unusual thrill had tickled his chest.

Tristan had felt it again, last night when he'd caught her scent in the woods. He, along with Henry "Cooter" Coots—the pack's chief sentinel, and a few others were out trying to round up Cybil, a large, ornery potbellied pig who'd escaped from Mary-Jane McAllister's farm.

Realizing Nel was nearby, he'd broken formation to get ahead of Cybil and cut her off before she encountered Nel. Cooter gave him hell later, but it had been worth it.

The ruckus Cybil created had frightened Nel. So had the sudden appearance of his wolf. Nel had called out for Tristan—the man—and the urgency to shift so that he could soothe her had caught him off-guard.

Wahyan law prohibited wolfans from revealing themselves to humans. The only exceptions were if the human was in mortal danger or was the wolfan's mate.

Nel was neither, so he'd done his best to assure her in his wolf form.

Once she overcame her initial fear, Nel had touched him. Or rather, his wolf. The electric charge from the contact had opened something between them. Whatever it was, the brief experience had felt incredibly intimate.

"Jaxen should've been here by now." Nathan Durrance wore a path between the front door and living room.

"Not unless they drove twice the speed limit, Dad."

Per protocol, any Wahya returning to the pack had to submit to a complete physical exam given by Doc Habersham, the pack's physician. Cooter had called nine minutes ago to report they were leaving the clinic with Jaxen, and the drive to Ruby's house took seventeen minutes.

"Sit down, Nate." Ruby clunked her empty porcelain teacup against the matching saucer. "You're making me nervous."

Tristan stood, collected Ruby's dishes and walked to the kitchen to pour her another cup. If she hadn't wanted a refill, she would've told him. Her silence was its own reward. It meant he'd done something right. Otherwise, she would've given him a tongue-lashing.

In the community, his position as a deputy commanded a certain amount of respect. The same was true of his sentinel status within the pack. However, Aunt Ruby cared little to nothing for either. To her, he was the tagalong little brat she'd had to feed and clothe whenever his parents forgot to do so, which was more often than not.

Truthfully, Tristan didn't *need* Ruby, but she was blood-kin. After Jaxen was banished, well, even before that, Tristan had been the one to look after her—not that she would ever admit to wanting or needing his help.

Still, he visited Ruby at least every other day to make her meals and do some cleaning. Mostly she napped on the couch and never did much more than complain.

Ruby's mate had died when Tristan was a child. Never entirely healthy, she had a predisposition to respiratory problems. Weak lungs, she called it. The older she grew, the more often she got sick, creating yet another job for Tristan.

"Here you go." He held out the cup and saucer for her.

Outside, car doors closed.

"He's here!" Ruby grabbed Tristan's arm and tried to stand.

Hot tea jostled over the edge of the cup and sloshed down on his hand. Biting back a few choice words, he sat the dishes on the coffee table, then helped Ruby to her feet.

Tristan's dad reached to open the front door.

"My house, my son." Ruby jabbed her cane at her brother's backside. "I greet him first."

Gut tightening in a viselike grip, Tristan gathered Ruby's discarded dishes and returned to the kitchen. She wouldn't think any more about hot tea tonight.

The front door creaked open and the porch squeaked beneath the thud of heavy footsteps.

Arms folded over his chest, Tristan leaned against the sink and waited for the show.

It wasn't a long wait.

"Mama!" Emotion choked Jaxen's voice. Arms fastened around Ruby's thin frame, he lifted his mother off her feet.

"You're home." She wept into his chest. "You're finally home."

A fist-sized lump formed in Tristan's throat.

"Ah, Mama. Don't cry." Jaxen set her down gently. "I'm back for good."

"Glad to hear it, son." Nate vigorously shook Jaxen's hand, then pulled him into a bear hug.

Tristan inhaled sharply and the lump in his throat dropped to his stomach. He couldn't remember the last time his father showed any affection toward him or called him *son*.

The buzz in his head drowned out the rest of the homecoming exchanges. He glanced at Cooter and Reed lingering in the doorway. At a curt nod from Tristan, the sentinels silently departed.

"Well, well." The edge in Jaxen's voice was expected.

Tristan unfolded his arms and straightened to his full height.

Expression hard, Jaxen strode into the kitchen. "It's been a long time since I saw your ugly mug."

Odd thing to say. They were the same height and build, with features so similar they could be mirror images of each other. The only significant physical difference was their eyes. Like Ruby and Nate, Jaxen's eyes were blue-gray and slightly squinty. Tristan had his mother's eyes, big and brown.

"I missed you, man." Jaxen clasped Tristan's shoulders in a brotherly hug.

Not at all what Tristan expected.

"Who punched you in the face?" Tristan asked, noting the fading bruise beneath Jaxen's eye. He hooked his finger in Jaxen's collar and pulled on the shirt. "Why is your shoulder bandaged?"

"Well—" Jaxen slightly lowered his head in a sly shake. "You don't think the bastards at Woelfesguarde would let me go without a proper send-off, do you?"

"The inmates or the guards?"

Something unsettling glinted in Jaxen's eyes. "Does it matter?"

It did to Tristan.

"Jaxen," Ruby called. "Come sit with me." She swiped the couch cushion beside her. "Tristan, bring us some pie."

Tristan cut the rhubarb pie into equal wedges, plated three slices and grabbed some forks. He passed out the desserts.

Jaxen shoveled a big bite into his mouth. "Damn! This is the best pie I've ever tasted. Did you make this, Mama?"

All smiles, Ruby chuckled. "No. I can't hold out to bake."

"I asked Cassie to make it for you," Tristan said.

"Cassie? Don't remember her. She yours?"

"Hardly." Tristan snorted.

"A lot has happened since you've been gone." Ruby patted Jaxen's leg. "Cassie is the Alphena-in-waiting."

"Ah, so she's Mason's mate."

"Mason is dead," Nate said bluntly, and Tristan felt himself flinch.

Jaxen stopped chewing and swallowed. His curious gaze lighted on Tristan and then fell back to his plate. "Sorry, man. I know you two were close."

Braced for a smart-mouthed jab, Tristan was thrown a bit off-kilter by the condolence. Maybe the hard-core incarceration had taught Jaxen to have a better perspective. At the very least, it had improved his surly attitude.

Tonight, he seemed almost chipper. Then again, who wouldn't be happy to be free of Woelfesguarde?

Nate handed his empty plate to Tristan, then leaned forward in his chair. "Jax, have you thought about what you're going to do now that you're home?"

"I have." Jaxen forked the last bite of crust and held up his plate toward Tristan. "Another slice, if you don't mind."

Annoyance nipping his pride, Tristan took the plate. Although Jaxen flashed him a bright smile, an icy gray zapped all the blue from his eyes. It was gone in a blink, and Tristan decided he'd imagined the color change.

"I picked up some trade skills over the years," Jaxen continued. "Thought I'd look for handyman work."

"Why not work for me?" Nate asked.

Tristan's first impulse was to protest. Ruby's hopeful look silenced him.

Obviously, she had asked her brother to give Jaxen a job. Tristan couldn't fault his father or Ruby for trying to keep Jaxen out of trouble. Besides, with his father and the construction crew looking out for Jaxen, Tristan wouldn't have to.

"You'd actually hire me?" Jaxen's voice held an uncharacteristic note of emotion.

"Why wouldn't he," Ruby said. "You're blood-kin."

Since his input wasn't requested or required, Tristan quietly withdrew to the kitchen. Tuning out the discussion on Jaxen's actual job skills, Tristan rinsed his father's plate, hand dried it and placed the dish in the cabinet. Next, he doled out his cousin's second piece of pie and returned to the living room.

"You'll start a week from Monday morning. That'll give you time to get reoriented." Nate grinned.

"I appreciate it, Nate. Thanks." Jaxen accepted the dessert from Tristan with a slight nod.

With nowhere to sit comfortably, Tristan stood next to the couch, close to Ruby.

"I want you to do your best." Ruby shook her fork at Jaxen. "No cuttin' up, and I mean it. Nate is giving you a serious job."

"I won't mess up this time, Mama." Jaxen kissed her cheek. "I swear."

For all their sakes, Tristan hoped Jaxen would make good on his promise. But he wouldn't hold his breath.

"If you work hard and demonstrate an aptitude for the business—" Nate cleared his throat "—I'll let you take over when I retire."

What the hell?

Though he stood perfectly still, Tristan felt as if he'd smacked head-on into a brick wall.

"Are you kidding?" Jaxen looked genuinely happy, in contrast to the stormy emotions swelling inside Tristan.

"I never joke about my business." It was the one thing Nathan Durrance loved more than anything. Except for his sister, Ruby. And, apparently, Jaxen.

Jaxen's attention swung to Tristan. "Is this all right by you, cuz?"

"Of course it is," Ruby interjected. "Tristan would rather ride around in a comfy *po-leece* car all day than do hard work."

The tops of Tristan's ears heated. Swiping a palm across his mouth, he swallowed the spew of words burning his tongue.

Jaxen set down his plate. "What happened to you becoming an architect?"

"Plans change." Tristan's lungs no longer seemed to process the air inside Ruby's house. "I have to go."

"Always rushing to leave. Family time don't mean squat to you, does it?" Ruby's disapproving gaze cut Tristan to the quick.

"I told you earlier, I'm on duty tonight." Tristan paused at the door. "I'll stop by tomorrow to fix lunch."

"Don't bother." Mouth scrunched, Ruby squinted at Tristan.

He gave her a curt nod and walked outside. Unfortunately, summer humidity had thickened the night air as much as the tension had indoors. Dark, threatening clouds floated across the sky, bright from a near full moon.

Damn! Why did that time of the month seem to come around faster when he wasn't looking forward to it?

"Hey, cuz, wait up." Jaxen leisurely descended the porch steps.

Tristan leaned against the grill of his truck.

"Hard to believe you ended up in law enforcement. Why weren't you one of the dozen sentinels who escorted me?" Jaxen spit on the ground. "Gavin's going a bit over-the-top, don't you think? A dozen, really?"

"Not my call. And I wasn't involved in your escort because I'm not your keeper, Jax."

"No, you're not. You're family." Jaxen hooked his thumbs in the belt loops of his jeans, his shoulders loose and posture relaxed. "Are you okay with your dad's decision?"

"It's his business. He can do whatever he wants." What irked Tristan was that his father hadn't bothered to discuss his plans with him, who by blood rights was the heir.

"Not what I asked." Jaxen shook his head, good-naturedly.

"Fine." Tristan sighed. "If you're serious about turning your life around, then I'll be happy for you to take over my dad's construction company when the time comes."

"Glad to hear it."

"But, toe a straight line or—"

"Or what?" An irritating grin spread across Jaxen's mouth.

"I'll make your time in Woelfesguarde seem like a picnic."

Jaxen laughed, hard.

Tristan pushed away from the truck and stood tall. "I'm not that little kid who idolized you. I will put you down without a second thought if I think you're going to hurt someone again."

Jaxen sobered and fell silent.

Tristan opened the truck door and climbed inside.

"For fuck's sake, Trist. We were kids."

Tristan didn't miss that Jaxen didn't express regret over the incident.

"You getting me banished kinda makes us even. Don't ya think?" Jaxen held the truck door so Tristan couldn't shut it.

"Not by a fucking long shot." Tristan yanked the door closed and rested his arm on the open window, keeping Jaxen in his line of vision. "For the record, you got yourself banished. I simply didn't lie to give you an alibi."

"Why don't we forget all the stuff that happened when we were kids? I'm ready for a fresh start, how about you?" Jaxen extended his hand.

Tristan's inner wolf prowled restlessly and his instinct warned against a truce until Jaxen proved himself.

"Come on, Tristan. Clean slate?"

"Time will tell." He cranked the truck engine.

"Watch yourself out there." Pregnant clouds drifted across the moon and a shadow darkened Jaxen's face, twisting his features into a grotesque mask.

Unease coiled in the pit of Tristan's stomach. "Always."

Chapter 5

Butterflies darted and fluttered in Nel's stomach as if they were auditioning for a Cirque de Soleil performance. Starting tomorrow, she would be responsible for the success or failure of the Walker's Run Resort's new children's activity program.

Although Penelope confidently managed her kindergarten classes, she never volunteered to take the lead in any of her school's events. She made a great assistant, but being in charge was something she never had the confidence to attempt.

"It's fabulous." She gazed at the colorful paper-ring garland swooping from the ceiling and crisscrossing the room. "I couldn't have hung it without your help. This old lady on a ladder is a Shakespearian tragedy no one wants written."

"Nonsense." Shane MacQuarrie stepped off the last rung and gave her a mischievous look. "You're in your prime and quite the catch, milady." He bowed low.

"Why, thank you, kind sir." Laughing, Penelope curtsied.

No older than his early twenties, Shane was too young

for her to have a romantic interest in him, but his easy manner and teasing banter had immediately put her at ease.

"Someone is in a really good mood today." Cassie leaned against the doorway. "I haven't actually seen you in a bad mood, but you seem more engaged."

"The gunk from the city is sloughing off." Penelope placed the extra construction paper on the supply shelf, returned the scissors to the plastic bin and secured the glue bottle in a drawer. "Or it could be the invigorating moonlit stroll I had Friday night."

"How can a stroll be invigorating? A run, yeah. But a stroll?" Shane folded the ladder.

"Would you do me a favor?" Cassie looked at Shane. "The light in my office is out. I put in a call to maintenance, but they're searching high and low for the ladder."

"No problem." He hoisted the missing ladder onto his shoulder.

"Thanks." Smiling warmly, Cassie touched his arm. "The bulbs are on my desk."

"Holler if you need me again." He nodded toward Nel and left.

"Sweet kid."

"You're right, but Shane wouldn't take that as a compliment." Cassie glanced around the room. "Looks great in here. All set for tomorrow morning?"

"As ready as I can be." Penelope gave one last look. "Thanks for providing the big round table. I think it will be more fun for the kids to sit in a circle and help each other rather than sitting alone at individual desks."

"You're going to be great at this."

"I hope so." After Penelope turned out the lights and locked up the room, she and Cassie walked down the spiral stairs to the main lobby. "Where's Brenna?"

"Sundays are daddy days. She's with her father, and her godfather and his two-month-old twins."

"Sounds like a handful. Where's the babies' mother?"

"Oh, Grace is on her way here to meet me for lunch and an afternoon at the spa. Would you like to join us?"

"I wouldn't want to intrude."

They stopped in the middle of the quiet lobby.

"If you were an intrusion, I wouldn't invite you." Cassie withdrew a cell phone from her purse. "Should I confirm three?"

"Yes, please." Penelope's fingertips and palms warmed and her nerves prickled nearly to the point of discomfort.

"Something wrong?"

"Um…" Penelope's breathing hitched. She glanced in all directions, but when the lobby doors swung open, her gaze locked on the uniformed lawman coming inside. Tristan stopped suddenly and looked directly at Penelope. Some of the tension drained from his shoulders. A tired smile disrupted his firmly set mouth.

Was he glad to see her?

Every feminine cell in her body danced.

"Penelope?" Cassie tapped Nel's arm. "Are you feeling okay?"

Okay didn't begin to describe the feeling of standing on a cliff, toes gripping the edge a second before leaping, or the rush of wind stinging her skin during the free fall right before she opened her wings to fly.

Not that she'd ever experienced those things, but Penelope couldn't think of any other way to describe how she felt in that moment.

"Yeah," she sighed. "I'm good."

Noticing Tristan, Cassie giggled.

"I've never met a man who could steal my breath with a simple look." Men as gorgeous as Tristan never took notice of Nel. Their gazes simply swept right over her without a moment's pause.

"He's headed this way," Cassie said.

"What?" Penelope's heart kicked into high gear, beating fast and furious, and flooding her body with so much giddy adrenaline that she nearly swayed from a wave of light-headedness.

Breathe, just breathe.

Halfway across the lobby, Tristan stopped, slipped his hand into his pocket and pulled out a cell phone. His smile turned downward as he held the device to his ear. While talking, he tipped his head back and ran his fingers through his hair.

Penelope figured the conversation was over when the hand holding the phone dropped to Tristan's side. His gaze returned to her.

Maybe next time, sweet cheeks.

He nodded in her direction, took a few steps backward, then turned on his heel and headed toward the corridor to Gavin's office.

"Did you hear that?"

Tristan had been too far away for Nel to actually hear anything he said, but his deep, Southern drawl hummed in her head.

"Hear what?" Cassie looked around.

"Someone called me sweet cheeks, just now." And when she'd been frightened by the wolf in the woods.

"Sorry, I didn't hear anything."

Maybe the higher altitude and fresh mountain air had induced some sort of auditory hallucination.

More likely it was her hormones running amuck.

"Why is Tristan here? Is there a problem with one of the guests?"

"Everything is fine. He's a member of the Walker's

Run Cooperative and helps manage the resort's security as well as the wolf sanctuary." Cassie pointed to a corner nook. "We can wait for Grace over there."

"Does he patrol the area around the rental cabins?" Penelope sat in a cozy overstuffed chair next to Cassie.

"Sometimes. Why?"

"Friday night, I walked one of the trails from the cabin and thought I heard his voice."

"He was on duty so it could've been him. What did he say?"

"Basically, he told me to sit up."

"Sit up?" Cassie's nose wrinkled and her brows drew together. "That's weird. Were you lying down?"

"Hunkered down. I fell trying to get away from an animal making terrible noise in the woods. Scared the daylights out of me."

"It was probably Cybil. The old sow sounds like an elephant stampede whenever she gets out of her pen. Her owner lives on the border of the wolf sanctuary. Usually the sentinels round her up before she makes it this far."

"Sentinels?"

"The Co-op's security team."

"Ah." Penelope picked at the drop of glue stuck to the front of her blouse. "Well, I didn't see a pig, but I did encounter a huge wolf."

Cassie's friendly expression blanked. "Can you describe him?"

"His coat looked like burnished gold, but really was a mix of warm, rich colors." Penelope's voice rose with excitement. "And his ears were absolutely delightful, like chocolate brownies with the edges dusted in white sugar. He was the sweetest thing. Didn't growl or bark at me, and he followed me back to the cabin to make sure I got in safe."

"He did, did he?" One of Cassie's red brows arched.

"He won't get into trouble, will he?" If the poor thing was put in heavy chains, forced to wear a muzzle or locked in a cage, Penelope would be heartbroken.

"No." A smile broke the serious mask that had formed over Cassie's features. "Our wolves aren't punished for being curious or for helping someone, but I'll need to talk with Tristan about the incident."

"Why?"

Cassie tucked an errant curl behind her ear. "From your description, the wolf you described matches Tristan's wolf."

"So, Tristan was nearby?"

"Oh, yeah." Cassie's curls bounced with her little head nod.

"Why didn't he answer when I called him? I could've been hurt and he didn't come."

"The wolf would've alerted him if you were in any danger. I can speak from a similar experience with my husband's wolf."

"I would've appreciated Tristan giving me a quick heads-up before sending his wolf to check on me. I nearly had a stroke before I realized the cutie wasn't going to bite me."

"Tristan probably had his hands full with Cybil." Cassie brushed her hand across her lap, as if wiping away invisible crumbs. "I think he would've given you an explanation if that phone call had come two minutes later."

"I wouldn't mind meeting up with him again. I haven't forgotten your warning, but he seems like a nice guy and someone fun to know. I could use some fun."

"There's always tomorrow night," Cassie said cautiously.

"What's happening tomorrow night?"

"Singles' night at Taylor's. It's a family-friendly road-house on the outskirts of Maico. The steaks are fabulous."

"Singles' night." Penelope's voice unintentionally deadpanned.

"It's not what you think."

"I'm thinking everyone there will be looking for a hookup."

"Some will, but it isn't sleazy or creepy. And there's no pressure to go home with anyone. It's a great chance to meet some nice people and have a good time. There's a band, a dance floor and excellent food. Come to think of it, that's pretty much every night at Taylor's."

Penelope wasn't a great fan of singles' night at the bars in Atlanta, mostly because she was uncomfortable in crowds and didn't appreciate drunken gropes from men who wouldn't give her a second glance sober.

"Might be your only chance to meet up with Tristan. He's always coming or going somewhere, but tomorrow night he'll be at Taylor's."

"Thanks for the tip." Penelope had always been too shy to attend singles' events alone. But, if Tristan was there maybe she wouldn't be alone for long.

Chapter 6

A full moon on singles' night, it wouldn't be hard to find a partner for the evening. Tristan, weary of the primitive drive for sex a full moon triggered, just wanted to get it over.

In his twenties, he'd been more appreciative of the biological urge. Now, in his midthirties, he'd become too tired or too bored to care.

Still, he had to be careful about coupling with the same female too often or risk inspiring false hope about future possibilities. Though he was always upfront about his commitment to singlehood, some women considered it their mission to convert him to the ranks of the happily mated. In his family, *happy* and *mated* were an incongruent pairing.

He lifted a frosted beer mug to his lips. Cold, dark ale slid down his throat and plunked into his empty stomach. The gnawing clench didn't ease and likely wouldn't until the full moon passed.

"Hey, Tristan." One of the she-wolves had broken away from her friends to sidle up to his table. A dark-haired beauty, her slightly upturned nose and pretty eyes spaced close together made her look exotic and mysterious.

"Sonia, you look lovely tonight." He focused on her face rather than ogling the swells of her breasts popping out of the low-cut neckline. At least twelve years his junior, she didn't appeal to him on a sexual level and it bothered him that some of the older males nearby were practically panting for her.

"Are you waiting for someone?" She-wolves didn't flush from embarrassment and they definitely weren't shy. But, Tristan heard the hitch in her breath as she waited for his response.

"Sorry, doll, I am." He lied, knowing he wouldn't bed her tonight or any night.

He hated that the process of selecting a moon-fuck partner had become so tedious and torturous. Some unmated wolfans had regular partners for the full-moon nights. The pair usually did not maintain a social relationship. They merely rendezvoused in the woods and took care of business as wolves. Tristan had considered doing the same, but hadn't had the time to discuss a possible partnership with the limited, unmated she-wolves his age.

"Aww." Sonia's voice turned soft and seductive. "Mind if I keep you company while you wait?"

"Not tonight." Or any other night as far as he was concerned.

Her smile turned pouty. "I'll be at the bar, if you change your mind."

I won't.

Tristan tipped his head, then picked up the beer mug and swallowed the ale without tasting it. Sonia sashayed toward her friends. She was the fourth she-wolf he'd turned down tonight. If he kept at it, he wouldn't get laid.

For the past two months, he'd missed the full-moon

fuck. The first time, Ruby had fallen ill and he'd taken her to the hospital. The second, he got called in to help a neighboring town's law enforcement deal with a multicar collision that had resulted in a dozen casualties.

Tonight, Tristan had no choice. He had to have sex or run the risk of elevated wolfan hormones awakening his beast.

An unexpected electric charge pulsed along his nerves. His heartbeat kicked up two notches. Before the restaurant doors opened, he made a guess at who would enter. Even though he shouldn't, he couldn't wait to see her.

Penelope cautiously stepped into the restaurant. Tonight, her hair fell in soft waves around her shoulders. She wore white jeans and a billowy black blouse that hid her generous curves.

Curves his hands ached to feel again and that had tormented him in his dreams.

Intense desire spread through his body like a wildfire during a drought. The full-moon effects were starting early.

A tumble with her might be foremost on his mind, but was definitely not on his agenda. He'd pegged her as a forever kind of woman and he needed to stay far, far away from her.

Her confident stance was slightly marred by her uncertain gaze as she eyeballed her surroundings. Though she failed to notice him, Tristan couldn't drag his attention from her.

The hostess greeted her and picked up one menu.

Here alone and not expecting anyone.

His evening just got better and more complicated. Not unlike felines, curiosity often got the best of wolfans. And he wanted to know why she'd specifically called out for him, Friday night.

Watching Penelope follow the hostess to a table, he scooted back from his own.

"Tristan!" A feminine squeal rang in his left ear. Slender arms lassoed his neck and a sloppy kiss dampened his cheek.

Damn!

He hated being blindsided. Keeping a tight cap on his irritation, Tristan focused on the woman making a concerted effort to squeeze onto his lap.

"Hello, doll." Tristan didn't budge an inch to allow her room.

He searched her vaguely familiar features but couldn't recall her name. Heavy perfume and cigarette smoke clung to her skin, so her scent was no help in identifying her, either.

"Long time no see," she said, all breathy and dramatically animated. "I hoped you would be here."

"And so I am." He consciously smiled, racking his brain for a name.

A name, a name, he'd give up his dinner to remember her name.

Well, maybe not. Wolfans loved to eat.

Shoving back the table, she managed to wedge herself onto his lap. Her arms draped his shoulders. Long, red nails raked his hair.

Huh!

Not one single spark. He felt absolutely nothing.

What the hell was wrong with him?

A full moon, a willing woman and not one flicker of interest. He might've suspected some type of dysfunction if not for his reaction to Penelope.

"What have you been up to since the last time I saw you?" Not that he cared, but her response might help him figure out her identity.

"Kenny and I divorced. The rat bastard skipped out on child support so the kids and I had to move back to Maico to live with my mom." Tears glistened in her heavily painted eyes.

Somehow, Tristan got the feeling her sorrow stemmed more from living with her mother than the divorce. Or maybe it was his skewed perception of family.

He would cry, too, if he had to live with his parents again. Neither loving nor caring, his parents could hardly be in the same room without a fight breaking out.

If they were human, a divorce would've sent them happily on their separate ways. As wolfans, a mate-claim bound them for life. Even if it was accidental, as it was in their case, the claim was irrevocable.

"Here ya go, Slick." Angeline slid him a glass of ice water he hadn't ordered. One perfectly curved auburn brow arched and she looked pointedly at the womanly octopus tangling him with her tentacles.

"Thanks, Sassy." He gave Angeline a bug-eyed stare. She had been his friend long enough to recognize the SOS.

Humor played on her lips and she actually looked ready to walk away without tossing him a lifeline. He squinted a dire warning.

Angeline's teasing gaze locked on Tristan, then dropped to the woman in his lap. "Long time no see, *Deidre.*"

The name exploded in Tristan's ears. In disbelief, he stared at the woman who had been his high-school sweetheart. Short platinum hair, steely gray eyes lined with thick black smudges, pouty lips painted dark red against a weathered canvas obscured the traces of the pretty girl he'd once dated. Tristan's heart gave a tiny squeeze. When he'd ended the relationship with Deidre, he'd truly wanted her to find happiness. The haggard look behind the heavy makeup suggested she hadn't.

"What do you think?" Deidre said to Angeline as the clamor in Tristan's ears faded. "Do we still look the same as we did in high school?"

"Um…" Angeline's head tilted as if picturing them then and now.

Clenching his jaw, Tristan felt his mouth pull tight and his brow wrinkle.

"Oh, yeah." Angeline laughed. "Now you look exactly like I remember."

"Thanks," Tristan muttered. Back then, he was an infatuated fool and believed he could beat his family legacy of high drama.

It didn't take long to learn that he couldn't. When his and Deidre's behavior began to mirror his parents', Tristan ended the relationship before the unthinkable happened and he accidentally claimed her. Under no circumstances did he want to be in a relationship that he couldn't escape.

"After all this time, we've found each other again." Deidre beamed. "It's kismet."

"I don't believe in that crap." The humor faded from Angeline's eyes.

"Deidre," Tristan interrupted before Angeline launched a tirade about fate and fairy tales and not so happily-ever-afters. "My leg is falling asleep, doll. Would you mind moving?" To another table? Another restaurant? Another town?

"How about some company for supper?" Deidre stroked his jaw.

"He's waiting for someone," Angeline said.

Hoorah for the wing-girl. Tristan owed her big-time for this one.

"Oh." Deidre's mouth took on an exaggerated pout. "Rain check?"

Tristan offered a noncommittal nod.

Deidre pressed her lips against his. He kept his lips closed instead of encouraging her kiss. Had to be a first for him.

When she finally vacated his lap and sulked away, the tightness in Tristan's body eased.

"Never expected that blast from the past, did you?" Angeline dipped a napkin in the glass of ice water on her tray and handed it to him.

"What's this for?"

"Wipe your mouth and cheek, unless you want to walk around branded with big red lips all night. Might scare off the real woman you've been waiting for."

"Thanks." Tristan used the damp cloth to clean his face. "But I'm not waiting for anyone."

"Sure you are." Angeline looked over her shoulder. "She's sitting alone near the restrooms."

"Penelope's just…" Exactly what was she to him? "A friend?" Possibly, if they ever got past the furtive glances across the resort lobby.

"You and I have been friends since we were twelve." Angeline leaned close enough to whisper in his ear. "You've never lit up for me the way you did for her when she walked in that door. Go get her."

"You know my situation."

"It's your parents' situation. Doesn't have to be yours."

Unfortunately, Tristan knew differently.

"Don't be a jerk and leave her sitting alone." Angeline bumped his shoulder. "She's got that vulnerable look and there are hungry wolves on the prowl tonight. One of them might get lucky enough to eat her up."

The low, warning growl vibrating in his throat caught him off guard, but apparently not Angeline.

She laughed and laughed.

"Don't you have work to do?" Tristan grumbled.

"Don't you?"

Chapter 7

Penelope barely heard anything over the panicked drum of her heart. She was so out of her comfort zone. How had she allowed Cassie to talk her into this?

In the ten minutes since she'd arrived, Penelope had kept her head lowered and avoided eye contact. Some habits were hard to break.

She picked up the menu. Her gaze skipped over the fried foods and sandwiches, and landed on the salads, but what she really wanted was that platter of chicken wings the server carted past her.

Taking a deep breath, she glanced around the restaurant. For singles' night, the crowd seemed relatively calm.

Oh, she could spot the hookups, all right, but the frenzied, frantic atmosphere of the few singles' bars she'd gone to with a friend from work was thankfully absent.

Through the crowd, she noticed a tawny-haired man at the bar and her heart fluttered.

Lately, her sex life had stagnated. Not that it was anything spectacular before. She'd been in a few relationships, but none of the men had rocked her world in or out of the bedroom and she really wanted to be rocked. Hard.

Hard enough to leave her sweaty and breathless. Hard enough for the headboard to chip the paint off the walls.

She'd settle for one good orgasm.

Oh, she could give them to herself when she indulged in fantasy, but she'd never achieved the same result with any of her boyfriends. Tired of fantasies, Penelope slid out of her seat and made determined steps toward the bar.

Tristan, the subject of her latest fantasies, tossed back a shot of something. If she wasn't such a lightweight drinker, she might do the same. "Courage," she muttered to herself.

The closer she came to him, the more militant the butterflies in her stomach became. Maybe that was why the zip of excitement she usually felt when seeing Tristan didn't manifest.

Penelope tapped him lightly on the shoulder. "Hi there."

He turned slowly. His gaze landed on her chest and lingered before sliding down the length of her body and then all the way up to her face, leaving an icky feeling on her skin.

Not the reaction she hoped for.

"Do I know you?" His blue-gray eyes were cold and distant, and no smile touched his tight mouth.

"No." Penelope forced a confident smile. "I thought you were someone else. Sorry to have bothered you." She turned to scurry back to her table.

"Hold on." Steely fingers cuffed her wrist and spun her around. "You are definitely not a bother, love." The man pulled her close, way too close for her comfort. "Join me for a drink."

"I have other plans." She employed the stern tone she used when disciplining the schoolkids in her classroom.

"Plans change." His grip remained firm but didn't

tighten. For a second, his gaze lost the hard edge and she glimpsed a shadow of loneliness.

She almost relented.

"Let her go."

Now Penelope's internal bells and whistles went off. Tristan stepped close enough that she went all gooey inside and had to concentrate on remaining cool and collected so she wouldn't melt into a puddle at his feet.

"We were just about to get to know each other," the other man said.

"Jaxen, this is Penelope. She's my date for the evening. That's all you need to know about her." The growl in Tristan's deep, sexy voice inspired all sorts of electric mayhem throughout her body. She shivered.

When his arm gently slipped around her waist, the ripple along her nerves twisted into a wild, interpretive dance.

"Let her go." With his right hand, Tristan clasped Jaxen's wrist until he released her, one finger at a time.

"No harm, no foul." Jaxen rubbed the red streaks Tristan's grasp had left on his arm. "Man, you need to lighten up."

Penelope glanced at her wrist. Jaxen's grip had not left a single mark.

"You need to mind your manners."

"Noted." The muscle in Jaxen's jaw twitched. He gave Penelope a wistful look, then showed them his back and ordered another shot.

"Did he hurt you?" Tristan gently turned her away from the bar.

"No." And she wasn't so sure Jaxen would have.

Tristan laced his fingers through hers. Warm, comforting heat spread beneath his touch.

"Is Jaxen your brother?" Penelope fell into step slightly

behind Tristan as he led the way through the swelling crowd. Mostly people moved out of his way and he made a direct path to a table near the dance floor.

"Cousin."

"You favor each other."

"Only in looks." Tristan's upper lip lifted in a silent snarl.

Apparently there was an unpleasant history between the two men.

"I hope you don't mind joining me, sweet cheeks." Tristan's warm eyes encouraged her company.

"Just so you know—" Nel sat in the chair he pulled back for her "—I like Nel. But I don't like doll, darlin', love, sweetie, sweetie pie or sweet cheeks."

He took the other seat. "Sweet cheeks is a compliment. When you smile, you look so damn sweet I want to eat you up."

"Oh." A light heat spread across her face, down the column of her throat and across her cleavage. "I changed my mind, you can call me sweet cheeks."

He glanced around the room before settling his gaze back on her. "I was working resort security Friday night and heard you cry out in the woods. Did you get hurt?"

"No, but I was scared. There was a terrible noise, then a wolf came up to me and…I thought heard your voice."

Surprise and disbelief blinked in Tristan's eyes.

"I know it was my imagination kicking into overdrive because I was frightened." Penelope fiddled with her fingers. "And I was really hoping to see you again."

"Yeah?"

She needed sunglasses to protect herself from Tristan's smile. She also needed to divert away from flirting with him because, well, she rather sucked at it.

"I was scared, Tristan. To know you were nearby and didn't help—" Her voiced cracked.

"Nel, when I heard you call out, it was impossible for me to get to you. My wolf accompanies me on patrol, so I sent him instead. I trust him with my life. I knew I could trust him with yours." Tristan's hand covered hers and the angst tying her stomach in knots dissolved into a calm, soothing assurance. "My wolf will never hurt you. I'll stake my life on that."

"What's his name?"

"Tristan." His brow creased. "With the population we have, it would become confusing to give separate names to the wolves."

"Everyone should have a name of their own."

"Trust me, he doesn't mind being called Tristan."

"He told you that, did he?"

"As a matter of fact, he did."

Penelope nearly giggled because of the teasing tent in Tristan's eyebrow and the broadening, impish smile he flashed at her.

"Am I forgiven?"

Nel studied his face. He had a strong brow that dipped over warm, deliciously decadent eyes, a straight nose of just the right proportion, high cheeks, a masculine mouth tempered by a delicate cupid's bow and soft-looking lips, and a powerful jaw shadowed by dark gold stubble.

How could she stay mad at someone with a face of exquisite perfection?

"Forgiven."

"Here ya go." The server placed a glass of white wine in front of Penelope. "Figured you'd rather have this here than at the table where you were."

"Yes, thank you."

"Ready to order?"

"A Caesar salad will be fine."

"That's an appetizer, right?" Tristan's gaze slid past Penelope and to the left.

"Um, no. It's supper."

"For a rabbit." He turned his attention to the server. "The usual, and add an order of grilled chicken wings."

"Want another beer? That one's probably warm by now."

Tristan handed the server the nearly full beer mug. "Water is fine."

"Sure thing, Slick." The server sauntered toward the kitchen.

"Slick?" Penelope asked Tristan.

"A nickname. Angeline and I have been friends for years. She calls me Slick. I call her Sassy."

Penelope felt a slight prick of envy. She'd lost her first friends when her parents died and she had to move. In college, she'd had some acquaintances and quickly lost touch with them after graduation. More recently, her small social circle included a few coworkers and the sister of Penelope's last ex.

"So, what's your usual order?" she asked Tristan.

"Sixteen-ounce rib eye, medium rare, a loaded baked potato and fried okra without the batter."

"You're going to eat all that plus a plate of chicken wings?"

"Nah, I got those for you. I saw the way you looked at the platter on the table next to us. Besides, after supper I'm hoping you'll be my dance partner. You'll run out of steam before the second song if you don't have protein in your stomach."

"I'm not a much of a dancer." Mostly because she'd never learned.

"Good thing I'm an excellent teacher." Tristan exuded

an easy confidence and openness Penelope would find sexy even without his perfect features.

"I bet you're excellent at a lot of things." Vivid visions of all the things she would like for him to do to her flashed through Penelope's mind.

"Yes." Tristan's smile turned wicked and decadence smoldered in his dark sinful eyes. "I certainly am."

Nel's body charged with awareness, heat erupted from her core, and raging desire flooded her senses.

With no experience to handle a man like Tristan, the safest thing to do would be to cut and run.

Unfortunately, her legs had turned to jelly.

Chapter 8

Anticipation coiled inside Tristan. He couldn't wait to get Nel in his arms, hold her close and work up a sweat. He'd be a liar to deny he wanted more, but dancing was all he dared.

Another quick visual sweep of the restaurant confirmed there were no simmering or escalating troubles, especially since Jaxen had left with Deidre. Even when he wasn't looking directly at Nel, Tristan was intimately aware of every move, every breath, every sound she made.

Methodically, she wiped her hands on a napkin and tucked it beside her empty plate. Her soft sigh sounded sad, disappointed, drawing his full attention.

"What's wrong?"

"Nothing." Her voice sounded tight and she avoided his direct gaze. "How much do I owe you for dinner?"

"Nothing, it's my treat." No one had ever mistaken a date with him before. Maybe he was losing his touch.

"Oh, okay. Um, thanks for dinner." She inhaled a slow, deep breath. Her spine straightened and her shoulders stiffened. "It's been a long day, so I'm going back to my cabin."

The sudden crash of disappointment left him speechless.

Damn. How did he screw this up?

They both stood and Tristan hooked his fingers through Nel's to make sure she didn't walk off.

"One dance?" He gave her his best puppy dog look.

"One," she finally agreed.

Despite the band's fast beat, Tristan pulled Nel close and set their own slow pace. He waited a few more beats before asking, "So, how did I mess up at supper?"

"You barely looked at me once the food arrived."

"I hadn't had a decent meal since yesterday." He was wolfan. Even when he wasn't starving, food was a pretty big deal.

"Hunger has nothing to do with roaming eyes."

"What?" Tristan halted their dance. Absolutely and unequivocally, he had not scoped out any woman tonight, aside from Nel.

She looked up at him, her eyes clear, guileless, and a direct window to the vulnerability she was trying not to show.

"I'm not the most desirable woman here tonight…"

To him, she was. To prove it, he tipped her chin intending to give her a gentle kiss.

But the moment her lips parted, Tristan's rational mind disengaged and primal instinct took control. He swept her mouth, probing, claiming, branding her as much as she probed, claimed and branded him.

Thankfully, she broke the kiss because he couldn't.

"You were saying?"

She touched her fingers to her lips as if they tingled as much as his did. "That was an unfair distraction."

"But it was good, right? Good enough to adjust your perception?"

"Do you find me boring? Because every few minutes you look away."

Tristan scratched his jaw. He was such an idiot for not mentioning it, but he'd done it for so long he no longer realized when he was doing it. "I'm partially blind." He enticed her back into his arms, but she resisted getting as cozy as they were before. "I have no left peripheral vision. Whenever I sense movement on that side, I look."

"Oh." Nel's expression softened and he hated the sympathy that pooled in her big, beautiful eyes. "I'm sorry for the misunderstanding."

"Don't be. I'm glad we cleared the air."

"Since we're on the subject of clearing the air..." Nel inched closer. "Is it my imagination, or have you also sensed this thing...this energy bouncing between us?"

He did, and wondered what it was. Even more so, he wondered what to do about it.

A fast country tune belted from the speakers. Penelope was swirling across the dance floor before her brain caught up with her body. Song after song, it seemed the rhythm never slowed. Neither did Tristan.

Penelope's laughter chased her all around the twirl Tristan spun her in until she landed back in his arms and he dipped her deep. Slowly, he brought her upright and flush to his body. She was panting too hard from exertion for her breath to hitch. Otherwise, it would have.

"You are a fast learner. No one will ever believe you didn't know those moves before tonight." Tristan seemed in no hurry to have her step back. His hands palmed her low back, holding her in place. "Ready for the next one?"

"I don't have the energy to keep up the pace." Her

sigh was really an attempt to catch her breath. When she'd vowed to make up for lost time, she hadn't meant to do it all at once.

"We can slow it down again." He drew her closer. So close her cheek rested against his chest.

Admittedly, they'd hit a rough patch during the evening. However, Tristan impressed her with his earnestness in discussing the problem and his honesty in solving it.

He was a true gentleman. Even now, squashed together as they were, his hands rested respectfully on her lower back, not copping a feel of her ass, which hopefully would not grow a size larger from the chicken wings she'd eaten at Tristan's insistence.

He didn't seem to mind she wasn't a size two, or even a ten, and she certainly appreciated the solid bulk of his muscular build. The face of Adonis, a body built for sex and a devilish Southern charm that could entice a woman to drop her panties without a second thought.

So what was he doing with her?

Yeah, they had some kind of inexplicable connection. Electricity sizzled between them and had from the start. She had no idea what it meant, but a definite idea of where she wanted it to lead.

Unfortunately, despite the kiss and smoldering looks Tristan gave her, he hadn't suggested anything more than a night of dancing.

Maybe her fantasies had colored reality.

"Hey!" Tristan's hand glided up and down her back. "You're all tensed up."

"Sorry. My mind wandered."

Tristan stared down at her. In the dim light his eyes looked puzzled, contemplative. "I must be rustier than I thought."

"Rustier at what?"

"Entertaining a date." He shrugged. "It's been a while since I've been on one."

"You're kidding."

"Nope." His smile flatlined. "I'm not celibate, by any means, but those aren't dates."

"What are they?"

"Hookups, for lack of a better term."

"So, why is this a date and not a hookup?"

Tristan's eyes warmed. "I'm not angling to bed you at the end of the evening."

"Why not? Aren't you attracted to me?"

"I think I proved I am when I kissed you." Tristan trailed the back of his hand along her cheek. "You aren't the kind of woman a man turns to for a one-nighter. You are a now-and-for-always kind of woman."

"You're assuming an awful lot about someone you just met."

"Am I?"

"Sometime in the future, I may want to settle down," Penelope said. "Right now, I'm stretching my wings and trying new things."

The band wound down to take a break.

"Damn." Tristan sweetly kissed her knuckles. "I hate for our evening to end, but I have Co-op duty tonight."

"And I have to work tomorrow. I guess I should go."

"Yes, Penelope. You should go. And when you get back to the cabin, lock the door and don't open it until morning." Tristan sounded so serious a sliver of alarm swept through her.

"Why?"

"It's almost midnight." He stroked his thumb along her jaw. Waves of fire and ice undulated beneath her skin. "The moon is full. And the wolves are restless tonight."

Chapter 9

"*What the hell is wrong with you?*" Cooter's voice drifted through Tristan's mind, but the words floated without meaning for a few seconds before Tristan comprehended them.

Nearly too late, he realized Cooter had stopped short. Tristan's snout would've ended up in Cooter's rump if the much older sentinel hadn't sidestepped. As a result, Tristan's shoulder grazed Cooter's ribs.

"*That's the third time you've run into me tonight,*" Cooter growled. "*Anyone else, and I would've chomped their ass.*"

"*I don't know why I'm so distracted tonight,*" Tristan lied. Since leaving Nel, he couldn't focus on anything but her.

After following her to the resort, Tristan had parked near Gavin and Abby's private entrance, and stripped down in the shadows of their private gazebo before shifting. He'd made a quick trek through the woods around the resort property to assure himself that there were no interlopers. Then, he'd snuck by Nel's cabin.

She was on the back porch painting, but he didn't

allow himself the luxury of watching. Forcing himself onward, he circled around Brice and Cassie's homestead and padded across the footbridge to Rafe and Grace's home.

Once assured his brothers at heart were safe, Tristan made the trek to the wolf sanctuary to meet up with Cooter.

"I scented a female on you when we started out." Cooter's dark gaze speared him. *"You did fuck her, right?"*

Tristan remained conspicuously quiet.

"For the second time tonight, I'm gonna ask... What the hell is wrong with you?"

"She's human."

"Never bothered you before, so what's the real problem?"

The pull toward Nel was nothing like Tristan had ever experienced. A part of him wanted to give in just to see what would happen, but after a couple of months of celibacy, he wasn't sure how much control he'd reasonably exercise in human form while with her.

"You've never hesitated where women are concerned. If they were willing and available, so were you."

"I'm tired or bored. Or maybe I'm sick."

"You aren't sick." Cooter snorted. *"You're acting like a lovesick pup. Don't tell me you've gone and found a mate."*

"Hell, no," Tristan snapped. *"I like being single. The best part is no conflict. My home is always peaceful."* Unlike the one he grew up in.

"Well, then, why do you spend so little time there?"

In truth, Tristan's apartment had never felt like home.

"I can handle rounds alone," Cooter finally said. *"Human or she-wolf, bed someone. You need a warm body to ground you."*

Cooter departed, but Tristan lacked the motivation to track a she-wolf. Instead, he turned toward the river. Keeping to the dark tree line, he followed the winding stream toward the resort. Once he'd retrieved his clothes, Tristan planned to text Angeline. Showing up at her apartment if she already had a bed buddy would be awkward for all. Part of him hoped she would be unavailable. He wasn't in the mood for skin-to-skin coupling with her, and she didn't like wolf sex indoors.

Maybe he should go see Doc. Tristan's annual physical wasn't due for another three months, but he'd rather know sooner than later if he'd contracted some sort of wolfan ague.

A light rain began to fall.

By the time Tristan reached the edge of the resort property, the tips of his damp fur were charged with static from the growing intensity of an imminent storm.

Staying in the shadows, he worked his way back down to Nel's cabin. She stood near the bay windows in the kitchen nook. A scarf tied back her hair and she wore a long, baggy shirt over black leggings. Her movements were poetic as she swept the paintbrush across the canvas. She frowned, chewing on the wooden end of the brush. Her head tipped to one side, then the other. In a flurry, she jabbed the paintbrush bristles into the color on her palate and made short furious dabs at the canvas. She switched brushes and employed long, sweeping strokes until a sweet smile curved her mouth.

"Irresistible, isn't she?"

Tristan startled at the intrusive voice in his mind. He swung his head left. Jaxen sat behind him, a toothy grin plastered on his muzzle.

"Why are you here?" Tristan knew his agitation carried telepathically.

"Reorienting myself with the territory."

"You're in a restricted area."

"So are you."

"I'm a sentinel. It's my duty to protect the Alpha family's property."

"What's your duty to her?" Jaxen pointed his snout toward Nel. *"Did you know your tongue was lolling while you watched her? You might've even drooled."*

"Bite me."

"You should say that to her." Jaxen's teasing laughter didn't earn him any favors with Tristan.

"Go home, Jax. I'm cold and wet." And irritably horny.

"Guess I'll take a rain check on that run you promised." Jaxen shook out his fur, slinging muddy water droplets all over Tristan.

"Bastard."

"What?" Jaxen bumped him. *"I thought you loved the water."*

"Clean water. Not mud." Tristan shook, splattering Jaxen in kind and grinned at his cousin's disgruntled growl.

The sky brightened with a flash of light and the on-and-off drizzle restarted.

Nel scurried around the kitchen. Her movements more frenzied with the increasing rumble of rolling thunder.

"Hey." Jaxen caught Tristan's attention. *"At Taylor's, I thought you monopolized her attention so I would stay away from her, but there's more to it, isn't there?"*

"Nope. We shared a nice dinner and some dances. That's it."

"So, you wouldn't mind if I struck up something with her?"

"Actually, I would." Tristan issued a warning growl.

"Actually," Jaxen mocked, *"unless you claim her, she's fair game."*

"I don't need to claim her to keep her safe." From the likes of you.

Although Tristan hadn't sent the entire thought, Jaxen seemed to sense the sentiment anyway. His teasing demeanor slipped.

"I've done a lot of things, but I've never hurt a female or allowed one to be hurt in my presence." Jaxen stood snout to snout with Tristan, his blue-gray eyes icy and turbulent. *"Do you know why I ended up in Woelfesguarde?"*

"You assaulted a human."

"That human *smacked his woman so hard she fell to the floor with a broken jaw. So I made sure he knew how it felt and fixed it so he couldn't ever do it again."*

"Nel is sweet and kind and sensitive. All of which makes her vulnerable to being hurt. Intentionally or not." Tristan slightly lowered his head, but kept his gaze firmly on his cousin. *"She's a friend, Jax, and I'm asking, as nicely as I know how, stay away from her."*

"You always did have trouble sharing your friends."

Tristan could almost taste Jaxen's bitterness, and the cold, unforgiving gleam in his eyes suggested Jaxen still begrudged the close relationship he'd had with Mason.

Jaxen bolted into the darkness.

One day, all the anger festering in both of them would erupt. Tristan only hoped Nel wouldn't get caught in the fallout.

A howling wind wailed against the kitchen window. Nel's heart beat a frantic rhythm inside her chest and she was seriously rethinking the wisdom of spending the summer in a cabin, all alone.

Especially if the raging storm outside was typical for the season.

Relentless rain battered the tin roof. Sleep would not come anytime soon. After starting a pot of coffee, Penelope padded into the living room. The sudden rainstorm vanquished the heat and a chill saturated the air. She pressed the button on the mantel and the gas fireplace came alive. Since it was summer, a fire wasn't necessary, but it was certainly cozy and comforting. And if the power went out, the firelight would prevent her from being consumed in darkness.

She hoped Tristan was home safe. The thought of him caught in this awful summer squall made her stomach churn.

The old scar on her arm began to throb, unleashing a wire-thin, white-hot current from her right shoulder to the tip of her middle finger. The neurologist had found no substantial cause for the pain that every bad storm seemed to incite. After assuring her that all the nerves had healed perfectly, the advice he offered was for her to see a shrink. He might've been right, but she fired him anyway.

Kaboom!

The cabin rattled and shook as though the sky above and the ground below had split open. Nel dropped to the ground.

The only thing remotely suitable to crawl under was the small round kitchen table, but the large bay windows presented too much of a risk if the wind shattered the glass. The best she could do was wedge herself between the coffee table—which was made from a giant section of a very old tree—and the leather couch and hope that the roof didn't cave in.

The lights flickered once and faded. If not for the glow of the fire, darkness would've swallowed her whole.

The longer the storm raged, the harder and faster her heart beat until Nel was sure she'd have a heart attack before the storm broke.

Bam! Bam! Bam!

Nel swore she heard someone call her name.

The sound had to be her imagination. No one in their right mind would be out in this dangerous weather.

"Nel! Open the damn door!"

Penelope flew to the front door, slapped the chain off the hook, twisted the deadbolt, yanked open the door and plowed into Tristan's chest.

Arms banded around her, and he shuffled her back inside and kicked the door closed.

"Are you all right?"

"Yeah. Just shaken." The strong steady beat of his heart against her cheek provided an anchor for her to ride out the turbulent emotions crashing inside her. "What are you doing here?"

"I saw you on the back porch earlier. When the transformer blew and knocked the power out, I wanted to make sure you were okay."

"I'm glad you did. I hate bad storms."

Slowly, the tension drained from his body, taking hers along with it. He didn't let her go until she was good and ready, and thoroughly cognizant of the state he was in.

"You have to get out of those wet clothes."

Penelope darted into the bathroom. When she returned with dry towels and a laundry basket, Tristan had kicked off his shoes and was peeling the plastered T-shirt from his torso.

"Oh, boy," Penelope whispered, staring at the sculpted

muscles beneath a smattering of damp, matted chest hair and the incredibly defined ripples along his abs.

He plopped the shirt into the empty laundry basket Nel placed on the floor. She handed him a clean towel to dry his hair, then he swiped his shoulders and patted his chest and stomach.

"Pants?" Her voice hit a high note Nel didn't know she could reach.

Tristan hung the towel around his shoulders. His gaze locked on hers, he unzipped his pants and began peeling them from his lower body.

Nel sucked in her breath.

He had those sharp indents along his sides, angled just above the hips that could only be described as an evolutionary perfection of the male species.

"I, um…" Her tongue felt too thick for her mouth. She glanced over her shoulder into the kitchen. "I made coffee before the power went out. Want some?"

Tristan's penetrating gaze never wavered from her.

"How do you like it? Black? Cream? Sugar?"

"Cream, no sugar." His drawl was slow and deliberate.

"Got it." Penelope darted into the kitchen to give him some privacy.

She still jumped every time the thunder boomed and her shaky hands made pouring coffee a possible burn risk. So she placed two mugs in the sink before filling them. Then she added two splashes of cream to Tristan's cup.

Holding a warm coffee mug in each hand, she marched into the empty living room.

"Tristan?"

He emerged from the dark hallway. His skin looked golden and shimmery in the dancing firelight. The planes of his face, some in shadow, some in light, made him appear dark and dangerous.

And sexy as hell.

Not that he needed ambient lighting to help in that department.

"I wrung out my clothes and hung them up in the shower." His eyes narrowed in silent interrogation.

If she'd been guilty of anything, Nel would've confessed in no time.

"When the power comes on, I'll put them in the dryer for you."

Tristan edged into the living room, the towel fastened low, but snugly, around his hips. The outline of his erection was visible despite the thick plushness of the towel wrapping.

Nel's mouth and throat went dry. Other places became wet.

Oh, boy!

Forging ahead, she held out his coffee cup. "Here's something to warm you up."

"I'm not cold." He accepted the cup anyway, his cautious, curious eyes tracking her every movement.

Nel sat on the couch and pulled her feet beneath her. She sipped her coffee, watching him above the rim as she drank. He sat next to her. Closer than expected, and that made her smile. He stared at the fireplace, his posture rigid, his breathing tight and controlled. Nothing like the relaxed, easygoing, self-assured guy she'd danced with all evening.

"You seem uptight. Was everything all right in the wolf sanctuary? You weren't hurt, were you?"

He wrinkled his brows and squinted his eyes. Slowly he turned toward her. He sat the cup that had yet to touch his lips on the sofa table behind them. "Penelope, what are you doing?"

"Trying to distract myself from the storm by having a conversation with you, but you aren't cooperating very much."

Thunder broke overhead, shaking the cabin. She squealed and splashed a little coffee on the front of her T-shirt. Tristan carefully lifted the cup from her hands and sat it next to his.

"I hate storms." She shrugged at his inquisitive gaze. "My dad used to read stories to me as a distraction."

"What kind of distraction are you looking for tonight?"

Nel's heart launched into her throat. Was he coming on to her? Or playing with her?

She couldn't decide.

"Jeezus, don't look at me like that."

"Like what?"

Tristan leaned forward, his arms poled on either side of her, his fists balled into the seat cushion. "Like you want me to strip you down, kiss every last inch of your bare skin and sink so deep inside that your breaths become mine."

"Didn't know that was an actual look." Nel swallowed. "But yeah. I want you to do those things to me."

"You sure about that?" He grazed his cheek along her jaw. Warm breath blew across her skin. Chill bumps surfaced everywhere. Fluttering rose in her belly.

Oh, yeah, she was sure.

Chapter 10

"You never should've opened that door." Tristan drew his finger along Nel's ribs and she shivered.

Despite his slow, methodical movements, his heart hammered against the palm she pressed to his chest and his muscles bunched as her fingers glided over his taut skin.

He nibbled her earlobe until she wiggled.

"Go to your room and lock the door," he sighed against her ear.

He pulled back and Nel watched the rawness of every conflicting emotion he had flicker across his face.

"Oh, no," she said. "I've spent too much time afraid to take chances. I'm not going to hide from whatever this is between us. If you want to call it quits, there's the door."

In case he had any lingering doubt about what she wanted, Nel pushed him down on the couch and kissed him.

Tristan growled her name. His hands gripped her ass, his fingers kneading the globes. She took that as encouragement, not a protest. His hands moved upward, beneath her shirt. His fingers skimmed her ribs and nudged up her bra so he could cup her breasts.

She broke the kiss. His eyes fluttered opened. Fierce, needful.

Nel glanced at the fire. She hoped the glow was dim enough to hide her imperfections. She whisked off her shirt, then unhooked her bra and dropped it to the floor.

A smile spread across Tristan's face before he lowered his eyes to look at her. His touch followed his gaze and when it returned to her face, his hand cupped the back of her neck, urging her closer. All the while his voice ran through her mind. *Kiss me, Nel. Kiss me now!*

Pure imagination. Still, she gave in to the plea, brushing her mouth across his in a featherlight kiss that made him groan.

"You're killing me," he said softly in a voice full of agony.

"I'm so sorry!" She sat back, grabbing her shirt and covering her chest.

"What the hell?" Looking cross and confused, Tristan pushed up on his elbows. "Why did you stop?"

"You said I was killing you. I got carried away and straddled you with my full weight." She couldn't be more mortified.

"Nel," he said softly. "It's just an expression. I was referring to this." He pointed at the tent in the towel around his groin. "I want you so badly, my cock is hard to the point of pain."

"Oh." Embarrassment replaced the heated flush in her skin. "My mistake."

"Do you think what we're doing is a mistake?"

"No."

"Good." He rolled to his feet and held out his hand to

help her stand. "Let's go to the bedroom and get completely naked."

"Can we stay here, next to the firelight?" With the lights out, the bedroom would be shrouded in utter darkness. Sex would be the last thing on her mind.

Tristan sank to the floor on his knees. "Absolutely." He gazed at her face as he hooked his thumbs in her waistband and inched down her pants and panties. She gripped his shoulders, stepping free of the clothes.

Her skin warmed as Tristan's gaze leisurely traveled every inch of her body.

"Beautiful, absolutely beautiful." He gifted her with a smile that heated something deep inside her.

She knelt in front of him. His hands gently roamed her curves as they kissed. He eased her to the floor, trailed kisses down her throat and along the valley between her breasts. His tongue teased her belly button.

When he kept going lower, she tensed. Even though they were about to have intercourse, his mouth on her sex was more intimate than she was willing to go with a one-night stand.

Tristan glanced at her curiously and she shook her head. He offered a warm smile before placing tiny kisses along her inner thighs. His hand took the place of his mouth on her mound. His long, strong finger stroked between her folds, teasing her opening, tormenting her nub.

She quivered and writhed beneath his touch. Tristan licked and nipped her skin as he stalked up her body. When his tongue lapped the lower part of her breast up to her hardened nipple, she groaned. Arching her back, she rubbed against his cock, which was hard, thick and leaking at the slit.

"Condom," she said raggedly.

Tristan pulled away only long enough to grab one of

three silver packets off the end table. He must've found them in the bathroom cabinet.

He ripped open the foil wrapper with his teeth and sheathed himself in latex. "You have no idea what it's doing to me to watch you watching me."

Repositioning, Tristan dipped his head to her chest and took her breast into his hot, wet mouth, twirling his tongue over her taut peak.

Nel lightly scraped her nails over his broad, muscular shoulders. Tristan hissed with pleasure. He released her breast to gaze at her. She leaned into him to kiss the hollow of his throat and then chased his Adam's apple with her tongue when he swallowed hard.

Tristan dotted light kisses across her forehead. He nuzzled hair, nibbled her ear, nosed along the curve of her neck. "I love the smell of your skin."

At the junction of her neck and shoulder, he playfully sucked her skin between his teeth and lightly nibbled.

Boom!

The unexpected thunderclap shook the cabin.

Nel jerked, slamming Tristan squarely in the face. He sat on his haunches, his hand covering his nose.

"I'm so sorry." She sat up. "Let me see."

He allowed her to pull his hand away. She gingerly traced the outline of his straight, slightly flared nose.

"It's a little red, but not bleeding. I think it is okay." She saw amusement and something indescribable flicker in his eyes.

"Here's a better test." They lay down, his body settling comfortably over hers.

He tipped her chin, exposing her throat. Instead of the kisses she expected, he breathed softly across her skin. "Yep, you still smell delicious."

Nel laughed. "Planning on eating me?"

Tristan's breath faltered. "I would have, but that wasn't on the menu tonight."

Nel stared at him, her body in a flux of desire and embarrassment.

"It's okay." He lightly traced his knuckles along her jaw, then gave her the gentlest, sweetest kiss she could've imagined.

Her lips parted and his tongue slipped into her mouth. Slowly, he deepened the kiss until she no longer knew where her breath ended and his began. By the time he broke the kiss, she was ready.

His lips peppered hot kisses down her throat and between her breasts. As his mouth slid down the plane of her stomach, his thumbs strummed her nipples.

Tristan groaned and slipped his hand between their bodies. He nestled the plump tip of his cock against her opening, which was already clenching in anticipation.

With one smooth, masterful thrust, Tristan buried himself deep inside her body. He growled when she locked her legs around his hips and tightened around his shaft. They rocked in a deep and steady rhythm.

"God, Nel." He watched her beneath hooded lids. "You feel so damn good."

He gave her a hard, possessive kiss, thrusting against her harder, faster.

Tension coiled low in her belly, building into a gnawing hunger that had never been satisfied during intercourse.

She bit her lower lip to keep from crying out prematurely. She'd been on the cusp of orgasm before, only to lose it when her partner rushed to finish.

Blocking out all thoughts, she focused on the feel of Tristan's bare skin against her, the shared heat between bodies in synchronized motion. How he filled her, utterly and completely, stretching her inner walls to the indistinguishable point between pleasure and pain.

Yes! Yes! God, yes!

"Nel," whispered like a prayer, drove her right over the edge.

She screamed in ecstasy, as wave after wave of indescribable pleasure bombarded her being. The entire world seemed to come undone. No longer cognizant of the floor, or pillows or even the cabin, all she could sense was Tristan, whose strong steady presence tethered her, otherwise she would've drifted into nothingness.

Breathing hard, Tristan stilled and pressed his head against her shoulder.

Body humming, Nel slid her fingers through his hair and kneaded his scalp. The tenderness of the moment and the sheer intimacy was not what she anticipated, but was greatly appreciated.

His breathing eased and he kissed her temple so sweetly, unbidden emotion rose in her throat.

His warm, comforting gaze searched her face. "You okay?"

"Mmm," was all she could voice.

He eased out of her. "Damn. The condom broke."

"What?" Panicked, Nel sat up and pulled on her shirt.

"It's not a big deal," he said calmly.

Maybe not, if they'd been a couple and had future plans.

But a broken condom was certainly a very big deal for two people who were practically strangers.

Heart pounding as fast as her mind was racing, Nel grabbed her clothes and ran to the bathroom illuminated by the emergency light in the ceiling. She locked the door, leaning against it to catch her breath.

"Nothing to worry about," she told herself. "No STDs, no accidental pregnancies."

Whoever said deep breathing calmed the nerves obviously had never been in this situation.

She turned on the faucet and snatched a washcloth from the linen cabinet. After cleaning up, Nel splashed cold water on her face and neck. The fluffy hand towel she dabbed over her moistened skin smelled earthy and masculine. Tristan must've used it when he hung up his wet clothes in the shower.

She held the hand towel to her face and inhaled his scent. A strange calm settled over her, chasing away the panic her imagination had incited. Feeling much more herself, Nel laid the hand towel on the sink counter and looked in the mirror. Despite the scare, Nel's face in the reflection appeared radiant. She had a faint rash just beneath her jaw and down the column of her neck, likely a whisker burn where Tristan had nuzzled her.

"What is that?" Nel pulled at her shirt collar and leaned closer to the mirror. The muted glow from the emergency light wasn't enough for her to decipher if the spot on her neck was a shadow or something else.

"Please don't be a tick." She opened the under-sink cabinet and grabbed the flashlight. Shining it on her neck, she looked in the mirror. Whew, not a tick. Just a little love bite.

Chapter 11

Tristan knocked his fist against his forehead. Tonight, he would've broken one of his own rules. Nel's delicious scent and the pillowy softness of her body had weakened his resolve, enticing him to cuddle with her and luxuriate in the glow of her satisfaction. Except, the broken condom had sent her scurrying to the bathroom in full panic mode.

Of course, she didn't know there was no reason for concern. He couldn't get her pregnant unless he claimed her, and he would never allow that to happen.

And he was disease free, so Nel was perfectly protected. Still, he should've been more careful.

He debated going after her, but that might make the situation worse. She'd come out, eventually, and they could talk.

Grabbing the thick white bath towel off the floor, he stood and wrapped the towel around his hips. Wolfan vision allowed him to navigate through the dark to the kitchen without difficulty. He pulled back the curtain on the back-door window. The thunder and lightning had stopped, so the worst of the storm had passed, but the rain still pounded and the power remained off. Leaving Nel alone in bad weather didn't sit well with him, but he had a rule. Never spend the night after bedding a woman, to avoid attachments and messy entanglements.

His stomach growled.

Food. He always thought better on a full stomach.

He opened the refrigerator and scanned the contents. Slim pickings. Rabbit food, mostly, but he could whip up a couple of omelets. He grabbed the eggs, onion, green pepper, tomato, mushrooms and cheese, and placed them on the counter. He searched the cabinets for a pan.

"Tristan?" A beam of light flashed in the living room.

"Here." He found a knife and began dicing the onion.

Penelope padded barefoot into the kitchen, shining the light on him. "What are you doing?"

"Making a snack." Tristan started chopping the green pepper. "Hungry?"

"I am." Though she sounded uncertain.

Unless sick or dying, Wahyas never hesitated when offered food.

"Should you be chopping like that in the dark?"

"I have good night vision." Excellent, actually. Wahyas could see nearly as well in the dark as they did in the light.

He scraped aside the pepper and went to work on the tomato. "The flashlight helps." Not really, but Penelope seemed to find comfort in holding the light.

"I thought you didn't like vegetables." She sat on one of the two stools tucked against the island.

"I don't like lettuce. Tastes like grass." He laid down the knife and turned on the gas stove. Dropped a pat of butter in the pan and set it on the burner. Next, he placed a medium-sized glass bowl in front of him and carefully broke six eggs into the dish. After a couple of pinches of salt and a quick shake of pepper, he added the diced vegetables and whisked thoroughly.

He poured half of the mixture into the hot pan and adjusted the flame.

When the egg mixture firmed enough, he sprinkled the sliced mushrooms and shredded cheese just shy of center and folded over the egg mixture. When done, he slid the omelet onto a plate and grabbed a fork. "Eat up while it's warm."

He turned back to the stove to make his.

Nel's footsteps trailed behind him and stopped at the refrigerator. "Want some orange juice?"

"Sounds good."

Tristan was acutely and intimately aware of every move she made. Almost as if his body had become hypersensitive to her presence. He sensed her increasing tension as she sat the half-filled glasses on the island bar.

He prepared his omelet exactly the way he'd made hers. Carrying his plate, he sat on the stool next to her.

Leaning toward her, he dropped his voice. "You're not pregnant."

"What?" she said quickly.

"It's not possible for me to get you, or anyone else, pregnant." Male Wahyas were sterile until they'd claimed a mate. "And I'm perfectly healthy—no diseases to worry about."

"I wasn't worried." The understated relief in her voice said otherwise.

"I should leave when we finish eating." Tristan barely tasted the forkful of eggs he swallowed.

"Are you kidding?" Nel looked up from her plate, eyes round. "It's raining a river outside. It's safer if you stay here."

Tristan wasn't so sure. Sex hadn't quelled the full-moon effects. Something about Penelope intrigued him, clouded his judgment, undermined his resistance.

"What made you afraid of storms?" Maybe not the best conversation to go with, but he couldn't think of anything else to say and he needed to keep his mind off the warmth of her skin, the softness of her body, the rhythm of their joining, the enticing combination of her scent mixed with his.

Penelope swallowed a sip of orange juice. "I was born in South Florida. The rain isn't what most of the country experiences. It can fall in sheets from a perfectly blue sky. The wind can whip up with tornadic force and disappear within minutes. Outer bands from a hurricane can bombard us for hours or days before the storm comes ashore. I was always afraid of storms. My dad said there was nothing to fear, but…he was wrong."

Nel's gaze fell to her plate. The painful emotion flickering across her face struck a deep chord. Tristan's instinct urged him to soothe her distress. Before he figured out what he needed to do, she shook her head and blanked her expression.

"We went to bed after listening to the weather report," she said, her voice distant and detached. "A hurricane was nearing the East Coast, but not expected to turn inland. A tropical storm behind it was expected to fizzle out."

Her breaths became choppy and she seemed to see straight through Tristan, as if looking directly into the past. "During the night, the tropical storm got caught up in the hurricane's outer bands. The sheer size and massive force of the combined systems created a megastorm. It changed directions. Before sunrise, it made landfall in the coastal town where I lived.

"Evacuation orders were given but by the time most heard the news, it was too late. My dad tried to get us to safety. We were on a back road because the highway was jammed. I remember the high-pitched howl of the wind. And the windshield wipers were moving so fast, all I could see was a blur and still they weren't fast enough to clear away the water. I heard a loud crack above us, like the sky broke open. Then glass flew everywhere and the roof caved in from the weight of the tree that fell on the car. My parents died." Her voice broke. "I was eleven years old."

Tristan put down his fork to clasp her hand, curled into a fist on the counter.

"It was a freak accident," she said, still in a trancelike state. "If we had stayed home, we would've all died anyway. Our house and most of the homes in our town were destroyed. Hundreds of people died—friends, neighbors, teachers. The doctors said I was lucky."

She rubbed the dark pink scar that curved along her forearm. "I don't believe in luck."

"You're a survivor," he said, completely in awe. Nel had emerged from her tragedy with a kind, sweet disposition and an innocence he found utterly captivating. Not many people had the courage or strength to keep life from callousing the heart.

He hadn't.

"If you don't stop looking at me like that—" Eyes still closed, Tristan lay curled on his side, his muscled arm hugging Penelope's pillow. The sheet they'd shared draped his bare hip. The towel he'd worn, tossed aside sometime during the night.

Oh, lord, he was temptation incarnate.

Smiling, Nel laid his folded clothes, still warm from the dryer, on the couch.

After their late-night omelets, they'd returned to the

living room and settled into a cozy, snuggly position on the couch while Tristan read her a thriller from the digital library on her e-reader. Somewhere around chapter four, Nel had fallen asleep. She had no idea how long Tristan had remained awake, but he'd slept right through her phone alarm that went off at 6:00 a.m. The lights were on and the rain had stopped when she eased out of his arms to get ready for work.

"How do you know I'm looking at you?"

"I can feel it." A devastating smile curved his mouth framed by dark gold whiskers. "It's as if your hands are stroking my skin."

Slowly, his eyelids lifted. Longing and much more heated his dark chocolate eyes. She wanted to bask in the warmth, submerge in the rich decadence.

"You're dressed?" He rolled to his back and stretched. The sheet pulled tight across his morning erection. "What time is it?"

"Seven fifteen." Usually she was at the resort around six forty-five to eat breakfast in the restaurant. This morning, waiting for Tristan to wake up, she'd opted for a piece of toast with peanut butter and a cup of coffee in the cabin.

"Shit!" Tristan bounded to his feet and the sheet slipped to the floor so fast Penelope didn't have time to look away.

Then she couldn't. It was like her body disengaged from her brain. She heard a distant voice commanding her to look away, but she couldn't. Absolutely could not turn her head or avert her eyes from the most perfectly sculpted man she'd ever seen.

He didn't seem to notice.

"My clothes!" The urgency in his voice faded as he turned toward the couch. He snatched his pants off the cushion. "Thanks." Balancing perfectly, he shoved one long, muscular leg and then the other into the pants' legs. His T-shirt went on backward and he had to pull it off and put it back on. He grabbed his cell phone and keys off the end table. "Ready?"

"Don't you need shoes?" She handed him his hiking boots. "They're still damp."

He stuffed his feet into them, foregoing his socks.

"Got somewhere to be?" She turned to lock the door as he bounded down the steps.

"My aunt has a doctor's appointment at eight. I need to shower and shave before I pick her up so I can go to work when she's done." Instead of racing to the truck, he waited at the bottom of the steps. When Penelope reached the last step, he wrapped his arms around her waist.

"I put my number in your phone," Tristan said, low and soft. His gaze lingered on her lips. The air between them charged and he leaned into her as if he wanted to kiss her. "Use it," he whispered in her ear.

She couldn't imagine why she would call him, except the obvious. A tingly excitement buzzed cheeringly along every feminine cell in her body.

Regardless of the high-intensity attraction toward him and the body-splintering orgasm he'd given her, Nel knew better than to get further involved with him. His attention was fleeting and she wouldn't risk her heart on a disaster waiting to happen.

"Goodbye, Tristan," she said, with a firm mind to mean it.

Chapter 12

Someone had slaughtered Mary-Jane McAllister's pet pig.

No, not slaughtered. Butchered. Mauled. Mutilated. There was barely enough left of Cybil to recognize.

No cleansing breeze penetrated the woods, so the sharp, coppery smell of blood and the putrid smell of bowel clung to the air. Tristan considered shifting to his human form to use his hands to cover his sensitive nose.

Damn! This wasn't expected on a midweek security drill.

"We need to tell the others." Shane nudged him telepathically.

To do that, one of them needed to howl. Shane's thin, wolf lips were pressed as tight and flat as Tristan's were. Neither wanted to open their mouths and have that stench imprinted on their tongues.

"You're the lead sentinel," Shane prodded.

"Yeah, yeah." Tristan trotted several yards away before throwing his head back and howling a call specific to the Alpha-in-waiting. Brice answered. No one would advance on Tristan's location without specific orders from Brice.

Of course, Rafe Wyatt never paid much heed to protocol, and being the fastest wolf in the Walker's Run pack he appeared on-site within minutes.

"What the hell happened?" Rafe padded around the eviscerated remains, his nose wrinkling from the godawful smell.

"Found her like this." Shane had backed far away and turned to avoid looking at poor Cybil.

The official cause would be listed as a wild boar attack. Truthfully, there were no wild boar within the sanctuary. Only a wolfan could've done this. Of course, Tristan couldn't help wondering if Jaxen was responsible.

Brice arrived, took one look at the scene and ordered Rafe to get Gavin and Doc, the pack's physician. Then Brice issued a call restricting Cooter from the area. Cooter was too close to Mary-Jane McAllister, Cybil's owner, to witness the carnage.

Other sentinels arrived. Tristan divided them into teams and sent them out to search specific quadrants for tracks or other signs that might lead them to the perpetrator. He and Brice remained with Cybil. The outrageous hog had long been considered family to their wolf pack and it seemed wrong to leave her remains unattended.

Doc, a human pack member and Rafe's adoptive father, arrived with Gavin on an ATV. Brice and Tristan shifted into their human forms. Gavin opened the storage box and tossed each a pair of coveralls.

"Cooter?" Tristan's voice cracked with emotion. He couldn't imagine how hard the news had hit their chief sentinel.

"He's with Mary-Jane," Gavin said gravely. "Rafe stayed with them."

Doc examined Cybil's remains. "I believe she was already dead when the attack happened."

"Are you sure?" Tristan's heart squeezed. It wouldn't make the mutilation act any less horrific, but it would be a relief to know that Cybil had died peacefully and not in the throes of terror.

"There would've been more blood loss." Doc sighed.

The spot looked pretty damn bloody to Tristan.

"Even postmortem, this was a vicious attack," Gavin said. "What would cause a wolfan to do this?"

"Rabies." Brice limped to the ATV and leaned against the seat, taking weight off his bad leg. "I saw something similar when I was in Romania. Except the animal wasn't dead before it was slaughtered and there was a lot more blood."

"In feral packs, that would be a problem." Doc laid a cloth over Cybil's remains. "Even starvation would be a possibility, but not in Walker's Run."

"Were Jaxen's vaccination records verified?"

All eyes targeted Tristan.

"Before Jaxen arrived, I called the medical director at Woelfesguarde myself," Doc said. "She gave him a clean bill of health."

"Have you noticed something in Jaxen's behavior that might suggest he could be responsible?" Brice asked.

Other than past experience? "No. I'm considering the timing and he does have a history of violence. I don't want him overlooked because he's my blood-kin."

"And I don't want to swing the spotlight on him unless we find something that warrants looking in his direction." Gavin narrowed his gaze at Tristan, his jaw set, signaling the matter was closed. "Doc, this morning you mentioned a viral outbreak?"

"Several other packs have reported summer epidemics of the wolfan flu. I hadn't seen it here until Jimmy Young came into the clinic a couple of weeks ago. Seems his family may have caught the virus while on a family vacation and brought it home." Doc removed his glasses and wiped away the beads of sweat beneath the rims. "Fever, chills, nausea, headache, nasty stuff. But I doubt anyone infected would have the energy to get out of bed, come into the sanctuary and do this."

"What if someone got sick while inside the sanctuary?" Brice asked.

"With a high fever, some disorientation or delusions…" Doc shrugged. "It is possible."

Anything was possible, even a snowball in hell. But Tristan wouldn't bet on the odds of that happening.

"I'll talk with the sentinels to find out who was in the sanctuary last night," Tristan said.

"I'm going to let Reed and Shane handle this." Gavin held Tristan's gaze. "You're overscheduled as it is. I want you to step back from some of your responsibilities."

"I did, last year." Tristan swallowed his rising temper. "You went ballistic."

"We were reaching a crisis point with Locke. I needed you in the sheriff's department."

"Now you don't?" Tristan folded his arms over his chest, his fingers digging into the muscles of his upper arms. "Or are you suggesting I'm not needed as a sentinel anymore?"

"Tristan." Brice gave him a gentle warning with a slow head shake.

Gavin didn't always make decisions Tristan agreed with, but as the Alpha, Gavin did garner his respect because in the end it was Gavin's job to do what was best for the entire pack. It was a privilege and an obligation that had been passed down the Walker bloodline for generations. Brice would inherit the Alphaship from his father, and eventually, Brenna would inherit from Brice.

The weighty responsibility wasn't one many wanted to shoulder, which was why the line of succession had been established generations ago and continued to be endorsed by the pack.

"You're running on raw nerves, Tristan," Doc said. "I think Gavin is simply suggesting that you relax. Do something fun. Give yourself time to recharge before you burn out."

Unfortunately for Tristan, time was a commodity he couldn't afford.

Hidden from prying resort guests' eyes, Tristan changed into the clothes he'd stashed in the Walker's private gazebo. The weight of the morning's events leaded his feet as he entered the resort through the security entrance. He slid his Co-op ID through the card reader to unlock the interior door to the lobby. A conglomerate of smells emanated from the kitchen, turning his tumultuous stomach.

Restless to the point of nearly crawling out of his skin, Tristan needed something to settle his nerves. Usually, he ran in the wolf sanctuary when out of sorts. Considering what he'd left behind there, he wasn't in any hurry to return.

Crossing the lobby, he instinctively looked for Nel. Coming or going, he'd grown used to catching a glimpse of her. After Monday night, he shouldn't want to see her again.

Still, he wouldn't say he regretted spending the night with her. And since he was in a rebellious mood, he cut past the dark lounge and headed for the spiral stairs, taking two steps at a time to the second floor and heading to the activities room, breaking another cardinal rule: never seek out a woman he'd recently bedded.

Unnoticed, he leaned against the door frame. A few long honey strands had slipped from the ribbon tying her hair and curled around her face. Padding around in her bare feet, she wore black leggings with a dark green V-neck top that gave a modest peek at her beautiful cleavage.

Longing broke in his chest.

Popsicle sticks and glue bottles scattered across the big round table. All hands were busy, faces scrunched in concentration as Nel bobbed from one child to the other, offering words of instruction, encouragement and praise in the same breath. Her movements were natural, unpretentious and captivatingly beautiful. She was in her element. And Tristan loved that she was.

"Do you like my basket?" A little girl tugged his arm.

"Madison," Nel called out. "You didn't ask permission to get up. Please return to your seat."

"I wanted to show him my basket," the child protested. "See?" She held it up to Tristan.

"It's lovely." He squatted next to her.

"Madison." Nel shot Tristan a glance that signaled he was encroaching on her territory.

"Uh-oh," Tristan said. "I think you should listen to your teacher before we both end up in the corner for a time-out."

The little girl's giggles filled the room as she trotted back to her seat.

Nel moved toward him and he stood, tucking his hands in his pockets to keep from touching her.

Her gaze roamed the length and breadth of him before settling on his face. Worry darkened her eyes. "What's wrong?"

"Nothing," he lied.

"Something must've happened. You're pale and tense. Are you okay?" She touched his arm.

"Yeah, I..." The dam broke inside him, and all the tumultuous emotions from the morning rushed him like a tidal wave. Barely able to catch his breath from the deluge, Tristan pulled Nel close and buried his face in the curve of her neck, allowing her scent to cleanse his senses. His coiled muscles relaxed. The tension thumping his brain eased.

"Miss Nel? Is he your boyfriend?" Madison called out.

Nel turned her head toward the class. "No." She wiggled free of Tristan's embrace, but took his hand. "I want all of you to put the finishing touches on your baskets. I'll be back in a moment and we'll start cleaning up."

A collective chant filled the room. "Miss Nel has a boyfriend. Miss Nel has a boyfriend."

"All right! Enough goofing." She pointed at them. "Everyone needs to be on their best behavior. I don't want to be disappointed when I come back." Nel nudged Tristan into the hallway and closed the door behind them, leaving it slightly ajar. "I don't know what this is about. But in the future, please refrain from hugging me like that in front of the children. It's distracting to them."

Her words lacked true anger.

"So, I can do this as long as the kids aren't looking?" Tristan's hands slid over her curves as he pulled her close and touched his nose to the sweet spot behind her ear and inhaled.

Damn, he could get drunk off her scent.

"Ummm...that's not what I meant." Cheeks pink, Nel pushed away from him and checked her watch. "I have a half hour before I'm done. If you aren't busy, we could have lunch in the dining room."

"I can't," he said truthfully. "I have to change for work, got a ten-hour shift today."

"Oh, okay."

"I'll take a rain check." He shouldn't have said that, but her sweet smile alone made him forget why a rain check was such a bad idea.

Chapter 13

"Hungry?" Standing on the dark porch, Tristan's heated gaze moved over Nel like slow-dripping molasses. "I called when I got off duty, but it went to voice mail. I gambled that you would still be up, painting." He held up two take-out bags.

Nel's stomach answered for her. Loudly and undeniably.

The brilliance of his self-assured smile nearly killed her, because her heart stopped beating and her lungs stopped processing air.

"I'll take that as a yes." Chuckling, he stepped inside.

Nel locked the door. "Make yourself comfortable."

The words were unnecessary. Tristan had already draped his uniform shirt over the back of the couch, his white undershirt was untucked and he was in the process of toeing off his work boots.

"I need to bring in my canvas."

"Want help?"

Tristan followed her to the back porch. She gathered the scattered supplies into a large tackle box.

"You painted this?" He stood in front of the canvas

of the MacGregor antebellum house. Surprise danced in his eyes.

"Yes, but the sunlight isn't quite right." She showed him the photo on her phone.

He held the device next to the painting. "There's barely a resemblance."

Her heart sank. "I know. It's terrible. I'll probably whitewash it tomorrow and start over."

"Don't you dare." He lifted the easel, canvas and all, off the ground. "It's beautiful."

"You said it didn't look like the picture."

"It's a hundred times better." He carried the easel into the cabin. "The photo doesn't capture the movement of the trees or the sunlight glinting off the leaves. The painting makes me feel like I'm there."

"Really?" She directed him to the kitchen nook, where a large round table was covered with a tarp and littered with art supplies.

"I wouldn't say it if it weren't true." He sat the easel close to the bay window and studied the other canvases in various stages of development. "How long have you been painting?"

"On and off since the accident. The shard of glass that cut my arm damaged some nerves and nearly severed a tendon. Art therapy helped me regain the use of my hand and provided a way for me to deal with the grief of losing my parents."

"Nel—" Tristan made a start toward her, and hesitated.

"It was a long time ago." She waved off the melancholy threatening to settle. "The food is getting cold. I'll get the plates and utensils."

"There's a couple of spoons and forks in the bag and I don't mind eating from the containers."

"Something to drink?" Nel opened the refrigerator. "Which wine goes best, white or red?"

"White works for me." Tristan snagged two glasses from the cabinet. "Have you had any showings?"

"I wish." Bottle in hand, Nel followed him into the living room. "But I haven't shown anyone my portfolio to be considered."

"Why not?"

"I'm not talented enough for a gallery."

"Have you seen your paintings?" Tristan plopped onto the couch, his long legs stretched beneath the coffee table. He unpacked half a dozen food containers from the bags he'd brought with him.

"This will feed more than two people."

"You have seen me eat, right?" He winked and a flush spread over her skin.

She peeked into the containers. "What is all this?"

"This one—" Tristan pointed to the far left "—is the classic pepper steak."

He waited for her to sample the dish. The flavor was decent, but not spectacular.

"This is the *pad see ew* with chicken."

"Um, this is good."

Next, she tried the shrimp fried rice, the pad thai, the duck noodle soup and the garlic pork.

"Which is your favorite?"

"I'm gonna pick—" Nel waved her hand over all the containers "—this one!" She grabbed the *pad see ew*.

Tristan stared at the box in her hand, an indescribable look on his face.

"What's wrong?"

"That's my favorite, too."

"You don't want to share, do you?" She waggled the container at him.

"Well, it is my favorite," he said lightly, with no effort to retrieve the box from her.

"What's your second favorite?"

"I'm not telling. You might swipe that one, too."

"I don't mind sharing if you don't." She scooted close enough their hips touched.

"Deal." He stuck his spoon in the shrimp fried rice and scooped out a large bite.

"Do you usually eat this late?"

"Depends on my work schedule. On average, I put in four or five ten-to-twelve-hour shifts a week. We're a small department, so our in and out times change to ensure twenty-four-hour coverage."

"I can't imagine much happens around here. Maico seems pretty sedate."

He shrugged, finished chewing and placed the rice container on the coffee table. "I need to tell you something."

She put her container of food next to his and swiveled on the couch to face him directly. "If you're secretly married, engaged, or committed to someone get ready to handcuff me for assault on a law enforcement officer because I swear I'll slap you."

"I'm not, but I can put you in handcuffs all the same." The huskiness in his voice sparked an internal heat wave to dampen Nel's skin.

He leaned closer, his searing gaze evaporating her breath. The air crackled from the energy passing between them. "It's still there, isn't it? This thing between us."

All Nel could do was stare and swallow the pocket of air caught in her throat.

"What is it about you?" He held her gaze, searching, probing, all the way to the depths of her being. "I couldn't keep you off my mind, all damn day."

"Really?" A rush of giddiness made her giggle. Too old for schoolgirl silliness, she stifled it immediately. Tristan was out of her league. Trying to handle him so that her heart wouldn't get involved was as foolish as a red-attired matador with a broken leg challenging an angry bull. A disaster in the making.

Tristan's arm slipped comfortably around her waist. A thrill of excitement looped through her belly. Gently, he nuzzled the curve of her neck and she found herself defying logic and snuggling into his warmth.

Rubbing her cheek against his head, she inhaled deeply. His masculine scent reminded her of the fresh smell of the forest with a subtle spice.

"You smell so good." The tremble of Tristan's deep voice rumbled in her chest.

"I was thinking the same about you."

His hand slipped beneath her shirt, warming her skin despite the sudden emergence of chill bumps. Her nipples pebbled and ached for his attention.

The soft puffs of Tristan's breath against her throat, where he nuzzled her, turned to whisper-soft kisses.

Oh, god.

Any second now, the clothes would come off and they would end up having sex again. Every feminine cell in her body celebrated. If not for a steady beacon of reason shining through the lustful fog, she might've surrendered.

"We have to stop." Nel slapped her hand against his chest. Even through his T-shirt, her palm mapped every detail of his muscled torso.

Tristan's kisses and caresses ceased and her body silently screamed in protest. He met her gaze. In his eyes, she saw a flash of disappointment, confusion and resignation.

"You're right." His voice was thick, raw and full of…

need? Desire? Regret? Nel wasn't quite sure, but she was surprisingly disheartened that he acquiesced without question.

He sat back. Those long, tapered fingers that had branded her belly now stroked his jaw, which was covered with a dark gold shadow from a day's growth of beard. Totally relaxed and absolutely scrumptious, he offered her a soft smile. Unlike the stellar flash-of-teeth smile that could turn the head of every woman within a hundred-mile radius, this smile was the real Tristan. Kind, intelligent, wounded.

This smile would be hard to defend against.

"You have something to tell me, remember?"

"There was an incident in the woods between the resort and the sanctuary. An animal mutilation of a family pet." The glimpse of his vulnerability became cloaked in an aura of serious professionalism. Even the cadence of his voice changed, as if some part of him had disconnected.

Maybe it was his way of compartmentalizing his job and his personal life.

"We don't know who's responsible yet. So don't go on the trails alone, especially at night."

"Was it one of the wolves?"

"Not one of ours." Something dark flashed in Tristan's eyes. "Until we catch the culprit, I don't want you painting on the porch at night."

"You think I would be in danger on resort property?" Nel picked up her wine glass to have something to do with her hands. "I thought security routinely patrolled the area."

"They do. But I'd rather know you're safe inside than worry you're outside where something might happen."

"You would worry about me?"

"Yeah, and if you feel uneasy or if something happens, call me. Immediately." He hooked his thumb beneath her chin and turned her face toward him at the same time she went to sip her wine.

"Great," she mumbled at the splash on her shirt.

"Any time, any day, for any reason." Tristan's palm cupped her cheek, distracting her from the damp spot on her chest. "Got it?"

"I, um…" She glanced away from the rich, vast depths of his dark brown eyes. And those lips, even frowning, were oh so kissable. "I need your number again."

"Why?" He leaned in close, his face absolute beauty in symmetry.

"I sorta deleted it."

"What?" An uncanny growl tinged his voice. "I wanted you to have it in case you needed help. On Co-op property, 911 calls are routed by dispatch to me. It saves time to call me directly."

"Oh." Nel's cheeks warmed. "I thought you meant for me to use it for a booty call."

"Yeah?" All traces of annoyance were wiped clean by a mischievous grin. "That works, too."

"Not for me," she said, more confidently than she felt. "One night was all this *thing* between us was supposed to be."

"It's still there. Or am I wrong?"

He wasn't wrong by a long shot. "Neither of us wants a relationship."

"It doesn't have to be one." The charming, enticing, tempting smile was back. "We could let this *thing* run its course, get it out of our systems and say goodbye when it's over."

"I don't think it's a good idea to encourage it."

Tristan frowned and she could almost hear the gamut of thoughts wheeling in his mind. "Maybe you're right."

He grabbed the food container she had abandoned and grinned. "Mine now." Without sparing her another glance, he shoveled a giant spoonful into his mouth.

"Hey." She elbowed him, then placed her glass on the coffee table. "Were you seducing me just to grab my chicken *pad see ew*?"

"It worked, didn't it?" Though Tristan's tone was playful, she glimpsed the longing and indecision reflected in his eyes.

Somehow, it made her feel better to know that her emotions weren't the only ones jumbled. Nel reached for the garlic pork and resettled on the couch with space between them. A moment later, Tristan refilled their wine glasses and subtly inched close enough to her that their thighs rubbed when either moved.

The electric charge between them ebbed into a comfortable pulse.

Despite the wisdom to not encourage the strange connection between them, Nel had the feeling that was exactly what they were doing.

Chapter 14

"Get cleaned up before your mom sees you." Tristan shoved Jaxen into the men's restroom inside the hospital.

He should've been grateful for the interruption in his late-night dinner with Nel. His fascination with her had gone further, his feelings deeper, than they ever should have.

Instead, he'd been irritated by his father's call for him to find Jaxen and escort him to the hospital to see Ruby, who had been admitted for a severe asthma attack.

Jaxen stumbled to the sink and turned on the faucet. He shot Tristan an ungrateful look in the mirror, then scrubbed the dried blood from his mouth and chin.

Tristan didn't look much better with a bruise darkening his left cheek.

Jaxen hadn't taken kindly to Tristan hauling him out of Mad Dog's, a biker bar in Hiawassee. But it was the accusatory interrogation into his whereabouts during the time of Cybil's mutilation that had incited the first punch, a left hook that Tristan hadn't seen coming. Stunned, but quick to respond, Tristan had slammed his fist into Jaxen's laughing mouth. Tristan wasn't proud to admit he might've goaded Jaxen into throwing a punch just to land one himself.

Neither took the fight further. They were too well matched in size and bulk. No one would've come out the winner tonight.

Tristan splashed water on his face and ran damp fingers through his hair.

Jaxen tucked his shirttail into his jeans. Tristan, still in uniform, cocked his head toward the door. "Let's go."

Exiting the restroom, they proceeded to the main part of the hospital and turned down the left corridor. The west wing was devoted entirely to the Co-op members and where Doc treated all Wahyas. They didn't receive a different quality of care than the human patients in the east wing, but the separation was a necessary precaution. A sick or injured wolfan could quickly turn dangerous, and the west wing barrier doors assured that the human patients and employees were protected.

Tristan slid his Co-op ID through the card reader next to the steel double doors and glanced up at the security camera. The locks clicked and the doors slowly opened.

"Hey, Tristan." The wolfan night clerk seated behind the semicircular counter beamed a smile.

"Nice to see you, Katherine." He nodded. Ordinarily, he offered the people he greeted a smile. Tonight he lacked the energy and the effort required. He wanted to get Jaxen to Ruby's room, find out her condition and leave.

He wouldn't return to Nel's place, though. He needed to decompress from her company and establish an amicable distance between them before he did something stupid.

"Jaxen Pyke?" Katherine stood. "Is that you?"

"None other." Jaxen flashed an over-the-top smile that made Tristan roll his eyes. "How are you, Katie-belle?"

She squealed and dashed around the counter to hug Jaxen. "You remembered!"

"Ah, love." Looking over the she-wolf's head, he winked at Tristan. "How could I forget a woman as pretty and warm as you?"

Tristan's stomach flopped at the insincerity he saw in Jaxen's eyes. But hadn't he been guilty of the same? Sweet-talking women to stroke his ego and take him to bed, if only briefly?

"Oh, stop." She laughed, lightly swatting Jaxen's chest. "You're just as incorrigible as your cousin."

Jaxen whispered something in her ear. Tristan knew from Katherine's posturing that Jaxen had secured a bed buddy for later.

"I'm going to see Ruby," Tristan said, walking down the corridor. He didn't need to ask which room. All he needed to do was follow the raised voices.

Just before he went inside, Jaxen bumped past him to enter first.

"Mama?" He hurried to Ruby's bedside, the loving son in overly dramatic action.

Tristan believed that Jaxen did love his mother, but the doting part was merely an act to garner praise from Tristan's father, who was in the room.

Steeling himself, Tristan entered. He always felt like a rabbit hopping into a hungry wolves' den whenever his family gathered.

"Jax get the better of you?" Nate scowled at his son. "Again?"

Tristan swallowed his response and like a tightly held breath it fisted in his chest. He was here to see Ruby, not to get into an altercation with his father.

"What did Doc say?"

"Same as always," Nate replied. "He's keeping her overnight for observation. Expects she'll be okay to go home tomorrow."

Tristan stepped to the end of the hospital bed, noting the IV line plugged into Ruby's thin, frail arm and the oxygen tubing beneath her nose.

In her younger days, she and Tristan's father had greatly favored each other in appearance. Now her dark blond hair had faded to a dingy gray, and her face was deeply lined and weathered.

"If I've told you once," she heaved, "I've told you a thousand times. I don't like it when you boys fight."

"We weren't fighting, Mama." Jaxen's voice dropped low and soft and placating. "You know I always look out for Trist."

Tristan's stomach lurched.

"He needs to learn to protect his left side." Jaxen sounded so sincere that Tristan wanted to puke. "He's got a dangerous job. I don't want some asshole taking him down because he didn't see the threat."

"That's my boy." Ruby gently patted Jaxen's cheek.

Tristan dropped his chin to his chest. Insanity was thinking that things could ever change. Even if he fixed the rift between himself and Jaxen, he could never fix what was wrong with his family. They thrived on conflict and turmoil, and for some reason, he didn't.

He eased out of the room, but the weight of the chaos remained on his shoulders.

"Tristan!" His father halted him in the hallway. "What was your fight with Jaxen about?"

"I asked a question he didn't like."

"About him taking over the business?" Nate shoved his hands into his pockets.

"If I wanted to punch someone about that, Dad, it would be you."

Nate nodded. "Guess I deserve that."

"I think it's a mistake, but it's yours to make."

"You've never shown any interest in my business."

"You never tried to involve me."

"You've made your own way, Tristan. Jaxen has no anchor. I want to give him something to work toward, something to be proud of."

"How's that working out?"

Nate looked past Tristan. "He needs someone to keep him on track."

"I'm not going to be his babysitter."

"When Jaxen's father died, I promised Ruby I would look out for him."

"You promised, not me."

"He's your blood-kin."

"By blood-rights, Jaxen is your responsibility. You are the oldest male in the bloodline. You made the promise," Tristan said. "Gavin asked me to be Jaxen's friend again. Not his keeper. That's a line I cannot and will not cross."

"As far as I can tell, you haven't been much of a friend to him."

"That river flows both ways, Dad."

"You need to get over what happened when you were kids."

"If you knew what really happened, I hope you wouldn't say that. But you've never been able to accept the truth about Jaxen and I'm tired of trying to convince you."

Tristan turned to leave. "Watch yourself around him, Dad. He just might push *you* off a cliff."

Chapter 15

"Hey, pretty lady."

Nel looked up from her sketch pad expecting Tristan. A man very similar in size and appearance knelt beside her. "Hi?"

"Remember me?" He smiled, bright and broad, but it didn't have the warmth of Tristan's smiles.

"You were at Taylor's Monday night. You're Tristan's cousin, Jaxen. Right?"

"Yeah." Jaxen's smile faltered slightly. "I didn't get a chance to catch your name, love."

"Penelope." She pushed the sunglasses from her face, clearly remembering that Tristan had told Jaxen her name.

"What are you doing alone in the middle of the park on such a fine day?"

Hardly alone. Though not bustling with the activity she'd seen shortly after her arrival before one o'clock, Maico's little town square, with its lovely green park, shady oaks and the old, Colonial-style courthouse, still had at least a half dozen benchwarmers enjoying the beautiful afternoon.

"My car is getting serviced across the street, so I decided to make some sketches of the park while I waited."

"Are you new in town?" Jaxen's gaze leisurely dropped to Penelope's chest and lingered.

"Yep, just here for the summer."

"If you're interested in seeing the local sights, I'd love to show you around."

"What is there to see?"

"Track Rock isn't too far of a drive from here." His gaze slid over her generous figure. "But it's quite a hike from the parking area to the petroglyphs."

"Too bad." She wiggled a lovely pair of sandals that showcased a fabulous pedicure. "I didn't pack hiking boots."

"No worries, love."

"Do you work around here?"

"Nah, I was headed to the pharmacy to pick up a few things for my mother. I'm co-owner of a construction company. When my uncle retires, I'll become the sole owner."

"That's great."

"It can be labor intensive, but I like working with my hands and building things."

"Amelia!" a woman yelled from across the park.

Nel and Jaxen both turned toward the laughing little girl running as fast as her little legs could carry her.

"Amelia! Come here!" the mother called again.

"Do you know her?" Nel asked as the child headed straight toward them.

"She's definitely not mine," Jaxen said.

The closer the child came, the clearer it became that Jaxen was her destination. He watched her draw near but made no effort to call to her.

"Tiskan!" she squealed. "Tiskan!" Arms outstretched, she ran right up to Jaxen.

He stared at her as if he'd never encountered a child before.

"I think she wants a hug," Nel prodded him.

"Hey, little lady." He patted the child's back with the palm of his hand. "Your mama's looking for you."

The little girl looked straight up at Jaxen and screamed. A blood-curdling and ear-piercing scream.

Jaxen stepped back.

Nel rubbed the child's arm. "It's okay, little one. Your mommy is coming. Look!" She pointed at the young woman rushing to her child, her breasts jostling as she ran.

Nel glanced at Jaxen watching the woman, a leering grin on his face until he noticed Nel studying him.

"Amelia! What's wrong?" The woman grabbed her child. "Did she step on something?"

"I don't think so," Nel answered. "She ran up and started screaming."

The mother picked up the child to soothe her. "Amelia is usually excited to see..." She paused, taking another look at Jaxen. "Oh, she thought you were Tristan. She loves him to pieces. I guess when she realized you weren't him, she got scared."

"No harm done." Jaxen flashed the mother a big smile, but Nel noticed the tightness in his jaw.

"It's really uncanny, though," the mother continued. "You look an awful lot like him."

"They're cousins," Nel said when Jaxen offered no reply.

"When you see Tristan, tell him Melly said hello." Mother and daughter walked away, hand in hand.

Jaxen looked at Nel. "I didn't know a kid could sound like that."

As a kindergarten teacher, Nel had heard worse from children with social skills delays or separation anxiety. "It can be surprising what comes out of their mouths."

Jaxen picked up the sketchbook that had fallen from Nel's lap when she was trying to comfort the little girl. "These are good," he said, flipping the pages too fast to actually admire the drawings.

"Thanks." Nel gathered her supplies into her bag.

"I need to pick up my mom's medication and check in on her." Jaxen didn't offer to help Nel stand. "Wanna meet up for dinner later?"

Generally, Nel didn't turn down a first date, preferring to get to know someone a little better before deciding her interest. Still, she hesitated in accepting Jaxen's offer. He didn't quite creep her out and he hadn't set off any internal alarms, but something just didn't feel quite right about him.

"Oh, you're so sweet, but I already have plans with my friend Marie."

Nel had been meeting up with "Marie Callender" in the freezer section of the grocery store ever since college.

"Another time, then."

With a friend as dependable as Marie, Nel doubted it.

"You look like death warmed over." Mabel Whitcomb, owner of Mabel's Diner, sidled behind the lunch counter and stopped in front of Tristan.

He felt like it, too.

His left eye and cheek were still swollen from the punch Jaxen threw last night, and he'd had a fitful night's sleep, periodically waking up craving Nel's company.

"Well, you look as lovely as ever, Mabel." Tristan

forced a smile for the elderly restaurateur sporting a red beehive hairdo and bright blue eye shadow.

"Hush your mouth." Smiling, she swatted at the air. "I'm wise to that silver tongue of yours."

"Doesn't stop me from trying," he teased.

"Your charm doesn't work on me. Turn it on some young lady who'll make you stop working yourself to death."

"I'm tired, Mabel, not dying."

"Life ain't all about work, sug. You have to do some living, too."

He pushed aside his empty plate. "A week from Saturday I'm going rafting with Youth Outreach."

"That's work. You're going to keep an eye on the kids, not have fun."

"Fun is for kids, not adults." He reached into his back pocket for his wallet.

"'Cause you're doing it wrong." She waved away his money. "Your lunch is always on the house. 'Preciate your service to the town."

Mabel tootled off and Tristan vacated his spot, dropping a fifty-dollar bill into the collection jar for the fire department's annual fund-raiser.

Stepping through the crowd waiting to be seated, he exited the diner.

Sunshine warmed his face. His missed the lazy summer days he'd loved as a kid. Despite what he'd led Mabel to believe, Tristan looked forward to a day of white-water rafting. The outdoors and exercise, something more stimulating than his wolf patrols, would do him good.

Laughter across the street caught his attention. Scanning the park, he saw Nel and Jaxen. Together.

What is Jaxen doing with her?

Jealousy reared and startled him. He'd never been jealous before and didn't like the distaste that filled him. He had no reason to be jealous. Nel could talk to anyone she wanted to. He didn't have an exclusive with her. In fact, he wasn't quite sure what he had with her.

Instead of jaywalking, Tristan crossed the side street to Wyatt's Automotive Services and waited for traffic to clear on the main road. He heard a high-pitched squeal. In the park, he spotted a toddler in a pink outfit clapping her hands. Amelia Franklin. The first and only baby he'd delivered.

On the side of the road. In a snowstorm.

She squealed again and bolted.

"Amelia, stop!" her mother yelled, but the kid beelined straight toward Tristan.

"Shit!" He darted between two cars and dashed across the other lane. As a wolfan, he was faster than humans but he didn't have superstrength or superpowers. If he got hit, it would hurt like hell or kill him. As her little feet padded onto the asphalt, Tristan whisked the child into his arms. Her laughter rang out as if they were playing a game.

A horn blew, long and loud. Tires screeched. Before Tristan could move, pain exploded in his right hip and leg. Cradling the child against his chest, he rolled up onto the hood of the car. His shoulder smashed the windshield.

Amelia started crying.

"Shhh," he cooed, ignoring his own pain. "You're all right, Melly. We're all right."

All the distant voices converged and boomed in his head. As Tristan sat up with the child, Amelia's mother rushed up to grab her.

"Thank you, thank you, thank you," Sarah said, crying hysterically from fright and relief. The child reached toward him, calling, "Tiskan."

"I'm okay, sweetie." He kissed her chubby hand. "Get her checked out at the clinic."

"I will." The mother hugged him and he gritted his teeth against the pain. "That's twice I owe you for her life."

"Tristan!" Nel pushed through the gathering crowd.

She didn't rush to hug him like Amelia's mom. Instead, she stood close and cupped his face. "You're bleeding."

"I am?" Funny, he hadn't tasted the coppery tang in his mouth until then. He spat. "Must've bit my tongue."

"Someone call an ambulance." Nel swung her gaze around the crowd.

"One's on the way," Jaxen said. "I hear the siren."

"I just need to walk it off." Tristan stepped forward. His entire right side felt consumed with fire.

"That walk is going to have to wait." Jaxen caught him before he collapsed. In Tristan's ear, he whispered, "One day, playing hero is gonna get you killed."

Chapter 16

"Good news." Doc Habersham smiled as he entered the treatment bay. "Nothing's broken. You get to go home."

"Why do I hurt so bad?" Tristan's breaths came in short, quick pants. Every muscle in his body tightened against the pain.

"Your right side is severely bruised."

"I've never hurt like this in all my life." Tristan looked at his friend Brice. "Gives me a new appreciation of what you went through."

"I barely remember it. Doc kept me in a medicated coma through most of it."

"Sounds good to me." Especially since every breath felt like a sharp knife slicing through his chest.

"You're bruised on one side, not mauled head to toe. Big difference," Doc said.

"Pain is pain." Tristan's skin was slick from sweat. The medication Doc had given him earlier had barely taken the edge off.

"The hospital pharmacy is filling your prescription. Take one pill when you get home and stay off your leg as much as possible. No driving and you'll be out of work for a few days, if not a week."

"Great," Tristan mumbled.

"Tristan?" Nel's shy, sweet voice called him from the doorway. "I've been waiting for hours and no one would tell me anything."

Doc and Brice gave him a curious look.

"Nothing broken, so I've been told." Grinning like a fool, he waved her forward. "Come on in."

Tristan introduced Nel to Doc and Brice but gave them no insight as to why he was so damn glad to see her.

"Are you going to need a ride home?" Brice asked, his gaze falling on Tristan's hand closing over Nel's fingers as she stood bedside.

"I'll take him." Nel volunteered, and for some reason Tristan preferred that she did.

"Call me if you need anything," Brice said as he left.

"I've written the discharge orders. You can leave when the pharmacy tech brings your medication." Doc hesitated at the door. "It's best if you stay with someone for a few days, or at least have someone check on you."

"I'll ask Angeline or Shane to drop by." It would be convenient, since they were neighbors.

"I'll send a nurse to help you get dressed."

"I can manage."

Doc left as the tech came in with the meds. He dropped them off and disappeared, leaving Nel and Tristan alone.

"Thanks for coming." Tristan used the remote to raise the head of the bed. "I didn't intend to interrupt your picnic with Jaxen."

"We weren't on a picnic." She helped steady him as he slowly moved one leg then the other off the bed. "I was sketching in the park. He was on an errand for his mother and came over to talk to me."

"Mind handing me my pants?"

Nel picked them up from the chair. "Maybe you should lie down to put them on."

"That would probably hurt worse." He took off the hospital gown.

"You're black and purple." Tears filled her eyes. "Tristan, you could've been killed. Right in front of me, you could've died."

"Ah, Nel." He tucked her against his left side. "I wish you hadn't seen it."

"You didn't think. You just ran and grabbed that baby."

"It was my fault she ran into the road. Whenever she sees me, she wants a hug."

"She's awfully young to be working your charm on her." Some of the sadness lifted from her smile.

Tristan grinned. "Technically, I could be her grandpa. I went to school with her grandmother. Man, that makes me feel old."

"Well, let's get you dressed, gramps." Nel slid his pants onto his legs, helped him stand to pull them over his hips and steadied him while he zipped and buttoned. She made him sit down to put on his shirt, and she put his shoes on his feet so he didn't have to bend over.

"You're supposed to stay off your leg, so I'll bring the car to the patient pick-up area and ask a nurse to bring you out in a wheelchair." Nel was out the door before he could say no.

Nel stopped in the parking lot of the Chatuge View apartments. "Please tell me you're on the first floor."

"Third." Tristan didn't open his eyes.

"Is there an elevator?"

"No." His chest heaved.

"Give me your keys."

"Pocket," was all he said.

"Which one is your apartment?" She reached into his left hip pocket and pulled out his keys.

"The right corner one."

"I'm going to pack some clothes for you. You can stay with me for a couple of days."

"Not necessary. Give me a minute and I'll make it up the stairs."

Like hell he could.

He'd already had a ten-minute nap on the trip from the hospital. One more minute, or two, wasn't going to help him make it up three flights of stairs.

"Stay put." She left the car running so he'd have air conditioning. Poor thing was sweating, probably from pain.

She hurried up the stairs and went into his apartment. Nothing like she expected, it was neat and orderly, the furnishings black-and-white modern. The couch looked stiff and uncomfortable, and the decorations were replicas of modern museum pieces.

In the center of the bedroom was a large, metallic bed. The gray comforter was wadded to the side. The room smelled like him. Funny, she'd not thought about his scent. Fresh, crisp, with a hint of spice.

Nel found a duffel bag in his closet. She picked out a week's worth of T-shirts, several pairs of board shorts and a pair of jeans. She also dropped in socks and a pair of white sneakers. In the bathroom, she collected his toothbrush, a razor, his comb and hair gel. She looked for underwear but didn't find any.

On the way out, she grabbed his phone charger.

Descending the stairs, reality hit. Tristan was supposed to have been a one-night stand. Now she had volunteered to care for him. It was crazy, really, but something in her couldn't leave him alone in this condition. Much like her aunt and uncle, Tristan's family didn't seem to care. No one had come to the emergency clinic to see him, and no one had called since she picked him up.

In good conscience, she couldn't leave him on his own with the risk of him falling and further injuring himself.

Nel tossed the duffel bag into the back seat and slid behind the wheel. "How are you feeling, trooper?"

"Deputy," he whispered. "I feel drugged. Apparently not enough, because I still hurt."

Nel drove carefully, trying not to hit any bumps along the way. When she reached the cabin, she grabbed the duffel bag and unlocked the front door, then returned to Tristan to help him out of the car.

Getting him up the four steps to the porch was quite a chore. They never would've made it up three flights.

She eased him onto the couch.

"Thanks," he panted. "Could really use those pain meds now."

Nel gave him a bottle of water from the fridge and one pain tablet. He downed the pill and guzzled all the water. He leaned back, closing his eyes.

"Before the meds kick in, we need to get you into bed."

A smile spread across his face. One eye opened. "Are you joining me?"

"Not a good idea. You need to rest."

"I could use a nap." His words began to slur.

"Can you stand?"

"Shhurrr."

She helped him to his feet. He leaned heavily on her as they walked down the hallway.

"Come on, let's get your clothes off."

His glazed eyes gleamed. "Yours, too."

He tugged her against him and kissed her with such

intensity and purpose she had a hard time believing he was under the influence. She broke the kiss.

With one hand, he whipped off his shirt and dropped it to the ground. "Your turn."

He reached for her. She took his hands and squeezed. "Sit."

Obediently, he perched on the bed.

"Give me your foot." He lifted the good leg and she pulled off his shoe. "The other one."

He grimaced, barely lifting his work boot from the floor. She eased it off his foot.

He unbuckled his pants and shoved them down his hips. She pulled them off his legs, ignoring his bouncing erection.

"You should lie on your left side and keep the pressure off those bruises."

He frowned, but rolled to his side. She stuck a pillow between his knees. "How's that?"

"I've felt better." His gaze followed her around the room as she picked up his clothes. "Like the night we were both naked."

"The doctor prescribed rest, not sex."

"Later, then." His eyes drifted closed.

Nel waited until his breathing eased to leave the room.

She retrieved the duffel bag from the living room, put his toothbrush and grooming items in the bathroom, then hung his clothes in the bedroom closet. She couldn't resist smoothing his hair from his brow. A soft smile lifted the corner of his mouth.

The dark bruise on his shoulder, spreading down his ribs, caused her throat to tighten. Seeing Tristan protecting a child as he smashed into the windshield of the car that had struck him had made her heart stop. Just that quick, she could've watched him die.

Easily another life snuffed out far too soon.

She kissed his forehead and left the room. Lingering too long would only make her jumbled feelings more convoluted. She needed to keep things simple, uncomplicated.

Yeah? Well that boat had left the harbor the moment they first met.

Chapter 17

Complete and utter darkness surrounded Tristan. No matter which way he turned, he could see nothing but black.

His throat closed around a cry of panic. Heart pounding to near rupture, he tore at the suffocating shroud, but the ethereal fabric slipped through his fingers as if it were air.

A faint voice trickled through the silence. Thank god, he wasn't alone. Relieved, he took his first non-panted breath since awakening in the abyss.

"Tristan?" The sweetly familiar voice came closer.

"Nel!" He had to find her. Fast. Before she disappeared forever.

"I'm here." Her voice swirled around him like colorful, carefree ribbons.

"Where? I can't see you." He turned in frantic circles. "I can't see anything!"

A phantom hand touched his cheek. Tristan grasped the specter's wrist, solid and warm to his touch, and rubbed his nose against the palm. The powdery-soft scent mixed with a touch of paint cleaner loosened the tightness in his chest.

"Nel," he murmured.

"You're having a bad dream." Her arms wrapped around him and his cheek nestled in the crook of her neck, allowing her scent to infiltrate every cell of his being.

How could this be a dream? Her presence was a very real anchor and he was damn grateful that he wasn't alone, she wasn't alone. They would face the void together.

Her fingers ran through his hair and gently kneaded his scalp. He had no idea how long she rocked him, but all the tension in his muscles seemed to pour out of his body, leaving him weak, exhausted and slightly chilled.

Slowly the darkness faded, leaving him with a slight headache. He felt a sluggish disconnect between where he was and where he had been, as if stepping between two dimensions.

"Are you okay?"

The genuine concern in Nel's voice broke open a longing so deep that pain sliced through his heart, sharp and breath stealing.

"Still disoriented?"

Tristan managed a nod.

"Are you prone to nightmares?"

"Not since I was a kid." And those were traumatic dreams of Jaxen pushing him off the rock.

"This one was pretty intense. Fighting the sheets. Yelling."

"Did I hurt you?"

"No. The first time I called your name, you sat up and looked around. I called again and you looked at me. Your eyes were open but you weren't awake, which was weird because you said my name."

"I couldn't see anything, but I was looking for you."

Nel squeezed his hand. "I told you I would be here if you needed anything."

Tristan appreciated her kindness more than he could express.

She eased from the bed.

He stretched his back and pain flared throughout his right side. Grunting, he tossed aside the tangled sheets and scooted to the edge of the bed.

"Where are you going?"

"I need to use the bathroom."

"Doctor Habersham said to stay off your leg." Nel ducked beneath his left shoulder, her arm sliding tentatively around his waist as he stood.

Normally, nudity didn't faze Tristan, but needing Nel's help made him feel vulnerable.

They took slow strides across the hall. Once inside the bathroom, he gripped the edge of the sink. "I can handle it from here."

She looked doubtful.

"Really, Nel. I'd rather do the rest alone."

Her brows drew together. "Let me know if you need me." She backed out, pulling the door mostly closed.

Tristan eased to the commode and relieved himself. He eyed the shower, wanting to clean the sweat from his skin, but didn't have the strength.

After rinsing his hands, Tristan wet the cloth he'd snagged from the linen cabinet above the toilet and lightly washed his body.

"Tristan?" Nel's soft voice turned his damp skin into goose flesh. "Are you okay?"

He shut off the water, hung the cloth on the side of the sink and opened the door. "I'm hungry." Having missed supper, *famished* was more appropriate.

"I figured you would be." She draped his arm over

her shoulders and lightly gripped his bare hip. The return trip to the bedroom was just as slow and laborious. After helping him into bed, she fluffed some pillows behind his back so he could sit up.

He liked how she saw to his comfort, liked the way her hair smelled when she leaned close. He lightly palmed her face, his thumb brushing over the plump apple of her cheek.

Her eyes darkened and soft, halting breaths parted her lips.

If he hadn't been in pain and half starved, Tristan would've hauled her into bed and spent the rest of the night in ecstasy.

"I should get your supper." She pulled away.

Alone, Tristan painstakingly reached for his phone to retrieve his messages. Rafe had towed Tristan's truck from the diner to his apartment. Gavin and Cooter both left instructions that Tristan was off sentinel duty until Doc cleared him. Sheriff Locke had left a similar message.

Melly's mother had called to check on him. So had his neighbor Angeline, Carmen—the director of Youth Outreach where he volunteered, and Shane—also a neighbor and fellow sentinel following closely in Tristan's footsteps. Even Deidre had called. Nothing from his family.

A small, dull ache gnawed at his heart. At least he wasn't a child alone in the hospital, frightened and blind.

Nel's soft footsteps in the hallway ended his dark thoughts. She came into the bedroom, a shy smile on her face and a tray loaded with food in her hands.

His mouth watered and his stomach growled.

"I heard the way to man's heart was through his stomach."

"Whoever said that was right." He patted the mattress.

Pushing the tray toward him, she scooted onto the bed. He left the tray between them, even though he craved her nearness.

She handed him a deluxe sandwich with meat and cheese spilling out of the ends.

"My favorite." He chomped into it.

"I noticed the Blimpie's flyer on your coffee table. When I called and said I was ordering for you, they knew exactly what you wanted and delivered it, too."

He swallowed. "I'm a regular."

"So they said." Nel slowly unwrapped her sandwich, stuffed with veggies. "I have a few places in Atlanta on speed dial. I'm not much of a cook."

"Oh, I love to cook, but it's a lot of hassle for one."

"What about when you have a girlfriend?"

"I don't have girlfriends."

"I bet there are a lot of disappointed women."

Tristan snorted. More than likely their disappointment would come from being *in* an actual relationship with him. His long-ago romance with Deidre had proven that he wasn't any more successful as a long-term partner than his parents.

He glanced at Nel, so quiet, unassuming. Kind.

If ever he could make a go of a mateship, it would be with someone like Nel.

"Pen-pe!" With her arms outstretched and slightly wobbly steps, a small child bounded across the lobby.

Though anxious to check on Tristan, who'd been sleeping peacefully when Nel left for work, she turned to look at the darling girl whose dark strawberry blond curls bounced in tandem with her short strides.

"I told you not to let go of her hand." Cassie frowned at her father-in-law.

"She's quick." Gavin chuckled. "Just like Brice."

"Hello, Miss Brenna."

"Pen-pe." She lifted her arms, her cherub face rosy and happy, her mouth slightly wet from teething.

"Don't you look pretty today." Nel waited for Cassie's nod of approval before picking up the child for a demonstrative hug and a big kiss on her soft cheek. Brenna squealed in delight and clasped her arms around Nel's neck. "Are you and your mom having lunch with grandpa?"

"No." Brenna's blue eyes sparkled. "Be-bes."

"My friend Grace is stopping by with her twins," Cassie said. "Brenna adores them."

Brenna sniffled, hiding her face against Nel's shoulder.

"You aren't pretending to be shy, are you?" Nel lightly tickled her.

Brenna's laughter echoed around them until she grabbed Nel's hand and brought it her nose.

"What's the matter, sweetie? Do I stink?"

Brenna shook her head. "Tiskan!"

"She's asking about Tristan," Cassie said. "She must've heard Brice telling me about Tristan's accident and that you took him home."

"Em see Tiskan." Brenna clapped her hands.

"I'm sorry, honey," Nel said to Brenna. "Tristan won't be here today. He's still sore from his boo-boo."

"Tiskan boo-boo?" Brenna's bottom lip protruded and her dark blue eyes rounded.

"He's all right, sweetie. I'm sure he'll come see you as soon as he can." Nel kissed Brenna's head and handed her to Cassie.

"Would you like to join us for lunch?" Cassie asked.

"Thanks, but I want to get back to the cabin and check on Tristan."

"He's at your cabin?" A slew of warnings, or advice, or maybe encouragements danced in Cassie's eyes. Nel didn't really know Cassie well enough to decipher, but there was definitely an intended message in the look she flashed.

"He never would've made it up three flights of stairs to his apartment yesterday," Nel said. "And the doctor said Tristan should stay with someone for a few days."

"We'll get lunch another time, then." Cassie's smile was warm and genuine. "And please let us know if Tristan needs anything. He wouldn't tell us himself."

"I will."

"Bye-bye." Brenna waved as she left with her mother.

"Brenna is quite taken with you." Gavin's narrowed blue gaze dissected Nel with laser-like precision.

Nel didn't know why; she had nothing to hide.

"As are the children who've attended the workshops this week," Gavin continued. "You have quite a knack for handling them. Not everyone does."

"I lost my parents at a young age," she said. "My guardians believed children were a nuisance. They never provided any encouragement, though they had an end-less supply of criticisms. So, for every child I meet, I give them as much love and encouragement as possible because it may be all they get."

"I don't think your gift ends with children, Nel. And it is a gift." Gavin's smile lightened the intensity of his eyes, but just barely. "Tristan was one of those children, ignored, neglected. He grew into a singular force only a fool would dare to reckon with, and as damn close as any man could possibly come to being an island unto himself."

"I don't understand your point."

"It may have been a simple decision for you to bring

Tristan to your cabin to help him recover, but for him to *accept* your help is monumental."

Nel's skin prickled at the notion of what Gavin might be suggesting, but doubted the feasibility of anything developing between her and Tristan, other than friendship.

"Don't look so pensive, my dear." Gavin touched her arm. "I simply wanted you to understand that your kindness toward Tristan is appreciated."

After saying goodbye, Nel hurried to her car and drove the short distance to the cabin. The closer she came, the faster her heart beat.

She practically bounded up the wooden steps to the porch. If Tristan's meds had worn off, likely he would be prowling around when he should be off his feet.

The television was on, the volume low, but the living room was empty.

"Tristan?" She heard movement. Then his low, deep voice touched her ears.

He sat at the kitchen bar. Cell phone to his ear. When he saw her, a soft smile lifted the corners of his mouth. His eyes, though, lacked their usual vibrancy.

"I'll be fine in time for the field trip." He nodded. "Yes. I'm sure. No broken bones." He paused. "No, I hadn't heard about Sam's dad."

Nel went to the refrigerator and pulled out a container of duck noodle soup and gathered items for a salad.

"I ordered a pizza," Tristan told her, hand covering the phone. "Half veggie, half meat lovers."

Nel's stomach growled. Who wouldn't want carbs over lettuce? She reshelved the leftovers.

"I don't believe in omens." Tristan continued his phone conversation. "Good or bad."

I'm going to change, she mouthed to Tristan.

"Carmen, hold on a sec." He caught Nel's arm as she passed by.

An electric charge skipped up her arm from the sizzle of Tristan's touch.

"Need something?" Nel's voice cracked.

He didn't seem to notice.

"We're short a volunteer to chaperone a Youth Outreach field trip in a couple of weeks. We're taking the kids white-water rafting and then into Helen for a picnic. Interested?"

Nel's heart didn't know whether to speed up or stop.

One, she wasn't a huge fan of being in water. She could swim—well, dog-paddle—to keep from drowning, but after surviving a deadly hurricane, recreational water activities weren't high on her list of things to do.

Two, Gavin's words haunted her. From his speech, it wasn't too hard to figure out that Tristan had never asked anyone for help. Without waiting to be asked, she'd just stepped in because he needed help and it was the right thing to do. Now he was actually asking for her assistance.

Sorta.

He might've meant it as an invitation, but she sensed that if another chaperone wasn't found, the outing might be canceled.

Tristan held her gaze. He offered no pleading puppy-dog look. Instead, his eyes seemed to say he expected her to say no.

The sliver of irritation it caused was enough to break the tie on her indecision.

"Sounds like fun. Count me in."

Tristan didn't smile, at first. His eyes widened in a flash of disbelief. "Are you sure?"

"You do want me to go, don't you?"

"Absolutely." Now he smiled.

His entire face smiled. Relaxed, radiant and way too much for her to handle.

"I'll teach you everything you need to know. We're going to have so much fun!"

Oh, yes, she would.

Right up until the moment her heart smashed against the rocks they would soon be rafting. It would happen; some things were inevitable.

Chapter 18

Tristan startled awake on the couch. Gripped around the remote, his hand rested on his stomach. Women on a midmorning talk show yammered about some vague topic he couldn't quite register. He must've fallen asleep once Nel had left for work. After having her to himself all weekend, he sorely missed her company.

He shoved himself into a sitting position. His muscles stretched and protested with an achy pain. At least the sharp stabbing had lessened over the last couple of days.

Maybe tonight he'd feel well enough to test the waters with Nel again. After all, they were sharing a bed.

He'd refused to let her sleep on the couch, telling her he would go home if she did. Nel was too kindhearted to let him leave.

With her warmth and intoxicating scent to soothe him, he'd had the best night's sleep in recent memory, despite the pain every time he moved.

Knock. Knock. Knock.

So it hadn't been the television that had awakened him, after all.

He swung his feet off the couch and slowly stood. The

soreness in his muscles made him feel old. He hobbled a few steps, then, as his muscles warmed, his gait became more fluid.

Another knock landed as he gripped the doorknob.

A tall blonde woman in a cream-colored Oscar de la Renta pantsuit stood on the porch.

"Mom?"

Suzannah Durrance delicately removed her ridiculously big designer sunglasses. "You look like shit. Go clean up." She waltzed past him.

Tristan closed the door, scratching his nearly three-day-old beard. Nel liked the scruffy look. Her eyes had warmed and a soft breath had parted her lips when she told him.

"Why are you here?"

"I should ask you the same." Suzannah glanced around the living room, the downward curl of her mouth deepening. She hated rustic decor and it annoyed her that the Walkers hadn't gone with her posher recommendations when they remodeled the resort and the cabins. "Really, Tristan. If you needed a place to recuperate, you should've called me."

"I can manage." He would've camped out in his truck before he went back to the home his parents shared in Walker's Run. And her Atlanta condo was too far to drive while taking pain pills.

"Why didn't you call me? I didn't know you were hurt until I spoke with Cooter this morning because I couldn't reach you. Running out in front of a car? I taught you better than that, Tristan."

Actually, his parents had taught him very little, except to never, ever claim a mate. They only had two modes whenever they were in the same room, fighting or fucking. Those two activities had consumed them during his childhood; they'd had no time to handle him.

"I saved a little girl's life."

"My son being a hero wouldn't have been a comfort to me if you were dead."

Tristan doubted he was much comfort to her alive. The only thing she loved was her interior design business in Atlanta. And maybe her artsy friends.

Suzannah thrived on being included in the inner circle of Atlanta's art scene. She never missed a gala or a showing, especially at the Michaud Galleria d'Art.

"Coffee." He headed into the kitchen. He needed a lot of caffeine, and maybe a shot of whiskey, to deal with his mother.

She strolled into the nook where Nel stored her artwork.

He poured a large cup of coffee and downed a giant swallow without offering his mother a cup. She only drank specialty-shop coffee.

"Whose are these?" She picked up the canvas of the MacGregor homestead. Nel's artistry made the decaying house appear warm and inviting. To him, all of her work was timelessly charming and enchanting.

"Nel painted them."

"Haven't heard of her." Suzannah leaned over to study another canvas. "Not really my taste, but stunning nevertheless. Reminiscent of Kincaid and Roberson." His mother turned to him. "Is she on contract? Showing anywhere?"

Tristan shook his head.

"What's her name again?" Suzannah's voice sounded distant.

"Nel." Her name formed a smile on his lips.

Come to think of it, her smile could stop his heart,

her scent drove him crazy and her touch was both comfort and torture. He'd never wanted a woman the way he wanted Nel.

Suzannah snapped her fingers in front of Tristan's face. "Sometimes you act just like your father, not listening to a word I say."

Tristan's blood chilled. Some traits couldn't be escaped. A sharp pain sliced his heart. He would never put any woman through the misery his mother endured. Especially Nel.

"These are unsigned." Suzannah waved at the canvases. "Does she want to be known as Nel or use her full name?"

"I'm not sure," Tristan said.

"She'll need to decide." Suzannah withdrew a slim phone from the designer purse hanging from her right shoulder and began snapping pictures.

"What are you doing?"

"You remember Gilbert Michaud," she said with a French pronunciation. "He's always looking for new talent for his gallery. I assume you know where to find this Nel person?"

"This is *her* cabin."

Suzannah's golden eyebrows arched in perfect formation.

"She's just a friend." The word turned to ash in Tristan's mouth.

"This might actually be good." Tristan's mother patted his cheek. "Since you're sleeping with her, you can help me secure an exclusive showing if Gilbert is interested."

Tristan sighed. Of course Suzannah couldn't stop thinking about herself for sixty seconds to consider the gravity of her wolfan son cohabiting with a human female, even for a few days.

"When will she be back?" Suzannah squeezed his sore arm. "I need to speak with her."

Tristan's protective instinct flared. He couldn't begin to count the number of times Suzannah had promised him something but didn't deliver.

"I'd rather you didn't." Even though he believed Nel was highly gifted, she was insecure about her talent. He didn't want his meddling mother's failure to follow through to strengthen Nel's doubts.

"First, show the pictures to Gilbert. If he is really interested in Nel's work, then we'll talk about arranging a meeting." And Tristan planned to be in attendance. He wouldn't allow anyone to pressure, coerce, or take advantage of Nel or injure her gentle spirit. Not even his mother.

Chapter 19

"Is this really a good idea?" Nel skimmed past Tristan, holding open the gate to the resort pool. The buzz of a dozen happy voices filled the warm air of the early afternoon. The smell of chlorine and pine tickled her nose.

"I've been cooped up for days. Doc said pool exercises will do me good."

"I meant waiting at least an hour after eating before we swim."

"That's an old wives' tale." Tristan chuckled behind her.

They slowly made their way across the concrete patio to a quiet spot in a shaded corner near the shallow end of the pool. She caught her hesitant reflection in the mirrored lenses of Tristan's new sunglasses, purchased in the resort's gift shop.

"You've nothing to worry about, sweet cheeks." The brightness of his grin rivaled the sun as he placed their towels on the table beneath a huge umbrella.

"I'm not worried for myself." Beneath his T-shirt, bruises still colored Tristan's skin and his movements were still stiff and halting. "If you start drowning, I can't save you." She wasn't that strong a swimmer.

"Fatalistic, aren't you?"

"Realistic," she corrected.

"I'm not going to drown and neither are you." He limped to the pool and sat on the edge.

One of the teenagers at the deep end of the pool cannonballed the water. Nel was far enough away that only a couple of drops from the spray reached her. A float divider separated the two sections of the pool and she hoped the other guests stayed on the opposite side.

"Come on, sweet cheeks."

Nel stiffly slipped off her cover-up and laid it beside their towels on the table. Self-conscious about wearing her newly purchased bathing suit, she walked with fake confidence to the spot where Tristan had gone into the pool.

"How's the water?"

"Not nearly cold enough." He swallowed and she watched his Adam's apple slowly inch down his throat.

Nel's cheeks flushed, but not from the heat of the sun. Dressed in a modest two-piece, she couldn't imagine why her appearance got him so hot and bothered. The halter top cupped her ample breasts, but flared nicely to camouflage her hearty waist. And the bottoms were full-cut boy shorts that slightly slimmed her hips and thighs. Nothing too revealing, and yet the look Tristan gave her was as blatant as if she were standing in front of him naked.

She sat at the edge of the shallow end of the pool and dangled her feet in the water.

"Don't move." He inhaled sharply and sank below the water for a full two minutes. It seemed longer, but she counted out the seconds. He resurfaced, shaking the water from his head. "Had to get my bearings again."

He waded toward her, the water hitting him at waist level. He laid his sunglasses beside her and then cupped the backs of her calves. "I'll be right here. You don't have to be afraid."

"I'm not afraid of the water." She simply didn't like it very much.

"Why are you so tense?" His damp hands ran the lengths of her arms, warming her despite the coolness of his palms.

"People are staring at us."

With a face and body like his, women naturally fawned over him. Even now, the gaze of nearly every woman, and a few men, at the pool were on him. And her by default.

She hated when people stared at her. After her parents died, hospital workers gawked and whispered just outside her room. When she started a new school, the students and teachers couldn't stop staring at the ugly scar on her arm. In high school, the cheerleaders pointed and laughed because she wasn't a stick figure like them. But it was the boys' slack-jawed ogling when her breasts had developed that she'd hated the most.

"That's because they know they're in the presence of royalty." Though Tristan's gaze roamed her every curve, she didn't feel ogled or objectified. Instead, he made her feel cherished, appreciated.

"My queen." Tristan held out his hand.

Nel's fingertips glided over his wet palm. The energy that crackled whenever they touched prickled against the pads of her fingers.

Tristan must have felt it, too. Chill bumps erupted on his arm, causing the tiny hairs along his skin to rise. His nostrils flared slightly. Awareness flickered in the depths of his unwavering gaze focused entirely on her.

A month ago, if someone had told her that not only would she meet an incredibly handsome man, but that they would become friends—no, definitely more than friends—Nel wouldn't have believed them. At times, the reality of it was startling.

She'd always fallen short in the eyes of the men she previously dated. Her hair color was wrong. She was too curvy, too tall, too plain. She dressed too casual.

She was too uptight.

Yeah? Well, if they'd had someone criticizing everything about them, they would've been uptight, too.

But with Tristan, Nel never felt lacking.

"Ready for your first lesson?" He gave her a soft smile. Even though he often presented people with a megawatt smile, his understated ones affected her the most, pulling at her heartstrings and stirring something deep within.

"Are you sure that you feel up to this?"

"Nel, I'm bruised. Not broken. I'm fine." His expression turned slightly cocky. "Better than fine, actually. I haven't felt this damn good in a long time."

He helped her into the water and led her away from the edge. "I thought this would be a fun way to get you wet." He scooped water into his large hands and dumped it on her head.

"Hey!" She splashed him and his laughter swirled around her as he slipped behind her.

His muscular arms caged her. "Take a deep breath. I'm going to dunk you."

"You wouldn't dare!"

"Oh, yes I would. I promised to teach you how to handle yourself when we go on the Outreach's field trip. If you fall out of the raft, your life vest will bob you to the surface." He lifted Nel off her feet. "Ready?"

A nervous excitement twirled in her stomach and

spiraled through her. Deep inside, Nel knew if she told Tristan to put her down, he would. She also knew she'd never been safer.

Nel gulped air, pinched her nose and nodded.

They splashed into the water, dropping down to the bottom only to shoot straight up. As soon as they broke the surface, Tristan spun her around. His hands wiped water from her eyes.

"Okay, sweet cheeks?"

"Yeah." She peeked open one eye and then the other.

Water dripped from the tip of his nose and jaw, and droplets clung to his long eyelashes. He shook his head vigorously.

"Watch it!" She shielded her face behind her arms to protect herself from the water pellets lobbed in her direction.

"I'd rather watch you." A soft growl tinged his husky voice.

Hooking his thumb beneath Nel's chin, Tristan tipped her face. Instead of a kiss, he grazed his jaw along her cheek.

Seeing her face after the accident…he'd never been so happy to see someone in all his life. And every morning since, waking up next to her curled against him was worth all the pain he'd endured.

If he had any sense, he'd get as far away from her as he possibly could go. He knew better than to commit to any woman.

He'd been resigned to his fate, until Nel came along and she'd made being a couple seem comfortable and effortless.

Except they weren't a couple.

He was merely a houseguest, platonically sharing her bed, while he recovered.

Maybe he'd succumbed to some sort of Nightingale syndrome, developing feelings for his caretaker. He hoped the cure was distance, which was what he expected to place between them once the rafting trip was over.

"What's next?" An expectant smile anchored the absolute trust in Nel's face.

"When you bob to the surface, you'll need to position yourself so that the river will carry you back to the raft. We'll start with the basic back float."

"I never liked floating in a pool. People jumping and splashing all around me, I was afraid someone would land on top of me and I'd drown."

"I won't let you drown." And he definitely wouldn't allow someone on top of her. Unless it was him.

He helped her maneuver into a prone position on top of the water. Her hand gripped his arm almost to the point of pain. "Relax, Nel. I won't let go."

Mine!

The booming voice was so loud Tristan jerked.

"What's wrong?" Nel broke position and stood.

"Thought I heard someone behind me."

Tristan shook off whatever it was that had sounded very much like his own voice. Repositioning Nel in the water, his free hand trailed down her back until he splayed his fingers at the base of her spine. His other hand rested on her stomach. "Close your eyes and just breathe."

She cut her gaze sharply at him. *Have you lost your mind?*

Clear as a church bell, her voice, an octave higher and tinged with incredulous sarcasm, rang through his mind.

He would've thought she'd said the words, but her jaw was locked tight and her lips never moved.

Perhaps he'd simply interpreted the look. He couldn't have actually heard her thoughts. Wolfans were only telepathic with their own kind when in wolf form. The only exception was when a mate-bond formed between a wolfan and his mate.

Nel was definitely not his mate. A mate-claim could only be established when a wolfan male bit a female while having sex, and he was careful to ensure that never happened. The last thing he wanted was to accidentally claim a female and spend the rest of his life suffering the miserable repercussions.

"You have to relax, Nel. Think of something you like," Tristan paused. "Imagine that you're painting. Think of everything involved. Go to that place and relax."

She continued staring at him.

"This isn't going to work if you don't relax." Knees bent, he hunkered in the water so that only his head and shoulders were above the surface. "I'm going to count backward from five. When I get to one, let your body go limp."

He counted slowly. On two, her eyes closed and her breathing shallowed.

The tension drained from her body, even her grip eased. Her trust humbled him. It also stroked his ego and he would do anything to maintain her faith in him.

Water gently lapped around her face and the outline of her body. Tendrils of hair that had come loose from her braid floated like a halo around her head.

The face of an angel and a body he wanted to worship.

God, she was achingly beautiful.

Not like the stick-thin, hollow-cheeked beauty glamorized in magazines. Nel's curves, soft features, and warm eyes were the substance of hearth and home. She was the comfort a man couldn't wait to get home to each night.

Longing gripped him body and soul.

Already he knew that he would never forget her warmth, her softness, the gentleness of her spirit. The taste of her skin. Nor would he forget her trust, her kindness, her genuine concern. He suspected memories of Nel would keep him warm on long, lonely future nights.

A loud splash landed just to his left. Tristan swept Nel into his arms and stood, but not before the tidal wave dumped huge amounts of water onto her. He spun away from the disturbance as laughter filled the air.

Nel coughed, wiping water from her face.

"Are you okay?"

She nodded.

Slowly he slid her out of his arms until she stood.

He turned on the teenager. "Get out!"

"Dude, it was just a joke."

"Don't play jokes on people you don't know, and don't horse around in the pool. It's dangerous."

"Yeah, right." The kid slammed his fists into the water, panning a wave toward Tristan.

Tristan stepped forward.

"Want a piece of this?" The kid beat his chest like a baboon.

The lack of respect some children had for adults never failed to amaze Tristan.

"What I want—" without touching the kid, Tristan backed him up against the side of the pool "—is for you and your friends to get out of the water."

"Says who?" The kid's face twisted.

"The one permanently revoking your pool privileges." Tristan whistled. Two sentinels wearing the resort's security team shirts stepped from their hideaways. "Round 'em up and see that they don't bother anyone else," he told them.

Without hesitation, the sentinel closest to Tristan walked over and hauled the unruly teen out of the water. The other guard stood at the opposite end of the pool waving the kid's complaining entourage out.

Tristan made his way back to Nel.

"They were just being kids."

"Being disrespectful isn't being a kid. It's being an ass." He tucked the strands of hair matted to her face behind her ear. "We don't tolerate that kind of behavior."

"We?"

"The Co-op."

"I thought the Co-op was a group of wolf enthusiasts."

"No." Taking Nel's hand, he led her to the in-pool steps and sat down. Instead of Nel sitting beside him, he positioned her to sit between his legs and encouraged her to lean against his chest. "We strive to give our wolves a safe environment to live in, but we're really all about family. Community. And we don't want our juveniles to turn into hoodlums who have no regard for others."

"I bet you're the king of the ball at Youth Outreach." Nel laughed softly and the tinkling sound washed over him in a warm, satisfying shower.

"More like the ballbuster." He loved the feel of Nel against him, how her head rested beneath his chin, her shoulders relaxed against his chest, how his legs molded around her hips and her hands absently stroked his thighs.

"Excusing bad behavior doesn't help them succeed in a world already stacked against them. Until I met Mason Walker, I was just like the kids I work with. No parental involvement, no positive role models. I had no one who cared, no one to show me a better way."

"Was Mason a volunteer at the Outreach?"

"No, he was the kid who found me after I fell from a rock and cracked my skull."

"Is that how you lost your vision?"

Tristan nodded. "Jaxen was there when it happened, but he ran off."

Nel stilled. "To get help?"

"So he says." Tristan held a breath in his chest and let it out slowly. "But he didn't. I would've died if Mason hadn't come along."

"Tristan, how awful." Nel twisted around, her gaze peering deep into his soul. "How old were you?"

"Fifteen." Two years older, Jaxen could've been legally charged by human law enforcement, had anyone figured out the truth. Then the Woelfesenat would've become involved, adding another dimension to the overwhelming situation Tristan had faced.

Suffering from dissociative amnesia, he couldn't actually remember anything that happened that day. Mason had filled in some of the missing details. Practicing his tracking skills, he had followed Tristan's and Jaxen's scents through the woods to the large rock they had climbed. They were arguing as Mason approached from a distance. Jaxen kept advancing on Tristan, who kept stepping back.

Realizing what would happen, Mason had bolted toward them. Momentarily losing sight of them as he rounded a huge tree, he didn't actually see Jaxen push Tristan off the boulder. But, he had watched Jaxen standing over Tristan's limp body without lifting a finger to help. Then, Jaxen shifted and left Tristan there without even howling a distress call to the sentinels.

The color had drained out of Nel's face. "How could he leave you there?"

Tristan supposed it was for the same reason Jaxen had pushed him. Despite the amnesia, Tristan knew that was how it happened. Even if the man can't remember, the wolf never forgets. Ever since that day, Tristan's inner wolf had considered Jaxen a viable threat.

"Doesn't matter now. Because of the accident, Mason and I became best friends. He always challenged me to be a better person and I like to think I am better than I would've been without his influence."

"He sounds like a great man."

"He was. He died a few years ago."

"I'm sorry for your loss." The compassion shimmering in Nel's eyes tugged at Tristan's heart. She resettled against him and Tristan felt his world starting to right itself. "With all the terrible things that happen to children, I'm amazed when anyone grows up to be a decent human being."

"That's why I volunteer. When I see the kids at Outreach, I remember me and Jaxen at their age. Then, Mason came along and I discovered I really could change my life. I want these kids to know that, too."

"I'm sure they do know." Nel glanced over her shoulder. A sweet smile played on her lips.

He resisted the urge to kiss her. Too much testosterone and wolfan hormones were flooding his body to stick to just one kiss, and they were in a very public place.

"Just like I knew you wouldn't let me sink." She relaxed into his chest. "You're a good man. With a very big heart. And I'd trust you with my life."

Mine!

This time, the declaration in his head synchronized with the steady strum of his heart. And in that moment, Tristan knew he would do anything to keep her safe. Even from himself.

Chapter 20

Hunched down at the river's edge, Tristan, in wolf form, lapped the cool, clean water. He wasn't on sentinel duty, even though he'd told Nel that he had a Co-op meeting to attend tonight.

Being in the cabin with her for nearly a week had wreaked havoc on his sensibilities. Whenever he was with her, thoughts of possibilities he shouldn't imagine kept popping into his head. He needed a good run to clear his brain and to help him get a handle on his hormones before he did something really stupid.

He shook the dribbles of water from his snout and trotted upriver with no particular destination in mind. The exercise stretched sore muscles and loosened the joints that had stiffened from inflammation and reduced activity.

Nudging a fallen tree branch, he unearthed a large bullfrog. It croaked and leaped, and Tristan jumped back. The back and forth between the two became a game that lasted several minutes until something barreled into Tristan's left shoulder. His right side hit the ground, and pain flared from his previous injuries. He rolled several times from the momentum of the tackle.

Laughter ran through his mind.

"Dammit, Jaxen. What the hell is your problem?"

"Lighten up. I'm just trying to keep you on your toes."

"It's not my toes I'm worried about." Biting back a groan, Tristan pushed up on all fours. *"I'm going rafting with the kids from the Outreach next week. I'd like to get there without the use of a stretcher or wheelchair."*

"You'll bounce back. You always do." Jaxen's steely gaze followed every step Tristan took to shake off the effects of Jaxen's body slam. *"How about we go for the run that we got rained out of?"*

"No more blindsiding me, Jax. I didn't like it when we were kids. I don't like it now."

"All right, but I'm just trying to help."

Tristan doubted that.

They loped side by side, weaving through the forest like old times.

The times before Jaxen had become an enemy. Or, at least, become someone Tristan was wary of, which was why, as they trotted, he made sure Jaxen stayed to his right and completely in view at all times.

"How's work?" Tristan asked to fill the silence.

"It is what it is," was Jaxen's only comment.

They only made a mile loop because Tristan didn't want to overtax his muscles.

"What's up with you and the curvy brunette? I heard you shacked up with her. Any truth to that?"

"Her name is Penelope and I haven't shacked up with her. She offered me a place to stay after the accident. I wasn't in any shape to climb three flights of stairs."

"By place, do you mean her bed?"

"Not your business."

Jaxen's laughter had no real mirth. *"Are you just fooling around, or does she mean something to you? Because she seems soft and sweet, and I could use some comfort from a woman like her."*

Ordinarily, Tristan wasn't possessive, but Nel brought out his protective nature. *"It's not personal, Jax."* Okay, it was. *"Pick any other woman and I won't compete, but stay away from Nel. She's mine."*

"So you've changed your mind about claiming a mate?"

They'd reached the trail that led to the resort's property.

"Good night, Jaxen." Tristan parted company without responding to the question because he had no idea how to answer it.

"Are you painting Cassie and Brice's wolf?"

Even though Nel hadn't heard Tristan come in, she wasn't startled by his sudden presence.

"I got the idea one morning watching Cassie play on the floor with Brenna."

"It's stunning, Nel. Contemporary, but it also has a fairy-tale quality to it."

"Great." Nel's confidence soared. "That's exactly what I'm going for."

"Will you paint my wolf?"

"I'd love to, but I need a better picture." Nel wiped off her hands and picked up her phone. "This one isn't very clear." She showed Tristan the photo she'd taken of his wolf one night when she'd seen him watching the cabin from the edge of the trail. "He hasn't been around lately, but I guess that's because you haven't been on patrol."

"Will you paint him watching you from the woods?"

"I'm not sure yet." She began closing up her paints

and cleaning her brushes. "When the idea comes to me, I'll sketch it out. I could show it to you to see if you like the concept."

"I'd love to see anything you create." Tristan moved behind her and rested his hands on her hips. Chills ran along her skin while heat flashed inside her body. "You're beautiful, Nel," he whispered in her ear. "But when you're painting, you're absolutely breathtaking."

"You give the best compliments." She hugged his arms snaking around her waist.

"Hmm." He nuzzled her hair and gently nudged the sweet spot behind her ear. The one that made her knees weak, her breath short and her sex clench.

Tristan kissed the shell of her ear, then slowly pulled his arms away and stepped back. "Hungry?"

"A little." Nel laughed because Tristan seemed to have a bottomless stomach and was always in search of food.

He went to the refrigerator and pulled out the sandwich meat, cheese and condiments. Nel retrieved the bread from the pantry.

Tristan always prepared whatever they ate and she enjoyed watching him whip everything together.

"How did the Co-op meeting go?" She took a bite of her sandwich.

"Actually, I went to run my wolf. I needed the exercise, he needed the exercise. I should've told you outright."

"Why didn't you?"

Tristan toyed with the crust he'd torn off his bread. "I didn't want you to worry."

"You didn't want me to fuss at you." Nel grinned over her sandwich and Tristan grinned back. "I'm not your mother or your keeper, Tristan. You can do whatever you want." Of course, that didn't mean she wouldn't be concerned. Maybe outright worried. But he obviously knew how to take care of himself.

Except for the rule about not running out in front of cars.

Tristan polished off his sandwich. "Go ahead. Ask. I know you want to."

"How do you feel? You didn't do too much running, did you? Are you sore? In pain? Is there something you need me to do?"

"Just keep doing what you do, sweet cheeks. It's nice to be fussed over." Especially since this was the last night he could indulge in her care and concern. Doc had released him to go back to work. Limited duty for the first couple of days and then without restrictions, which meant he'd see a lot less of Nel.

Tristan's heart squeezed. It hadn't taken long for him to get used to Nel's company. He wondered if he would adjust to being alone again, just as quick.

The restlessness he felt suggested he wouldn't.

Chapter 21

"Happy birthday, Brenna!"

The little girl's strawberry blond curls bounced in pigtails as she nodded her head. "I this many." She stuck her index finger toward Nel's face.

Cassie put the child down. "Go tell Daddy that Nel is here."

Her cherub face grinning, Brenna toddled off as instructed.

Cassie looked a little tired. "Her grandfather gave her too much sugar this morning. We keep expecting her to run out of steam and crash for a nap. Oh, no. She's too stubborn for that—just like her father."

"I hope I'm not late…" Nel began.

"Not at all." Cassie's brow creased. "Where's Tristan?"

"He started back to work, but he'll stop in later." Nel hadn't seen him for a few days, but he had texted. "Several deputies are on vacation, so he won't stay long."

"Bren will be disappointed. He's one of her favorite people. But so are you, and we're glad you came."

"This is for Brenna." She gave Cassie a brightly colored present. "And…" Nel picked up a large package wrapped in brown paper. "This is for you. My way of saying thanks for the opportunity at the resort and your kindness."

"Thank you." Cassie smiled, accepting the gift. "Come in."

She followed Cassie into a spacious living area that opened out to a gorgeous wood-and-tile patio.

Brice, leaning against the bar between the large kitchen and living room, lifted his glass of iced tea. "Want something to drink?"

Nel nodded and he headed to the cooler. Gavin Walker sat in the leather recliner, his shoes kicked off. He looked more casual than Nel had ever seen him. Abigail Walker, his wife, sat in a rocker holding one of Grace's twins—Reina—considering the bright pink bow fastened in a gelled blond curl on top of her head.

Grace dozed quietly, leaning against the shoulder of her husband, Rafe, who held Ryan—the other twin—whose hair was as red as Rafe's own.

Brenna had climbed onto the couch beside Rafe and was rubbing the baby's back.

Cassie set Brenna's present on the coffee table, which held only a few other gifts. Even though the child's parents and grandparents seemed well-off, it was heartwarming to see that they weren't extravagant or overly indulgent with Brenna.

"Look what Nel gave me." Cassie waggled the package at Brice.

Nel sat on the love seat and smiled her thanks as Brice handed her a drink.

"What is it?" he asked.

"A token." Nel shrugged. "Something on Cassie's desk inspired me and I thought this was something she might like to have."

Nel hoped they liked it. Really, really hoped they liked it.

She gulped her drink but it seemed to lodge in her throat because her heart was in the way.

Cassie carefully removed the paper. She and Brice simply stared. Nel's mind raced and her heart dived into her stomach.

Wordlessly, Brice showed the others the painting of Cassie in a white linen shift, with her red curls spilling over her shoulder, sitting in a moonlit forest with a black wolf beside her gazing into her face.

Abigail Walker gasped; her hand flew to her mouth. Gavin Walker got up from his chair and walked over to inspect the painting. Rafe's gaze settled on Nel. She could barely breathe, uncertain what everyone's response meant.

He tipped his head toward his sleeping wife and quietly spoke to Nel. "Grace will want one of her with my wolf."

Brenna hopped over to Nel and pointed at the painting. "Mama, Dada's woof." She climbed into Nel's lap.

Within seconds the child fell asleep and the entire room heaved a sigh of relief.

"It's a lovely work of art," Gavin Walker said. He took the canvas from Brice, allowing him to wrap his arms around Cassie, who had started crying.

"Thank you, Nel." Emotion choked Brice's voice. "We love it."

"I know someone else who'd love a portrait like this one," Abigail said. "Would you consider taking orders?"

"That's very kind, but I'm not a professional artist." Nel's cheeks warmed. "I paint for fun."

"A talent like yours would be appreciated and admired here, Nel." Gavin Walker propped the painting on the bar counter and returned to his chair. "Please give some thought to Abby's suggestion."

"I will, Mr. Walker."

Brenna snuggled against Nel's chest. Her lips parted slightly and her nose whistled softly as she breathed.

"She's taken quite a liking to you," Brice said softly to Nel. He sat in the chair next to the love seat. "I think Tristan has, too."

"I've taken a liking to them, too," Nel said lightly, although her heart pinched. It was going to be hard to say goodbye come the end of summer.

Tristan rapped his knuckles against the door twice before walking inside. From the echoes of Brenna's squeals of delight, he suspected everyone was on the back patio.

He glanced around the old log-cabin home redesigned with a sprawling first floor and second floor. Hard to believe it used to be little more than a two-bedroom shack.

He'd helped Brice with the design. Tristan loved architecture and his parents once hoped he would become an architect. They had grand dreams of building a Durrance family niche in the housing market with his dad's construction business, his mom's interior design firm and Tristan's structural designs.

Unfortunately, he liked the idea of architecture much more than the actual work.

Needless to say, his parents never understood why he chose a career in law enforcement.

His plan had been to gain some practical experience locally before Mason announced to the pack that he'd been offered an apprenticeship with the Woelfesenat. Tristan had had no aspirations for a seat on the international wolf council, but a position on their security force, well, that had been a different story.

Of course, Mason's murder changed everything. Tristan didn't have the heart to pursue a career with the Woelfesenat when his best friend never had the chance to do the same.

Most days, Tristan was happy with his path. Days like today, though, when he'd almost missed an important event because of his work schedule, it rather sucked.

He eased outside, no one aware of his arrival. Cassie, Grace and Abby were lounging comfortably in the seats around the unlit fire pit. Gavin, Brice, Rafe and Shane were gathered around the grill. The twins were rocking in their dual swing sets.

Anticipation built as he searched for Brenna and Nel.

A light breeze tickled his nose. He shifted his sense of smell from the sizzling meat on the grill and homed in on the buttery-sweet, feminine scent that reminded him of honeysuckle. The canter of his heartbeat kicked up its pace. A child's innocent laughter danced on the air before he made visual contact.

Sunshine highlighted the honey tones in Nel's hair. She held Brenna's tiny hand as they slowly and deliberately climbed the wooden steps from the river.

Nel looked so sweet, she made Tristan's heart ache with a yearning for *home*.

Instantly, he knew why he'd been so irritable lately. He missed Nel.

Brenna saw him first. Observant little scamp. She squealed, "Tiskan!" and started to dash toward him, but Nel held steadfastly to her hand.

"No running until we get off the stairs."

The commotion caused everyone to turn in Tristan's direction and they called out greetings.

Tristan said his hellos, then strolled to the edge of the patio and went down on one knee. Opening his arms, he welcomed the toddler with a giant hug, then picked her up and kissed her cheek.

"Dial down the charm," Nel teased. "She's too young for you."

God, her smile warmed and exhilarated him.

"What can I say," he said. "It's a gift."

A gift, Tristan was beginning to realize, he no longer wanted to share with a multitude of women. Just one.

He set Brenna on her feet and she ran to show her daddy the rocks she'd collected.

"Thanks for texting me a reminder." He draped his arm over Nel's shoulders and they walked leisurely toward the others.

"You've been busy." There was a touch of sadness in Nel's voice.

"Something wrong?" He halted their stroll.

She shook her head, but didn't meet his gaze.

"I've missed you." Nel's voice infiltrated his thoughts.

"I've missed you, too."

Her cheeks pinked and her eyes widened. "I didn't say anything."

"I could tell what you were thinking." He laced his fingers through hers. "I told you that your face is very expressive, Nel. You're easy to read."

The voice he'd heard was pure imagination. Wolfans were only telepathic with each other in wolf form. They couldn't hear a human's thoughts unless connected through a mate-bond. And he doubted the feasibility of one forming between him and Nel. No one in his family had ever bonded with their mates. Tristan didn't expect to be the exception, though for the first time he wished he could be.

Chapter 22

"How about that dinner I promised you, love?" The cadence of the masculine voice behind Nel at the deli counter was close, but not quite Tristan's deep timbre.

Nel turned around. Jaxen's smile was a mirror of Tristan's but nothing in his gray eyes warmed her to the soles of her feet the way Tristan's chocolate-brown ones did. "Sorry, I have plans."

It was Tristan's first night off since he'd returned to work and he had promised to make her a home-cooked dinner as a thank-you for taking care of him for nearly a week. It really hadn't been a chore. He'd cleaned up after himself, once he was able to hobble around, and there were no dishes to wash because they'd ordered in every night. Nel wasn't much of a cook. The most she could do was boil water.

Best of all, he didn't complain when she opted to paint rather than watch television. He simply joined her on the porch with a book. Sometimes he read in silence, sometimes they discussed whatever topic came to mind.

She had enjoyed having someone to come home to

and who was as happy to see her as she was to see him. His presence had kept the loneliness at bay.

She had missed him terribly.

"Another date with Marie?" Jaxen stared pointedly at the frozen meals in her cart. Since Tristan had returned home, she was back to eating prepackaged meals for supper.

"Not tonight."

"We could make a date for tomorrow."

Nel knew Tristan's interest wouldn't turn into anything serious, but getting involved with Jaxen was something she couldn't stomach. Especially after learning what Jaxen had done to Tristan when they were teenagers. "Thanks, but no."

A tingle spread through her body and she sensed Tristan's approach before she saw him round the corner, basket in hand. She felt, more than saw, a subtle tension creep into his body.

"The butcher butterflied the chicken breasts for me," he said, depositing the basket in her cart. "I picked up some fresh asparagus and red potatoes. How's the deli coming with the thin-sliced ham and Swiss cheese?"

"I placed the order a few minutes ago. It should be ready soon." Nel noticed he'd also picked up a premium bottle of chardonnay.

"He's your other plans?" Irritation briefly flashed in Jaxen's eyes.

"I promised to make Nel supper," Tristan said casually, though his jaw was clenched. "It's the least I can do for her hospitality and company."

There was an awkward pause.

"Why don't you join us, Jaxen?" There might've been a hint of sarcasm in Tristan's voice. "We'll have plenty of food, wine. It's casual, so you can come with what you're wearing."

The air immediately became charged. He and Jaxen stared at each other until Jaxen finally declined the offer and left.

"Why did you invite him?"

"Because I knew he'd say no." Tristan shrugged.

The deli clerk signaled their order was ready and Tristan reached for the freshly packaged ham and cheese.

"He asked me out."

"Did you agree?" Tristan's knuckles tightened on the cart as they left the deli.

"No. Something about him doesn't feel right."

Tristan gave her a curious look.

"When I'm with you, I feel comfortable. Around him, I'm on edge."

"He's made some bad choices in life. I don't think he feels comfortable himself."

"I feel bad about turning him down."

"Don't." Tristan unloaded the items from the cart onto the conveyor at the checkout. "Trust your instincts, Nel. They'll never steer you wrong."

Oh, really?

Well, she couldn't help but wonder if Tristan would still believe that if he knew her instincts were telling her not to let go of him.

"Not too shabby, chef."

"Couldn't have done it without my sous chef." Tristan added the garnishing touches to their plates, looking too damn sexy wearing an apron and a crooked smile.

Nel was just about to light the candles on the table-sized kitchen island when he tucked the wine bottle beneath his arm and picked up the plates and silverware. "I'd rather eat in the living room."

Nel gathered the candles, the corkscrew and the glasses, and followed him.

"It seems weird to eat in the kitchen when we always eat here." Tristan set the coffee table and dropped the large sofa pillows onto the floor.

Nel dialed down the brightness of the living room lights to a soft glow. After depositing her items on the table, she wiggled herself comfortable on the pillow. Tristan opened the wine, filled the glasses halfway and handed one to Nel.

"Here's to good times." Tristan clinked his glass against hers and took a long swallow.

Over the rim of her glass, Nel watched the fluid movement of his neck muscles. Every move he made was graceful. Even when he hobbled, there was a certain poetry and stealth in his steps.

The artist in her more than appreciated his beauty and grace, but the woman in her saw the kind heart and gracious soul hidden beneath his physical appearance.

"Dig in." He nodded at her plate of chicken cordon bleu, steamed asparagus and roasted red potatoes.

She cut a bite of the lightly breaded chicken breast stuffed with cheese and ham and popped it into her mouth. The flavors blended beautifully. "Delicious." She swallowed and licked her lips.

Grinning, Tristan cut into his meal.

"Seriously, this is fabulous." She took another bite. "Where did you learn to cook?"

"In college I took a few cooking classes off campus. Thought it would impress the girls."

"How did that work out?"

"I learned to cook." Tristan remained focused on his plate. "It's not a lot of fun cooking for one, though."

"It's much better when you have a grunt to wash and chop the veggies."

"Yep." He munched a stalk of asparagus.

They ate in amicable silence; she kept stealing glances at him as often as she noticed him stealing glances at her. Each time, her heart would race because it knew that when he left, things between them would inevitably change.

She finished every bite, amazed that he had plated the perfect amount of food. Not so much that she'd be overly full, not so little she'd want seconds. He finished at the same time she did, even though his plate had held more.

He emptied the last of the chardonnay into their glasses, handed Nel her glass and took his own in hand. He toed the coffee table away from them, stretched his legs and crossed his ankles. Then he draped his arm over her shoulders as they reclined against the couch.

"Dinner really was fantastic," she said quietly.

"It was fun making it with you." He met her gaze, but didn't hold it. The glimpse he gave her was so full of raw emotion that a lump formed in her throat. He leaned his head against the couch seat.

"So, you're back to full-time duty without restrictions?"

"Yep." He nodded. "I have twelve-hour shifts for the next two days, then I'm off again."

Nel bit back the urge to plan something for his day off. "Don't overdo it."

"Thank you for caring." Tristan's fingers caressed her jaw and then he was leaning in for a kiss.

It was whisper soft, like a feather christening her mouth. She sighed and he deepened the kiss, his tongue parting her lips in a gentle probe. He shifted his weight, urging her down onto the floor pillows. Expectation curled in her lower belly but a nag swirled in her mind. A clean break would be better than complicating matters by having sex, which would only leave her begging for more.

He nibbled her lower lip then soothed the sting with his tongue. Propped on one elbow, his other hand trailed down her arm. Chills spread across her skin.

His kisses blazed a trail to her ear. He flicked the lobe then gently sucked it into his mouth. He nosed the sweet spot behind her ear.

"God, Nel. You smell so good." His hand slipped beneath her shirt. Warm, strong, patient, he stroked her skin.

"Tristan," she breathed. "We can't do this."

"Why not?" He nuzzled her neck.

Her nose filled with his clean, masculine scent, making it hard for her to think clearly.

His fingers wiggled beneath her bra cup and he began kneading her breast. Electric pulses shot through her body and converged in her sex.

She flattened her palms against his chest, curling her fingers in the fabric of his shirt. "This isn't a good idea."

"Sure it is." He chuckled in her ear. The deep, throaty sound reverberated through her body, a deep, sensual throb.

He lifted his face to hers, clenched in hesitation. His smile faded and his disappointment pinched her heart.

"No pressure." He began pulling away. "You feel so damn right to me, Nel."

Truthfully, it felt right to her, too. Nel grabbed him and kissed him with all her might.

"Thank god," he whispered against her mouth. He

yanked off his shirt and she palmed his muscled chest. His smile returned, as dazzling as ever.

Slowly, he unbuttoned her blouse as he kissed her deeply. He unfastened the snap of her pants, then pushed them down her hips and pulled them off her legs. He cupped her mound, rubbing lightly so the friction from the lace maddeningly teased her clit.

"Show me where you like to be touched," he whispered against her skin.

Her fingers closed over his. She slipped their hands beneath her panties and guided his strokes along her folds in a familiar rhythm.

Tristan never wavered; he kissed and caressed until she was lost in the sensation of his touch and breathless. Unhurried, he continued to stroke her. As the incredible pressure built, his fingers slid inside her and the heel of his hand ground against her clit.

"God, you're so wet. Do you have any idea how good you feel to me?" he panted.

His kiss turned urgent, needful. The thrust of his fingers harder, faster.

"Oh, god," she cried out as ribbons of pleasure pulsed through her body.

A faint ringing sound grew louder, dragging her away from the splendor.

"Tristan."

"Hmm." He kissed beneath the curve of her jaw.

"Tristan!"

His eyes opened, his gaze unfocused. "What, baby?"

"Your phone is ringing."

"Get up!" Tristan kicked the rickety metal cot.

Jaxen opened one eye, then the other. "Someone's in a bad mood." He slowly sat up, swung his feet off the cot and stood. His nose twitched. "Guess I interrupted something, huh?"

Boy, did he. And it had damn near killed Tristan to leave Nel tonight. "Start walking before I decide to leave your ass here."

"My mom and your pops would definitely not be happy if you did." Laughing, Jaxen vacated the jail cell. "See? A misunderstanding, just like I said," he told the deputy holding open the door.

"Don't be an ass." Tristan shoved Jaxen forward, then nodded at the deputy. "Thanks, Hank."

"The sheriff will want to talk to you tomorrow," Hank said.

"I'm sure he will."

Tristan walked to the truck with his hands clenched to keep from throttling his whistling cousin. Doors closed, engine cranked, he finally popped Jaxen's arm. "What the hell is wrong with you?"

"Look in the mirror, man. I'm not the one going ballistic. Maybe you should get checked out."

"I told you to stay away from Nel. Instead of listening, you asked her out."

"You never answered my question. Without a mate-claim…" Jaxen stared out the window, whistling.

Tristan had a thought to haul Jaxen's ass back inside, toss him behind bars and throw away the key. "Stay the hell away from Nel. Or I will boot you so far out of the territory the Hubble telescope won't be able to find you."

"Chill out, man. I've never known you to get this bent out of shape over a woman. So, what's up with you?"

"I had to leave her to haul your furry ass out of jail. What were you thinking? Breaking into one of my dad's model homes?"

"I had a key, and Deidre and I wanted a place to be alone." Jaxen snorted. "Didn't know there was an alarm."

"Do you have any idea how this is going to look to my boss?"

"Believe it or not, I consider you being a deputy a perk. If not for you, I might've been in there all night." Jaxen flashed a cocky grin and patted Tristan's shoulder. "Thanks, cuz. I owe you."

"I don't want you to owe me. I want you to get your life straight. Stop screwing up. Become a productive member of the pack."

Well maybe not that last one. Tristan didn't mind if Jaxen became a productive citizen, but he preferred it to be in some other place.

"Your mom is sick again. I can't believe you left her alone. What if she needed something?"

"She has your number."

"Unbelievable."

Tristan pulled out of the parking lot and drove to Ruby's place. Jaxen strolled into the house as if he didn't have a care in the world. Tristan stomped in behind him.

"What took you so long?" Nate stood in the living room. His gaze fixed on Tristan.

Tristan held his tongue. Anything he said would incite an argument and he was too tired for a fight.

"Did they hurt you?" Bundled in her rocking chair, Ruby lifted her arms.

"I'm fine, Mama." Jaxen hugged her.

No matter Jaxen's flaws, he did love his mother.

"Go on to bed, Ruby. I'll sort this out," Tristan's father said.

"I'll sit right here." Ruby coughed hard. "I wanna know everything that happened."

Tristan didn't want to be culpable or complicit, so he went into the kitchen to make a pot of herbal tea.

Ruby didn't look at him when he handed her a hot cup of lemon zinger.

"Tristan will take care of the sheriff and Gavin tomorrow." Nate glared at Tristan as if that had some power over his actions. "Jaxen has a key to the office. He was there to do some work."

"Good luck with that story, because according to the arrest report, Jaxen was caught in one of your model homes, not the office. And the only work being done was downing a bottle of bourbon while making out with Deidre Hall," Tristan said to his father, then looked at Jaxen. "I bailed you out because Ruby was upset. My involvement ends there and I will explain that in detail to the sheriff and Gavin. Get in trouble again, and you're on your own."

Chapter 23

Nel's ears rang from the incessant buzz of chatter. If anything was louder than a bunch of kindergartners on a field trip, it was a busload of teenagers.

Tristan and Carmen, the Outreach's administrator, rounded up the mob, separating them into two groups. Boys and girls.

Moaning and bitching were in full swing.

Butterflies zipped around her stomach, diving and soaring in panic. She'd never dealt with teenagers. Throw in her inexperience with rafting and she felt a disaster was waiting to happen.

Tristan's encouraging smile when she caught his attention kept her from bolting back into the bus and cowering behind the last seat.

Nel took a moment to settle her nerves. She'd survived a category-five hurricane. She could do this.

The soft roar of water in constant motion floated above the blended voices. The sun was bright but despite being summer, the air was slightly cool.

The outdoors smelled fresh, clean, invigorating, and it did nothing to quell her nervous stomach.

The rafting guides walked up to Tristan and Carmen. Soon they'd be getting the how-to and what-not-to-do speeches.

"Mary," Nel said to the girl who'd whined the entire trip. "Put your phone away. You can't have it out when we're in the water."

The teenager rolled her eyes. "I'm bored. Why don't they have Wi-Fi here?"

"We're not at an internet café." Nel's teacher voice held authority. "Put the phone away and don't take it out again until we're back on the bus."

Once the safety training was completed, Carmen began separating the two groups into four and a very unhappy Tristan pulled Nel aside.

"There's a problem with the larger rafts. We're going to do this on four smaller ones."

"And you're worried because?"

"There will be one chaperone in each raft." An aggravated sigh heaved Tristan's chest. "We won't be together, but there will be an experienced guide with you."

Nel's stomach dropped, but she swallowed her fear. None of the kids needed to witness her panic.

The rafting guides were professionals, probably rafting for most of their lives. She would likely be safer with them than on the I-75 in rush hour. "I'll be fine."

Tristan helped her put on the life vest. His gaze lingered on her skin like a tender caress. Emotion warred in his eyes. He didn't want her to be alone. He'd promised to be by her side, to be watchful, to be her assurance.

She squeezed his hand. "This will be fun."

He nodded, his smile tight.

Everyone lined up at the launch platform. Nel and her group of girls loaded into the raft in the positions assigned. Nel was in the back center and had a good view of all her kids.

She focused on them. Their safety was paramount, and none seemed too concerned that they were packed into a giant rubber float and were about to drift into a body of endless rushing water that had carved a path through the rock of the mountain.

The guide barked orders. Nel had to snap her girls to attention. Excitement rose as the raft launched. She felt like her ass scraped the rock bed as they started. Chatter ceased as the gentle ebb of the current hooked them, drawing them to the center of the flowing river.

It would've seemed like a peaceful drift down the stream if she hadn't known what lay beyond the bend. If anything had been within reach, Nel's fingers would've been clenched around it.

She glanced at Tristan in the raft ahead of them. He sat angled, watching his charges and sneaking quick peeks at Nel. Each time a relieved smile lifted his lips, a warmth would flash through her, easing her anxiety.

Mary wiggled in her seat. "I'm getting splashed."

"Duh!" Her friend laughed. "We're on a river."

"Sit still and tough it out," Nel said.

Laughter and squeals of delight from the other girls drowned out Mary's dramatic sighs.

Nel began to relax. Tristan continued to keep an eye on them, his reassuring smile broadening when she gave him a thumbs-up.

The guide in the back called out confident instructions for the paddlers as they neared the first rapids.

Nel's gut tightened and her heart raced, a little fear mixed with excitement.

They bumped and jarred over the first minor hurdle

to the screams of teenagers having fun. Except for Mary, shrieking at her wet clothes and hair.

Nel made a quick head count and released a sigh of relief. All were safe in the raft.

Before long, the guide called out again. "Bump!" Everyone leaned forward, and those with paddles placed the T grips on the floor, pointing the flat paddle end in the air. They hit the rocks and a wall of water cascaded into the raft. Mary screamed in frustration and stood instead of shifting back into the proper seated position. The guide yelled. Nel reached for her, but the raft dipped and jarred.

Losing her balance, Mary grabbed Nel's wrist. They both pitched forward.

Time slowed to a crawl.

The wind licked Nel's damp skin as she tumbled from the raft. The roar of rushing water sounded faint and lulling against the hard, fast, steady beat of her heart. A hard splash sliced through the sound and then she was cocooned in a blanket of cold water.

Panic erupted. She wanted to breathe, to gasp for air, but some sane part of her brain prevented it. She flashed back to the accident that killed her parents. The lightning, the storm, the rushing water of the flash flood.

She forced the memories from her mind. She needed a clear head, not only for herself, but for Mary.

Sunlight hit her face. She forced open her eyes as she bobbed in the water. The life jacket had done its job.

Mary, slightly more than a yard away, screamed and flailed her arms.

"Calm down and put your legs up! We'll float!"

Mary drifted close enough for Nel to grab her. "Do this." Nel flipped her feet into position. "Do it now!"

Mary did as instructed. Nel aimed her feet toward the raft. The guide and paddlers had slowed for them to catch up. Nel used her free arm to steer them. Mary clung to the other.

When they reached the raft, Nel clasped the side and pushed Mary's bottom upward as the others hoisted the girl into the raft. Then it was her turn. She didn't have anyone to push up her ample bottom, but with the others' help, she managed to wiggle into the boat without slipping.

"You did good," the guide told her.

Good?

What she'd done was damned amazing.

Tristan stood at the rafting dock, squinting against the sun and straining his neck to see downriver. Unfortunately, his wolfan vision didn't enable him to see around the bend.

When Nel had fallen out of the raft, Tristan's heart had leaped from his chest. Despite the debilitating flash of panic, he would've dived in after her if she hadn't bobbed up almost immediately.

Nel had remembered the safety instructions and gotten Mary and herself back to the raft without incident.

Tristan couldn't have been more proud.

Even so, his anxiety hadn't eased and wouldn't until Nel reached dry land and was tucked safely in his arms.

The distant rumble of laughter reached him before the raft came into view. Nel was all smiles.

Instead of relief, all Tristan felt was the scurrying sting of imaginary insects crawling beneath his skin. And the coiling of a python around his chest and stomach.

He needed, actually *needed*, to feel Nel in his arms, to breathe her scent into his lungs. Hoping to curb the trembling, he fisted his hands.

The raft drifted toward the landing at a leisurely pace

in the stream's calmer current. Tristan was no longer interested in the rest of the field trip. He just wanted Nel, a nice secluded spot and no clothes between them.

When the raft reached the dock, Nel gave him a thumbs-up. Tristan helped unload the kids off the raft, and then Nel. When his fingers clasped her hand, relief mixed with a healthy dose of desire flushed out the dread and anxiety.

"That was fun!" A broad smile curved her luscious mouth; a healthy flush brightened her skin.

"She's a trouper," the guide said.

"You have no idea." Tristan unfastened Nel's life preserver and slipped it off her shoulders. Despite her hair plastered to her head and wet clothes sticking to her body like a frumpy second skin, she had never looked more beautiful.

He dropped the life preserver onto the ground and cupped her face, his thumb strumming her rosy cheek. "Are you okay?"

"Fantastic." Confidence sparkled in her eyes.

The need to touch her, kiss her, make love to her nearly crushed him. Had they been alone, he would've surrendered without a fight.

Nel was unlike any woman he'd ever known. Caring, sensitive, ferociously brave. Now that he knew her, he couldn't imagine ever growing tired of her company, her touch, her sweetness, her creativity. Her nearness was a comfort. Her touch nirvana. Her taste addictive. Her scent divine.

"You gave me quite a scare." Tristan lifted her hand and pressed his lips against her knuckles.

"I knew what to do, thanks to you." She grinned. "You're an excellent teacher."

"Remember," he teased, "I'm excellent at a lot of things."

"Indeed, you are."

As if it was the most natural thing in the world, they walked hand in hand to where the group had gathered.

Carmen did a head count. Everyone was present, except for Mary. Even after a few calls, the girl didn't answer.

"I know she got off the raft," Nel assured them. "I should've kept an eye on her afterward."

"This isn't your fault. She was told to stay with her group."

As Carmen began to put everyone into teams to start a search, Mary strolled out of the women's restroom in dry clothes.

"I got this," Tristan told Carmen. He kissed Nel's temple. "Go change. We'll meet back here in ten minutes."

Nel gathered her girls and led them to the changing room.

"Mary," Tristan said sternly. "Here. Now."

The girl rolled her eyes and took her time strolling toward him.

"You were reckless on the raft," he said, keeping his annoyance out of his voice. "You could've been hurt and you could've hurt someone else."

"Chill, man." She popped her gum.

"You could end up in a bad place if you don't learn to follow the rules."

"Yeah, okay." She sighed. "Is that it?"

"I know your family is going through a difficult time. It's hard to adjust to change, but your attitude, not your circumstance, is what will keep you from making and keeping friends. Everyone here has gone through hardships. Yours isn't special, so stop acting like an ass. Otherwise people will treat you like one."

Mary glared at him with the same icy-cold gaze her

mother, Deidre, had given him when they were dating and he'd done something that had pissed her off.

"There's opportunity in starting over, Mary. It's yours to make or lose. Choose wisely."

Tristan sent her back to the group gathering at the rendezvous place. He watched Nel chatting with her charges.

Mine.

The thought drifted through his mind.

He shook his head.

If only she could be.

Chapter 24

The scent of corn dogs, popcorn and cotton candy saturated the air. Throughout the fairgrounds, loudspeakers piping country music from the band performing in the outdoor pavilion competed with the calls, bells and whistles of carnival games. With the whooshes of rides and their riders' screams, and the hum of conversation from everyone who'd come out for the Fourth of July celebration, it was a wonder Nel could hear her own thoughts.

"Which prize do you want?" Tristan stopped in front of a gaming booth in the middle of the midway and gave Nel a wink.

She couldn't believe that after nearly a week of twelve-hour shifts and overtime he'd chosen to bring her to the festival instead of catching up on sleep.

Licking cotton candy off her thumb, Nel eyed the rotating tables of milk-bottle pyramids. "You know these games are rigged, right?"

Tristan waggled his eyebrows. "Which one?"

Nel looked at the collection of stuffed animals suspended from the rafters. "That one." She pointed at the small wolf with coloring similar to Tristan's wolf.

The game attendant unhooked the prize and set it on the counter. "Six wins and it goes home with the lady."

Tristan took out his wallet.

"He's just going to take your money."

"And I'm going to take that wolf." Tristan paid for six balls and lined them on the counter. He picked up the first, rolling it methodically in his hands. His expression set in serious study, he walked around the entire booth ignoring the taunts and goads made by the game attendant.

"That's one," Tristan said before Nel's mind had had time to register that he'd thrown the ball, never mind that he'd actually knocked over one of the pyramids.

The game attendant's jaw dropped. Shaking his head, he moved toward the tables.

"I'm not done." Tristan passed behind Nel, his hand gliding along her lower back, and a widespread thrill passed through her.

"I was going to clear the table," the attendant said.

"Not necessary." Tristan picked up the second ball. "Just stay out of the way."

He stalked around the booth, making five more throws. Each struck its target just as quickly and precisely as the first.

"Why did you pick that one?" Tristan asked as they walked away with Nel's prize.

"He reminds me of your wolf."

"Is that so?"

"Yep." Nel tucked the stuffed animal into her bag so his head was peeking out. "Besides, if I woke up in the middle of the night and saw one of those psychedelic ones on my dresser, I might have a heart attack."

"I wouldn't want that to happen."

"Me, either."

"Tristan!"

He and Nel stopped, turning toward the woman advancing on them. "I can't believe you're here with *her*!"

"Who I spend time with is none of your business, Deidre."

"Mary nearly drowned because of her!" Deidre jabbed her finger at Nel.

"That's not what happened," Tristan and Nel said in unison. Only his voice remained level, while Nel's rose a few octaves.

"When you picked up Mary after the field trip last week, Carmen and I explained what happened. We gave you a copy of the incident report that Nel, Carmen, myself and the rafting guide signed." Calm and authoritative Tristan showed no signs of the panic Nel felt as a result of Deidre's accusation.

"Nel, in all likelihood, saved Mary's life." Tristan laced his fingers around Nel's hand. "You should be thanking Nel, not attacking her."

Deidre's mouth twisted into an ugly frown. "Keep her away from my daughter, or you'll be sorry." Her gaze snapped to Nel. The sharp, icy stare caused Nel's stomach to churn as Deidre looked her up and down.

Following a derisive grunt, the angry mother turned abruptly and left.

"I dodged a bullet with that one." Tristan squinted in the direction Deidre had stomped off. "She used to be my high-school sweetheart. I can't imagine what my life would be like if I hadn't broken up with her."

Nel coughed. Tristan and Deidre together was an unpleasant association she did not want to dwell upon.

"Except," Tristan continued, "I wouldn't have met you."

He looked at Nel. An understated smile tugged at the corners of his mouth, and his eyes, vast chocolate pools, warmed.

Nel's body heated and it wasn't from the summer sun shining in the bright blue sky. Tristan had a way of making her feel special. Of course, that was all part of his charm.

She needed to be careful not to get swept away by his compliments and attention. Or she'd be the one who was in danger of drowning in her own foolishness.

"This is so exciting." Nel clapped her hands and held them to her mouth. "I've never even been on a plane."

Too bad her excitement wasn't contagious. Tristan gripped the edge of the giant basket, trying not to flinch every time the burner fired.

"How high will we go?" Nel asked the pilot.

"Around twenty-three hundred feet."

Great, just great.

He must be out of his damn mind. He hated heights, but the look on Nel's face when she'd seen the hot-air balloon ride that the Chamber of Commerce was sponsoring made it impossible for him to say no.

Nel continued chatting with the pilot, but the roar in Tristan's ears prevented him from hearing the actual conversation. He took slow, measured breaths to relax and tried to focus his thoughts on how much fun Nel was having rather than about how horrific their deaths would be if they plunged to the ground in a fiery ball.

"Everything okay?" Nel squeezed Tristan's arm.

"Yeah," he said, not feeling okay at all. His stomach tingled uncomfortably, like there were ants scurrying inside his intestines.

"It's such a beautiful day." She leaned on the basket's railing, her face lifted to the sky.

Tristan kissed her temple, praying they would make it safely back to earth once they launched.

His heart raced as one by one the ties fell away. By the time the basket bumped from the ground, Tristan felt like he would have a full-blown heart attack.

If Wahyas were meant to float in the sky, they would've been born with feathers and wings. He wasn't even a fan of flying in a plane.

Pure joy radiated from Nel as they rose higher. Tristan did his best not to look like a scaredy-cat. The first time he'd flown on a plane, he'd been happily sedated. The next time was an absolute nightmare. A large cold front had moved in over Atlanta about the time the plane had started to descend. With no way around it, they'd had to fly straight through it. The cabin shook so hard the overhead compartments spilled their contents, the oxygen bags dropped and Tristan swore the rivets were loosening.

The plane had landed hard, jarring and bouncing passengers in their seats as they slid to a long, screeching halt. But for several long seconds he hadn't been sure they would actually stop.

Cooler air pricked his skin the higher they rose. Nel listened aptly to the pilot's monologue on the view.

"Beautiful, isn't it?"

Tristan didn't take his eyes off Nel's rapturous glow. "Breathtaking."

An impish grin plumped her cheeks. "The world looks perfect from here." She turned back around. "From this perspective, you can't see all the things going wrong. The bad decisions, the heartbreak, the sickness and disease. Everything looks calm, peaceful. Hopeful."

He sensed a brief moment of melancholy coming from Nel, and then felt a rush of gratefulness.

"It's good to be alive." She rubbed her bare arms dotted with goose bumps.

Tristan uncurled his stiff fingers and loosened his grip on the rail. Reaching for Nel, he pulled her in front of him, sheltering her with his body. When she was tucked safely against him, he fastened his hands back on the rail and rested his chin on the crown of her head.

Mine.

Instead of a loud and insistent declaration, the word hummed in his head.

Nel was right. Up here, everything was perfect.

Black velvet stretched across the expanse above them. If not for the twinkling pinpoint brilliance of innumerable stars, Nel thought the darkness would have swallowed them whole.

Hundreds of people reclined in lawn chairs or sat on blankets on the south side of the hill that faced the water. On the small island, not quite in the center of the lake, the outline of figures appeared in the muted glow of lantern light.

Nel hadn't been this excited, or had this much fun, since her parents took her to a carnival when she was five.

"They're almost ready," Tristan assured her.

"How can you tell?"

He was silent for a moment. "Timing. I'm usually out there helping. From the moment they step off the boat, everything they do takes a specific amount of time. It's practically a science."

"I'm glad you're with me and not out there tonight."

"Me, too." Tristan nuzzled her cheek. Warm fuzzies danced beneath her skin.

She loved how cozy and comfortable she was with Tristan. And how relaxed and in tune with her he seemed.

"Here we go."

No sooner had he said the words than a boom echoed

over the water. She tipped her face to the sky as an explosion of red, white and blue filled the heavens. Sparkles of green and ribbons of gold followed.

Every time color burst in the sky, Nel's heart swelled.

When she'd accepted the summer job at the resort, Nel had wanted to make a definite change in her life. Never had she dreamed someone like Tristan would be part of that transformation.

Sinfully handsome, Tristan could have, and probably did have, any woman he wanted. That he wanted her and all her flaws, well, it was indescribable.

He nibbled her ear and a sense of him filled her spirit. Maybe it was imagination or wishful thinking. All she knew for sure was that she'd never felt more content. She'd heard the saying "You complete me," and it always irked her. She didn't need anyone to complete her. As an individual, she was complete. What she felt with Tristan was more like a painting suddenly taking on three dimensions. The painting itself was perfectly complete, but the textured layers added richness and depth.

The last vibrant color burst faded from the sky, leaving thick, smoky scars in the black expanse, obscuring the starry twinkles.

Nel wished for five more minutes. But, if given the extra time, she would've wished for five more. And so on and so on.

She hated for the day to end.

Tristan made no move to gather their things.

"Man, I wish I didn't have to work tonight," he sighed.

Nel laughed. "Bet that's the first time you've ever wished that."

"Never had a reason to wish for it, until now."

Tristan walked Nel to her car. "Be careful. Unfortunately, there will be drunk drivers on the road tonight."

"I'll be careful."

Neither made a move to part.

"Do you want to make plans to do something next week?" she finally asked.

"I haven't decided if that's a good idea or not." He seemed as conflicted by their evolving situation as Nel. Was this *thing* between them only a summer fling? Was it wise to continue their course? What would happen when it came time for her to return to Atlanta?

"Should we say goodbye, see you around?"

Tristan frowned.

"I didn't like the sound of that, either." She tugged on the front of Tristan's shirt. "I like spending time with you. But if you want us to stop now, that's okay. It's been fun." Really, really fun.

Tristan's frowned deepened. Dark emotions simmered in his eyes.

He slanted his mouth over hers, kissing her soundly. Possessively.

His heat warmed her as he held her against him. Slowly, his hips rocked against her and the rigidness pressed into her stomach. Not only did she feel safe and protected with Tristan, she felt wanted.

"Good night, Nel," he panted hoarsely.

She practically floated on clouds back to the cabin. Because *good night* was definitely not a last goodbye.

Chapter 25

"Hey, Nel. Got plans this afternoon?"

Nel put up the last of the supplies from Friday morning's workshop and turned to see Cassie and Grace standing in the doorway. "Not really." Tristan was working, so she expected another quiet afternoon of painting. "Why?"

"We're going shopping." Cassie smiled.

"Where? I haven't seen any malls in Maico."

"We're driving down to Commerce for the afternoon," Grace said.

"And you want me to babysit?"

Grace laughed. "I told you she'd think that."

Cassie shook her head. "We're childless for the afternoon. The kids are at the Co-op child-care center."

"We thought it would be fun to have a girls' afternoon out."

"Wanna come?" Cassie prompted Nel with an affirmative nod.

"Absolutely." Although she loved painting, a break from another solitary day in the cabin would be nice.

Nel hadn't seen Tristan in over a week. When off-duty from the sheriff's office, he was covering extra shifts for the Co-op's security force because a nasty virus had left the team shorthanded.

"Great," Grace said. "Cassie is chauffeuring."

Nel locked up the classroom and accompanied them to the valet stand.

"Why don't you have Jimmy drive your car to the cabin?" Cassie suggested. "When we get back, I'll drop you off at the cabin on my way home."

"I didn't use the valet service."

"I'll drop it off, just the same," the young valet said.

"Jimmy does it for me whenever I leave with Brice," Cassie told her.

"Just the car key, please." Jimmy held out his hand.

Nel fished the key off the ring and handed it to him.

"I'll treat your car as if it were my own." Jimmy grinned.

"I hope that's a good thing."

A champagne-colored minivan pulled up.

A sandy-haired young man exited the vehicle. "Are you sure you don't want me to call Shane?"

"No," Cassie and Grace said in unison.

Cassie walked around the vehicle to get in. Grace and Nel climbed into the passenger's side.

As they drove off, Nel asked, "Why would he ask to call Shane?"

"Shane is like a pesky little brother," Cassie said. "He believes it's his mission to keep an eye on us when our husbands aren't around."

"Why?"

"Brice and Rafe told him to." Grace cracked a smile. "They're overprotective."

"With good reason," Cassie said grimly. "But that's all in the past and there is no cause for them to worry about a trip to the mall."

"Except maybe the credit-card bill." Grace laughed.

Nel didn't have anyone to account to. Though she didn't want a man who hovered over her every move, it would be nice to have someone who cared about her well-being.

"How do you like teaching at the resort?" Grace asked.

"It's a lot of fun," Nel admitted. "The hours aren't bad, either. Neither are the perks."

"The Co-op takes care of its members and its employees," Cassie said.

"Tristan said the Co-op is like a huge extended family."

"It is," Grace piped in. "It was daunting at first, but I've grown to love the Co-op community."

"Me, too," Cassie said. "I don't have any family of my own."

"Hey," Grace protested. "I'm family." She looked back at Nel. "Not by blood. We're heart sisters."

"Must be nice." Nel felt a twinge of jealousy. She had a few friends, but none she would consider a heart sister.

"Gavin mentioned that the Co-op's charter school will be hiring soon." Cassie glanced in the rearview mirror at Nel. "Would you be interested in a position?"

"I have a job in Atlanta," Nel said.

"Do you have family there?" Grace twisted in her seat.

"An aunt and uncle, but we're estranged. Permanently."

"Family isn't just the people you're related to by blood." Cassie gave Grace's arm a sisterly squeeze.

"Good thing. My parents were overseas during my pregnancy. The Co-op was a godsend. They brought food and cleaned the house when all I could do was puke out my guts from the morning sickness." Grace ran her fingers through her blond ponytail. "Good times."

Nel longed to experience the support and concern of

so many people. Scared and alone was not a position she ever wanted to be in again, especially if she were sick.

Maybe it wouldn't be a bad thing to give thought to Cassie's suggestion. The people, so far, seemed open and friendly. The Walkers had been good employers. She loved the area. And she'd painted more in the last few weeks than she had in the last two years.

Then there was Tristan.

A warm, cozy feeling ebbed through her body. He'd added a certain spice to her life. Going back to her bland existence would be difficult.

Different than anyone she'd dated, Tristan appeared genuinely interested in what interested her. She loved the way he watched her paint and praised her talent, and especially how he gently thumbed the streaks of paint from her face and hands. Not to mention the fire in his eyes that could heat her body and rev her up faster than anyone.

But as much as she enjoyed his company, he was a hardwired bachelor. Eventually she would want to marry and have a family. But how could she fall for someone else, if her heart wasn't in it?

"Even if I did relocate here," Nel said, looking at the scenery flashing by the car window, "I'd have to marry a Co-op man to be included in everything."

"You and Tristan seem pretty cozy." Cassie's reflection in the rearview mirror targeted Nel. "I've never seen him take more than a split-second interest in someone."

"We're friends."

"Tristan doesn't look at his friends the way he looked at you at Brenna's party or the Fourth of July festival," Grace said.

"You should explore that." Cassie grinned. "The two of you fit together well. You're very in sync."

"It does feel—" Nel paused "—comfortable." But that could be in part due to their understanding that whatever was between them would only last the summer. She valued his friendship and didn't want to risk losing him over a romantic blunder on her part.

"Tristan and I have different lifestyles." He was so busy with work, family and volunteering, there simply wasn't much time for anyone else in Tristan's life, at least long term. Nel had taken the back seat in her previous relationships. She wanted to break old patterns, not repeat them.

"Tristan?" Nel's heart stumbled over its beat at the sight of him leaning against her car in the resort parking lot as she was leaving work. Only Tuesday, she hadn't expected to see him until Thursday afternoon when he'd planned to take her fishing.

Still in uniform, he looked so tired that he could barely stand. His hair was mussed, his eyes were bloodshot, rough stubble covered his jaw and his mouth was pulled down so tight his lips had lost color.

"One of the kids I mentor," he said in a ragged breath, "OD'd."

Nel's heart clenched. "Oh, Tristan." She took his hands in hers.

"I was at the hospital with him all night."

Before she asked about the teen's condition, Tristan subtly shook his head.

Nel didn't know the kid but the weight of Tristan's loss and sorrow caved her chest.

"Want to get away from here for a while?"

"Sure." She had no particular plans for the afternoon. "Do I need to change?"

Tristan's gaze moved over her summer dress down

to her feet encased in white tennis shoes. "No, you look great."

Nel knew she didn't. Comfortable, but not great.

Still, his eyes warmed with interest and if his heart hadn't been hurting he might've kissed her.

She turned off the lights and locked the door to the activity room. Tristan hooked his arm around hers. They walked silently to his truck and he helped her into the vehicle. She didn't offer any words of comfort. She knew there were none.

But she did know one thing. "It wasn't your fault. He was lucky to have you in his life, even as it ended."

He didn't meet her gaze, but he did let go of a heavy breath and she could see the tension in his shoulders loosen.

Tristan drove to his apartment. "Mind if I shower and change before we head out?"

"Please do." Her tease was rewarded with a tentative smile.

He led her up the stairs and into his apartment. It looked exactly the same as when she'd picked up his clothes.

"Your decorating taste surprised me." She sat on the black leather sofa.

"Not mine, my mother's." Tristan removed his weapon and secured it in a locked box he stored on a shelf in the hall closet. "She's an interior designer."

"Does she know you at all?" Nel said without thinking. "Sorry, I shouldn't have said that."

"Don't be," Tristan said without censure. "And, no, she doesn't know me very well. Make yourself at home. I won't be long."

He headed into the bedroom, and a few minutes later Nel heard the water running in the shower. Trying not to picture him naked and slick with water, she picked up an *Architectural Digest* magazine off the coffee table. Two articles were dog-eared and one design had X's and circles with scribbled notes as to what Tristan would change.

Someone knocked at the door.

Nel answered, surprised to see the resort's chief of security. "Mr. Coots, come in."

"Call me Cooter." Removing his hat, he eased inside. "Everyone else does."

"Please have a seat." She waved toward the couch, feeling a bit awkward since this wasn't her home. "Tristan will be out in a few minutes."

A strange look flashed in Cooter's eyes and then it was gone. "Pardon my intrusion."

"We just came in ourselves."

"You and Tristan have become quite friendly, I hear." His congenial smile didn't match the suspicion in his eyes. "With you taking care of him and all."

"We're friends," she said, ignoring the compulsion to explain further. They were adults and she didn't need to provide justification for her actions, or Tristan's, to anyone.

"Would you like something to drink?"

"No, thank you, ma'am."

Nel gritted her teeth. Although *ma'am* was a polite social term in Southern communities, she hated the use of it when applied to her. Especially since Cooter was at least thirty years her senior.

"Is this a social visit or business? I could ask Tristan to hurry, if you need him."

"I'm a patient man," he said in a Southern drawl. "I can wait."

Nel didn't believe in telepathy, but she sent a few thoughts Tristan's way, urging him to hurry. She went to the kitchen and got herself a glass of water, just to have something to do.

The shower cut off. Less than a minute later, Tristan strolled out wearing nothing but a towel fastened around his waist. His hair and skin were damp, as if he'd rushed out.

"Cooter, why are you here?" Tristan's voice sounded rougher than normal.

The older man stood. "You weren't answering your phone. Gavin has a new security plan for the Co-op he wants to discuss with us."

Nel's heart sank. She was looking forward to spending the afternoon with Tristan and he needed the break.

"Can it wait?"

"Gavin wants this taken care of ASAP."

"It's okay, Tristan," Nel piped in. "I can take a rain check."

"I don't want a rain check," Tristan snarled, but not at her. Glaring at Cooter, Tristan stalked so close to the man, they nearly chest bumped. "If what Gavin wants has to be done today, recruit Reed. He wants more responsibility and he's up for the challenge."

"Tristan—"

"No." He cut off Cooter. "I pulled a twenty-hour shift because one deputy is on vacation and two more were sent home with food poisoning. As I was getting off, I got a call that one of the Outreach kids had overdosed. I've spent the last nine hours at his bedside because we couldn't locate the boy's mother.

"She showed up ten minutes too late. So, no, goddammit, I don't want to sit through another one of Gavin's long-winded security meetings where neither of you give a damn about what I have to say."

Tristan opened the door. "I'm spending the afternoon

with Nel. If Gavin has a problem with that, he can replace me."

His entire body trembled and he balled his fingers into his palms. His face darkened, leaving no trace of his usual amicable, flirtatiously friendly demeanor. Instead, he looked dangerously angry.

"As you wish." Cooter slipped on his hat and stepped outside. "Nice meeting you, Nel."

Tristan slammed the door, stretched his arms, pressing both hands against the frame, and thumped his head against the door.

Nel pressed the palm of her hand against the small of his back and a jolt of electricity shot through her. Tristan whipped around, hauled her against him and kissed her harshly and possessively. His hands urgently roamed her curves.

Nel yielded without complaint and she felt pretty sure they'd spend the rest of the day in the bedroom. If they ever made it out of the living room.

Suddenly, Tristan jerked away from her, his eyes fierce and his face strained.

"Nel, we can't do this," he said, his voice thick and raw with emotion. "I can't do this right now." His face contorted and he squinted at her. "I need to get out of here and do something fun."

"Having sex with me isn't fun?"

"That's not what I meant." He took her face in his hands. "When we make love, I want to be in the moment with you, not trying to block something out."

Warmed, Nel slipped her arms around Tristan and pressed against his torso. "Whatever you need."

"I'm beginning to think…" His voice trailed off. "I should get dressed."

Nel watched him disappear into the bedroom, her

heart suspended midbeat. She didn't even dare to breathe, afraid to disperse the ethereal sentiment drifting through her soul because when his spoken words had faded, his voice in her mind continued.

I'm beginning to think...all I need is you.

The sun dipped low behind the hazy blue mountain range, setting the sky afire with streaks of burnished orange. Nel stood on the observation deck of Brasstown Bald, the highest peak in Georgia. A summer wind, cooled by the higher altitude, nipped her skin and whipped strands of her hair around her face.

Tristan moved behind her, caging her between his arms. His body blocked the restless wind and his heat warmed her down to her soul.

They'd shared a perfect afternoon.

First, he'd taken her on a scenic drive, stopping for a hike through the woods to Track Rock, where he showed her the petroglyphs carved in ancient rocks. She'd even found an old stone arrowhead walking back to the truck.

On the trip back to Maico, they stopped at this local scenic attraction to mill around the exhibits and take in the gorgeous scenery.

"From the road," Nel began, "this mountaintop looks bald."

"Hence the name, Brasstown Bald." Tristan chuckled in her ear.

"How did it get this way? Over-forested? A fungus? Fire?"

"No one is really sure. The top was bare when the settlers came." Tristan's voice dropped. "There is a legend, though."

"Really?" Nel turned in his arms to face him. "A good one, I hope."

"There are other balds in the southern Appalachians, some right next to fully vegetated mountaintops. I've read several ecological and environmental theories, but I'm partial to the Native American legend."

"Yeah? How does it explain what happened?"

"Before the Anglo settlers invaded, the Cherokee Nation was attacked by terrible flying beasts with a huge wingspan and long, sharp talons. The beasts terrorized the villagers and stole their children.

"A council convened to discuss ways to capture or kill the creatures. After many days, they decided to clear the mountaintops of trees so the bird demons would have nowhere to roost. But the raids continued.

"The villagers built a tower and set up scouts to warn of impending attacks. Eventually, one of the scouts noticed the creatures entering and leaving from the inaccessible cliffs on the mountain.

"Two men attempted to climb down to the den. Unfortunately, they found the task insurmountable due to the smooth, perpendicular walls that protected the giant nest. But they were able to count at least a dozen or more hatchlings feeding on the villagers' stolen children."

"That's horrible."

"Ever hear of Hansel and Gretel?"

"Good point. Continue." Nel leaned back into the warmth of Tristan's chest. His arms wrapped around her waist.

"The villagers urgently prayed to the Creator. Suddenly, thunder roared across a clear sky. Out of nowhere, hundreds of lightning bolts struck the ancient cliffs in succession.

"The earth shook with a mighty force, black trails of smoke curled into the heavens and earsplitting shrieks caused the villagers to fall to the ground, holding their ears.

"Silence fell. The bird demons' reign of terror was over."

Silence fell between Nel and Tristan, too. Silence of the amicable kind, not the numbing silence a victim experiences once an ordeal had passed.

Tristan nudged her ear. "Hungry?"

"Not after that story." In protest, her stomach growled.

"Come on. I know a great place."

She loved the way he captured her hand, so naturally and without deliberate thought. His fingers curled through hers as if it were the most natural thing in the world.

She shouldn't like it so much, but she did.

The men she'd previously dated had been awkward and shy, like her. Even a little clumsy when it came to affection. Or they had been so terribly self-absorbed in their own nerdish world that she felt like an outsider in their relationship.

It was all so easy with Tristan. Probably because he'd had plenty of practice. She felt a twinge of jealousy, though she really knew she shouldn't.

Tristan never made her feel inadequate or not up to his standard. He seemed to genuinely appreciate her company. Maybe even appreciated her.

"You can add mountain climbing to your list of new experiences."

Nel stopped midstride. "Mountain climbing?"

"Sure." He pointed at the paved incline they were now descending. "This bald is the tallest mountain in Georgia. We walked all the way to the top."

Pride pearled in her chest. "Wow. I climbed a mountain."

"You certainly did, sweet cheeks. You certainly did."

Chapter 26

Nel awoke in the pillow-soft comfort of Tristan's over-size mattress. Instead of taking her to the cabin after supper, he'd brought Nel to his apartment to watch a movie. It was a silly comedy neither of them would've normally watched, but it contained no violence and no one died, so it was exactly what Tristan had needed. They'd even shared popcorn and soda and a box of Junior Mints.

Nel had eventually fallen asleep while Tristan spoke with Carmen on the phone about the funeral for the boy who overdosed. She rolled to her side, hugging his pillow. It held his clean, masculine scent.

After doing a full-body stretch, she threw back the covers and climbed out. Her toes curled in the thick carpet. Exiting the room, she padded into the living room wearing one of Tristan's soft T-shirts that hung to the tops of her thighs and caressed her skin as she walked. The yummy smell of bacon and coffee delighted her nose.

She plopped onto a bar stool to watch the chef at work. Earbuds in his ears, he swayed and bobbed to some unknown tune. He glanced behind him, tossing her a saucy wink. Finished with the bacon, he placed the strips on a plate of paper towels to drain.

Tristan tugged the earbuds from his ears. "Morning, sweet cheeks."

After he poured her a cup of coffee, he leaned across the counter to give her a kiss.

"I could get used to this." She blew over the rim of her mug.

"Me, too." Tristan met her gaze.

Nel wondered if Tristan was warming to the idea of a relationship. She certainly was. He opened the oven a few seconds before the timer buzzed, pulled out a ceramic pan and set it on the counter.

"Smells delicious. What is it?"

"Crème brûlée French toast." He lifted a small pan from the stove and poured the contents over the French toast. "With raspberry sauce."

"You're amazing."

"I try," he teased without cockiness. He plated the food. "I wanted to serve you breakfast in bed."

"Mmm." Nel licked her lips. "Tempting, but we should probably eat here. If we get distracted in bed, the food will get cold and I'm really hungry."

"I see your point." Grinning, he grabbed two forks from the drawer and sat next to her as they ate.

"Feeling better today?"

Tristan had not mentioned the boy's death to her again after leaving the resort. Still, there were moments yesterday when Nel knew Tristan was wondering if there was something he could've or should've done for the kid.

Tristan gave a noncommittal nod. His gaze lifted from his plate and warmed her skin with a slow sweep of her face. "Are you worried about me?"

"I am." Nel cared about him. Deeply.

From the start, she'd known better than to allow her heart to become emotionally invested in Tristan.

Everyone had warned her that he wasn't the type of man to settle down. Yet, the more she got to know him, the more she wanted to believe the naysayers were wrong.

Tristan had a lot more depth to his personality than people realized. Kind, intelligent and sincere, he never made her feel intimidated or lacking.

"Don't blame yourself for an outcome you had no control over. You can't save everyone, even though you want to."

"Figured that out about me, huh?" His hand slid over to hers and he toyed with her fingers.

"It wasn't hard." She offered him a smile.

Too bad Tristan wasn't interested in a long-term relationship. When the summer ended, it would be hard not seeing him. Hard not to call or text.

He probably had the routine down pat.

"What's wrong?" Concern filled Tristan's eyes.

"Nothing." Melancholy would not ruin their time together, no matter how short-lived.

"If you don't like breakfast, I can make something else. Or we can go out."

"Breakfast is delicious." She smiled at him. "If we went out, I'd have to put on my clothes."

Tristan's gaze darkened. "I could make it my goal to keep you naked for as long as possible." He cupped the back of her neck and pulled her closer as he leaned forward. He teased her with a light touch of his lips before he devoured her mouth. He tasted of coffee and raspberries.

"You were asleep when I came to bed last night." He caressed her thigh, drawing his hand beneath her shirt and along her bare hip.

Heat whipped through her and pooled low in her belly. Anticipation tightened her nipples.

"I'm awake now."

His fingers danced over her abdomen and down her sex, slipping through her folds.

"I love how wet you get for me," he breathed heavily.

She loved that he could affect her like that.

He pulled away from her. "Bend over the bar stool."

"Seriously?" They had a bed, a couch, the floor.

Still, she did as he asked, easing one leg off the seat, then the other. They stood so close together she could feel his heat.

Tristan reached over his head and yanked off his T-shirt. He was a solid wall of perfectly sculpted muscle and tanned flesh. He unbuttoned his shorts and shoved them down. His large erection bounced free.

Her body ached for his hands caressing, stroking her body, his tongue sweeping her mouth, sucking her breasts, laving her folds, his cock filling her, possessing her, driving her to the point of explosive pleasure.

She couldn't move of her own volition; her bones had turned to the consistency of pudding. He turned her around, urging her to bend over the bar stool and grip the legs for support. Her breasts and belly pressed into the hard wood seat, the hem of the T-shirt rode the curve of her bottom.

"You have a great ass." Tristan's warm hands gripped her globes, kneading the flesh. His knee parted her legs, wider and wider.

She swallowed her breath as his fingers slid through her wetness, teasing her opening using the pad of his finger to trace the outer rim.

Oh, god, close. So close.

Impatience grated in her voice as she panted his name.

He wouldn't let her come, at first, drawing out her pleasure until she finally came undone with explosive abandon.

Still reeling in the waves of ecstasy, she felt the plump head of his cock against her folds. He was gathering her wetness before entering. Her knuckles whitened from her tightened grip on the bar stool.

His body curved around her. "Ready, sweet cheeks?"

"Mmm-hmm," she murmured, since speech had deserted her.

Positioned at her entrance, he teased her with false starts. Her groans of aggravation invoked a deep, sexy growl from Tristan.

When he finally pushed a tiny way inside her, she wanted to scream and would've pushed back, sheathing him further, if his legs hadn't immobilized hers.

At his mercy, she would have to endure the sweet torture as he pulled out, entered her again, inching deeper. By the time he filled her completely, she was seeing stars.

He held himself deep inside her and his breaths fell ragged and harsh against the back of her neck.

Good. He deserved to be as on edge as she was.

"I can't do this slow," he panted.

"Then don't." She gulped.

His sexy laugh was drowned out by the sudden rush of blood to her ears when Tristan began thrusting hard and his sac slapped against her folds. His fingers dug into her hips. The pressure in her sex built to such an intensity Nel felt her body would come undone as wave after wave after wave of pleasure pummeled her senses.

Tristan gave one last thrust and growled. He took several long breaths, then bent over her. "Okay, sweet cheeks?" he asked quietly.

"Uh-huh," she murmured.

He didn't withdraw the minute he was finished, and she liked the intimacy of those extra few moments because she could feel Tristan's presence deep within her soul.

He nuzzled her neck, nibbling up to her ear. *God, I love this.*

"Me, too." Nel sighed.

"What did you say?" Tristan stilled, his heartbeat freezing midstrike.

"Me, too." Nel turned her flushed face over her shoulder. Contentment shimmered in her eyes. "You said *God, I love this* and I said *Me, too.*"

Tristan eased out of her, a smile planted on his face. Something wasn't right. She shouldn't have heard his thoughts.

They couldn't communicate telepathically unless joined through a mate-bond.

A zip of excitement lit up every nerve, every cell in Tristan's body. He didn't dare hope it was possible. Independent of a mate-claim, a mate-bond only formed between true mates, binding them together in body, mind, heart and soul. No one in his family had ever developed the ethereal bond with a mate.

Tristan gave Nel enough room to stand and turn around. She tugged down the hem of the T-shirt and he yanked up his shorts.

"We seem to be good together," she said cautiously. "Or am I totally off?"

He honestly didn't know how to answer.

"Got it." She flashed a brave smile but Tristan read the hurt and disappointment in her eyes. "I need to get dressed."

She turned away.

"You're not off, Nel," he said, catching her wrist. "But I don't know if this is a good thing. My family's relationship track record is pretty shitty."

"So, you're afraid to try," she said, playfully thumping him dead in the middle of his chest.

He didn't like how clearly she saw his weakness.

"I wasted too many years afraid to try new things," she said, chin up and shoulders squared. "I didn't think I was good enough, smart enough or pretty enough to go after what I wanted."

"If I ever meet the people who made you believe those things, I might strangle them."

Probably not the direction she intended the conversation to take, but Tristan didn't find Nel lacking in anything.

There was a pregnant pause between them.

"If you always do what you have always done, you'll only get what you've always had." She shrugged.

Tristan really wanted something different. He was tired of filling his life with work so he wouldn't have too much time to dwell on how empty he felt.

Nel filled the void. Going forward without her seemed unbearable. Shakespeare was wrong. It wasn't better to have loved and lost than never to have loved. Because deep in his soul Tristan knew if he ever lost Nel, he simply would not be able to go on.

Taking her hand, he led her to the couch. He sat and propped his feet on the coffee table. She scooted beneath his arm and snuggled against him.

"Let's see how the rest of the summer goes." Maybe Nel hearing his thoughts had been a fluke. The possibility of a mate-bond forming seemed too far-fetched for him to accept.

He wanted Nel and so did his wolf. But wanting someone didn't guarantee they wanted you, too. Nor did it guarantee happiness even if they did.

His parents lived with that truth daily. Some people said they were too angry with each other over the accidental claiming to allow the ethereal mate-bond to form.

Others thought a mate-claim was a crapshoot because they didn't believe mate-bonds existed. Having seen it at work in his friends' mateships, Tristan certainly believed in the possibility but he simply didn't have faith that he would be one of the fortunate ones.

As far as he knew, no one in his family ever had a happy mateship. They seemed to thrive on conflict and he had made the choice not to live that way.

Nel snuggled against him, her eyes drifting shut and her mouth curved with a satisfied smile. Tristan pressed his cheek against the top of her head. A feeling of contentment and protectiveness welled inside him.

He'd never actually craved any particular woman, but he certainly craved Nel. He loved her kindness, her bravery, her innocent nature. And the need to join with her, to possess her, to pleasure her, had kept him awake during the night.

And now that he'd given in to the overwhelming instinct, his mind howled *Mine, mine, mine* with every beat of his heart.

The strange thing was that Tristan hadn't felt the overwhelming instinct to bite and claim Nel as they made love. He kinda thought he should have, especially if Nel was his true mate.

Instead of having to battle his inner wolf to maintain control, he'd never felt more at peace.

Except for the little prick in his conscience that nagged him to tell Nel the truth about who and what he was.

The doorbell rang.

Nel sat up, eyes blinking rapidly. Tristan handed her the throw he kept draped across the back of the sofa.

With Nel modestly covered, he answered the door.

"Hello, Mother."

Suzannah swept into the apartment. "Why can't you answer your phone? You know I hate coming here. Really, Tristan. You can afford to live somewhere other than this dump."

"This apartment building isn't a dump," he sighed. "It's historic." Of course, the term was loosely applied. However, he did love some of the old architecture. "Besides, you decorated the apartment for me, remember?"

"Yes, yes. Once I get inside, I'm fine. It's the hideous three-level walk-up that stabs my eyes." Suzannah finally took notice of Nel, sitting on the couch, a soft glow of sexual satisfaction radiating from her.

No one could mistake what she and Tristan had been up to this morning.

"Are you feeling well, dear?" She looked at Tristan with a curious gaze.

"I feel great, why?"

"I've never known you to bring your sexual partners into your home."

Nel's cheeks reddened and she stood. "I'll be in the bedroom. Getting dressed."

Suddenly, Tristan's inner wolf wasn't so happy. Or peaceable.

He waited for the bedroom door to close before he interrupted his mother's prattle.

"Don't come into my home and disrespect her again."

Suzannah moved closer to Tristan, squinting at his face. "Did you do something stupid?"

"No." Tristan swallowed. "I'm always careful."

"Good. No woman should have to put up with what I do."

"Mom, why are you here?"

"I'm looking for the artist you shacked up with a few weeks ago. She wasn't home. Do your sheriff thing and find her."

"I don't need to find Nel, I know exactly where she is."

The natural arch of Suzannah's blond eyebrows sharpened. "Are you sure you haven't done something stupid? You're not acting like your normal self."

He'd never felt more like himself. "I'm happy."

"I do have eyes, dear. Very good ones. You've always had a cheerful disposition, but this is something more. You seem…" She looked puzzled. "What's the word I'm looking for?"

"I don't know, Mom. *Content*, maybe?"

"That's it!" She poked his arm with her index finger. "Content. It's so very odd for you."

"Maybe because my screwed-up family is usually driving me insane?"

"Don't be rude. I raised you better."

"You didn't raise me at all."

Suzannah flinched as if his words had slapped against her face. "Everyone has regrets, Tristan. Probably no one's are greater than mine."

The bedroom door opened and Nel emerged neatly dressed with her hair brushed and loosely braided.

"Hello, dear." Hand extended, Suzannah stepped forward. Her calm, collected demeanor on perfect display. "So delighted to meet you. I'm Suzannah Durrance, Tristan's mother."

Nel cautiously accepted the handshake.

"I must say, I admire your work. It's very quaint and likely very marketable."

"I don't understand. You've seen my work?"

An uneasy feeling gnawed Tristan's gut.

"Tristan showed me."

"What?" Nel's sharp gaze cut to him. "You know I'm sensitive about my art."

"Mom found your paintings when she came to see me at the cabin. I didn't actually show her."

"I took pictures of your work and shared them with a friend who is a gallery owner in Atlanta. He's interested in seeing the actual pieces and asked me to arrange a meeting."

"I don't know what to say." A flurry of emotion flickered across Nel's features.

Tristan held her tightly. He couldn't be more proud. She had tremendous talent and he wanted the world to see it. He only hoped that when they did, her success wouldn't take her beyond his reach.

Chapter 27

Nel gripped the armrest as Tristan's truck jostled along the unpaved road toward a destination she would swear was right dab in the middle of nowhere. The engine strained at the upward climb. Tristan didn't appear to be nervous or uptight about the steep incline. Maybe she shouldn't be, either.

She returned her gaze to beyond her rolled-up window. The trees around them were tall and skinny, and the tops bristled with a thick canopy of leaves that blocked a good deal of sunlight.

"How did you ever find this place?" The location was so far off the highway she doubted it appeared on any map.

"Jaxen and I used to roam all through these woods." Tristan's grin said he was remembering good times. "I fell in love with the place the moment I saw it. Couldn't wait to get my license so I could drive up here. It's a long ride on a mountain bike to fish."

In the back seat lay Tristan's fly rod, a well-stocked tackle box, a net and a bucket. Along with a wool blanket and a fairly large picnic basket.

Tucked in the bag near Nel's feet were her sketch pad and pencils—and a book, just in case fishing wasn't her forte.

Ahead of them, the woods began to thin and the road began to level.

"Almost there." He tossed her a wink. "Excited?"

She nodded. "I love picnics."

"There's not much better than relaxing outdoors and having a nice meal."

"So, what is better?"

He shot her a quick look that blazed so hot her skin flushed from the heat. Images of Tristan's kisses, his hands kneading her flesh, steamed her vision.

She flicked the AC vent toward herself.

"Close your eyes and keep them closed." Instead of being commanding or demanding, Tristan's voice sounded playful, so she complied. "Don't open them until I tell you, okay?"

"Got it."

The truck bounced a few times, and a slight centrifugal force caused her to lean left. The ride smoothed out and they glided to a stop. "I'd better not see those beautiful eyes peeking at me when I get out."

He placed a gentle kiss on her lips.

"You won't," she sighed against his mouth.

His door opened and he climbed out. The door closed.

Anticipation made her anxious but she kept her eyes tightly shut. Her heart thudded at the crunch of shoes nearing her side of the vehicle. Silence fell, except for the beating of her heart, which pumped a steady stream of excitement into her core. Alone in the woods with a blanket and Tristan...

Her door swung open.

"Did I see you peek?" he teased.

"No, deputy. I did just as you asked."

"Good. I wouldn't want to arrest you for failing to comply."

"I wouldn't mind the handcuffs." The words leaped from her mouth without forethought.

Tristan stilled. His hand rested against her hip where the seat belt was clipped.

Nel's cheeks warmed. She wasn't sure where that comment had come from or why she said it. Handcuffs weren't among the few sex toys she had used. Somehow, with Tristan, Nel didn't think she would mind. She trusted him.

The thought rang clear as a Christmas church bell.

She trusted him.

"Ah, Nel." He nuzzled her cheek. "You know how to bring a man to his knees, don't you?"

Really, she didn't. Her sexual experiences had been quite tame.

She wanted to open her eyes to see Tristan's face, but he sweetly kissed each eyelid, then sighed.

He helped her from the vehicle and escorted her several feet before they stopped. The roar of water nearly deafened her.

Tristan stood behind her, his arms hugging her waist, his chin resting on her shoulder as his cheek pressed against hers. "Now, open your eyes."

She did and her breath caught in her throat.

The roar she heard came from a simple but stunning waterfall.

"I've never seen anything more beautiful in my life."

"I thought so, too, until I met you," Tristan whispered.

Heat and need fluttered in her sex. Here and now would be the perfect place, but Tristan glanced away.

"We should unload the truck."

Well, damn. For a renowned ladies' man, he sure missed a lot of the silent invitations she sent him.

Her heart clenched. Maybe he was losing interest. After all, summer was winding down and she would return to Atlanta soon.

Tristan handed her the picnic basket and blanket without so much as a second glance. He grabbed his fly rod, the bucket and his tackle box. He walked several yards downstream and announced, "This is probably the best spot."

Nel laid the blanket on the slightly damp ground. "What's first?"

"Fishing." He grinned. "That's what we're here for, right?"

"Right," she said, unenthused. Sports, including fishing, had never interested her much. But neither had mountain climbing or white-water rafting, until she'd gone with Tristan.

He sat cross-legged next to her on the blanket. After opening the tackle box he fingered through a small bin of lures. One by one he held them up in a beam of sunlight, turning each to inspect it from every angle. His brows creased in concentration, his lips pressed firmly together in a dissatisfied grimace until one prompted a toe-curling smile.

"This one." He held it toward her. "What do you think?"

Nel had no idea, so she said, "Perfect."

He showed her how to tie the fly onto the fishing line and provided detailed explanations that wafted in one ear and drifted out of the other. Periodically she nodded intently.

She couldn't care less about the details, but joy danced in Tristan's eyes as he explained, and she would have to be insane to douse his happiness.

Once everything was to Tristan's satisfaction, they pulled on their wading boots and carefully eased into the stream. Tristan stood behind her, his left arm curled around her waist, his right arm aligned with hers and his hand molded around her hand gripping the fly rod. After receiving more instruction than she'd ever wanted about fishing, she nodded her readiness.

Tristan slowly pulled back their arms and flicked their wrists. The line whipped over the water. He repeated the action until the lure settled in the exact spot he wanted. Fishing seemed serious business, so Nel didn't interrupt his concentration. Instead, she relaxed against him, his heat taking the edge off the chilling effects of the water.

Something she could only describe as serenity seeped into her spirit. Not only did she feel Tristan's presence against her, she felt him deep inside. As if he were rooting into her soul.

She wondered if Tristan felt the same.

After several fruitless casts, Tristan angled Nel slightly and redirected where the hook and bait landed.

She felt a tiny peck on the line. Still holding her hand in his, Tristan teased the line until a solid jerk reverberated up the rod.

"Here we go!" Tristan reeled in the line, brought the fish up and scooped it into the net he had fastened around his hips.

"My first fish," Nel squealed. "It's a big one, isn't it?"

"Yep. You might have just out-fished me." Tristan grinned. "A few more and we'll have supper."

The fish flopped in the net. The large eye on the side of its head stared straight at her. Its open mouth gaped, its gills flared in the air it couldn't breathe. "We're going to eat it?"

"Never ate fish?" He laughed.

"I've eaten fish." Never one that she'd caught. "But I don't think I can eat that poor thing." Its panicked fish face would forever haunt her dreams.

She bit her lip. This fish was trophy sized. Tristan would never want to give it up, but she had to ask. "Can we put him back?"

She held her breath.

"I'll tell you a secret." He removed the hook from the poor fish's mouth. "I usually put them back."

Relief poured through her.

Tristan released the fish into the water and it darted away too quickly for anyone to change their minds. He kissed Nel's temple. "Want another go at it?"

"I'd like to sketch for a while. You don't mind, do you?"

"Not at all, sweet cheeks." He helped Nel back to the riverbank and waited for her to get set up, even going back to the truck for the pencils that had fallen out of her bag.

The sun glinted in his hair as he waded back into the water, fly rod in hand. He went out a little farther than he had taken her. His movements were symmetry and beauty. She hoped to capture his essence on the page. When the end of summer came, it might be all she had of him.

The warm sunlight filtering through the trees reflected off the stream. Even though he wore sunglasses, Tristan's eyes grew tired from the glare. He'd caught and released more than a half-dozen trout. Nel's hesitation to consume her catch struck a deep chord with him. She was sweet and tenderhearted to her very soul. He loved that about her.

His heart skipped a beat and he snuck a peek over his

shoulder. Her head bowed over the sketch pad, lost in whatever she was drawing, and she couldn't look more beautiful.

Mine. Mine. Mine.

The sentiment droned in his head and he had no desire to fight it. Her essence was a balm to his aching loneliness.

He wanted more with her, but she seemed content with the way things were between them. Not once had she brought up the matter of what they would do once summer ended.

Nel tucked a ribbon of hair behind her ear and gazed up at him. Catching him staring, she flashed a smile that plumped her cheeks and his cock.

He longed to show her the truth about his wolf but if Nel had no desire to continue a relationship, the revelation might be too much for her to handle.

Although, she had handled more in her life than most would ever suspect. Beautiful, with a quiet resilience, she really didn't need him to be her champion.

The twinge inside him said *he* needed *her.*

She sat up, straightening her back. Her expectant look twisted everything inside him.

He reeled in his line and waded ashore.

"Want to see something spectacular?"

"You bet!" Her eyes glittered. She closed the sketch pad, slipped it into her canvas bag and stowed her pencils.

He reached for her hand and helped her stand. Leading her along the riverbank to the waterfall, he laced his fingers through hers, loving the feminineness of her hand.

"Do I have to close my eyes for this one?"

"That would be dangerous." He lightly squeezed her fingers.

Her happy expression faltered as her gaze rose toward the waterfall. "We aren't going to climb up that and jump, are we?"

"I wouldn't recommend it." He laughed softly.

"Oh, good." The cheerfulness in her manner returned.

He led her slightly past the waterfall to a narrow ledge that widened into the opening of a cave. Nel's mouth dropped open once they were inside.

Eyes wide, her gaze fixed on the curtain of water falling over the larger opening. "We're behind the waterfall!"

"Yep!"

The sunlight reflecting though the water cast a rainbow of colors inside the cavern. Steam wafted from a hot-spring pool, a rarity he had stumbled upon when he was a kid.

Back then, he'd come here seeking solitude when his parents fought. As a teenager, he'd come when he and Deidre fought. Now he came whenever he needed a clear head, or when lonely or frustrated. He spent more time here than in his apartment.

When he'd set out this morning, he hadn't planned to show Nel his secret getaway. But now he wanted the memory of being with her here as much as he wanted his next breath.

"It's beautiful," she said, almost reverently.

"Glad you like it." Tristan peeled off his shirt and dropped his shorts.

"What are you doing?"

"Skinny-dipping in nature's hot tub."

He sat on the natural edge of the spring, dropping his legs into the perfectly heated water. "Join me?"

"Naked?"

"I'll leave that up to you." Tristan slipped into the water.

"Are there amoebas or bacteria in there?"

"None that will harm you." Tristan treaded water.

At Nel's hesitation, Tristan relented. "You can sit on the edge and dangle your feet. You don't have to climb in, Nel."

Though he really wanted her to.

"Will you turn around while I undress and get in?"

"Absolutely not." His body instantly hard and hot, Tristan closed the distance to the edge. "I'm not taking my eyes off you while we're near water."

One little skid on the slippery rock and…

After a long pause of apparent contemplation, Nel turned away from him and began removing her top.

"Don't be shy, sweet cheeks," he teased softly. "I've already seen you naked."

She gave him a quick peek over her shoulder, then wiggled her arms beneath her shirt. Seconds later, she dropped her bra onto his pile of clothes.

Her blouse was the next to come off, followed by her pants and panties. She took a deep breath before turning around.

He kept his gaze firmly fixed on Nel's face while willing his body and his inner wolf to behave. He wanted her safely in the water and comfortable before he gave in to instinct.

She tiptoed to the edge of the pool and sat.

"Ready?" Tristan swallowed hard, his gaze taking in her luscious curves and full breasts.

"Ready," she said, although her voice didn't sound as if she were.

He tucked her arm over his shoulder and helped her slip into the water, carefully, so she wouldn't sink below the surface. "Hold on to me if you want," he said. "We need to get to the other side. There's a natural ledge in the rock we can sit on."

They swam leisurely toward the opposite ledge. "Let me know if the water is too hot."

"The temperature is perfect."

They reached the ledge and he made sure Nel was comfortable before situating himself next to her.

"It's not fair." Nel's mouth turned into a pout. She pointed at his chest. "I'm all exposed and you're not."

Tristan grinned at the water lapping her breasts. The dark rose nipples hardened into tight points. "I don't mind one bit."

"I'm sure you don't." She crossed her arms over her chest.

"Ah, sweet cheeks. Don't hide yourself from me." He tugged her hand free and wrapped her fingers around his stiff cock. "I love seeing you naked."

"Really?"

"God, yes." He breathed heavily. "The proof is in your hand."

"Tristan?" No words were necessary. Her face was an open book.

"Ride me, Nel."

Without hesitation, she climbed onto his lap, gently pumping his cock as her hand glided up and down his length. Electricity fired through his body, every cell primed and ready. Except his head, which bumped against the pool wall as he fought closing his eyes in pure delight.

He'd promised Nel he wouldn't take his eyes off her.

He might not be able to keep that promise, but he wouldn't let go of her for anything in the world.

One hand clamped on her hip, he cupped the back of her head and brought her forward for a kiss. She devoured his mouth. Usually, he was the aggressor, but here and now she plunged and claimed with abandon.

She released his cock to thrust her hands through his hair.

He trailed his hand down her spine, stopping to squeeze the fullness of her ass. He reached between her thighs to stroke her sex.

"Oh, god," she softly panted in his ear.

He slid between her folds and found her soft, satiny and clenching.

"Tristan?" she groaned, pulling back. Her scent saturated his senses.

"What, baby?" He stilled his fingers, sliding his hand back to her hip.

She leaned back, leaving enough space to slip her hand down his chest and wrap her fingers around the base of his cock.

She gave him a hot, seductive look. Her lips parted.

The tip of his cock brushed her mound and he saw stars as she took him inside her and slowly inched down his shaft until he was completely sheathed.

Chapter 28

Having Tristan inside her felt more right than anything had ever felt in Nel's life. She moved slowly, clenching and milking him for every single delight. His hands roamed her ass as he nibbled her jaw, down her throat and along her collarbone.

He lightly kneaded her breast, strumming his thumb across her nipple at varying intervals. Each time he did, she lost track of the rhythm she was working to maintain.

She was overthinking. The times Tristan had brought her to orgasm, the only thing she'd been focused on was how good she felt when he made love to her.

"Everything okay?" He peered at her through hooded eyes. His breath came out in soft pants.

Tristan was lost in the sensory pleasure and she was the one who'd put him there. A surge of feminine power shot through her.

Slowly, she lifted herself off his lap. Tristan's face turned upward, his glassy eyes following her ascent. She leaned closer, the tops of her breasts grazing his chin. His gaze dropped. A wicked smile danced on his lips.

His tongue teased her nipple. A lick, a swirl, a nip. Fire

shot straight to her sex. She clutched his head against her chest and he sucked her breast into his mouth. Pressing into him, she wanted to feel him against every inch of her body, inside and out.

He kissed the valley between her breasts and she arched, giving him more access. With every stroke, every caress, he worshipped her, branding her skin with his decadent kisses.

Her sex ached with a hard-edged need to be filled. She clasped his face and he released her breast with a pop. She kissed him hard at first, but he gentled her, leisurely stroking his hand down her back and over her bottom.

He urged her down again, teasing her with the tip of his shaft through her folds.

She took him inside her, her body sighing at rejoining his. When he was fully seated, Tristan whispered her name like a prayer. His hands cupped her backside and he lifted his hips in a slow, easy rhythm that she continued.

She loved the way he responded to her every sigh and moan. She loved it even more when she elicited them from him.

There was comfort in the gentle, steady rhythm. This was nothing but plain, simple sex, but Tristan touched her more deeply than any other lover ever had.

He wasn't simply making love to her body, he was making love to her soul.

She curled around him, burying her face against his neck. His arms wrapped her tight, secure. She'd never felt safer.

He protected not only her person, but her dreams. Her heart applauded him. She had to be careful, though. Careful not to fall in love. If she did, she'd end up with a broken heart.

Tristan's hand rested at the base of her neck. *Stay with me, Nel.*

Clearly, she heard his voice but he couldn't possibly have spoken since his tongue was down her throat. He completely possessed her.

Nel no longer sensed where she ended and he began.

Intense pressure converged at the crux of their joining. The pace of their rocking changed. Tristan's grip on her hips tightened, urging her to grind against him harder, faster.

Nel closed her eyes, surrendering to the mounting waves of pleasure. Her body undulated from the climactic force. Tristan's hold on her was likely the only thing that kept her from floating away.

Tristan's body hummed with deep satisfaction. He buttoned his shorts and pulled on his shirt.

Nel's hands shook as she worked the clasp on her bra. He stepped over to help and instantly felt her jumble of nerves. Standing behind her, he fastened the hooks and gave her a quick peck on the cheek. Then he picked up her blouse from the ground and helped her into it.

"What's wrong, sweet cheeks?"

"This might've been a bad idea." She turned her face away, but he hooked his thumb beneath her chin forcing her to look at him.

"I don't see how." Unless she had decided to end things with him.

Maybe he'd lost his touch.

"We didn't use a condom," she said quietly. "I didn't even stop to think about one."

Neither had he. He always had condoms, although, aside from Nel, he hadn't had need of them in a while.

He hadn't brought her here for sex. He'd merely wanted to share his favorite spot with her.

And it had been spectacular.

"I'm not on the pill. I'm leery of putting artificial hormones into my body."

"No worries, sweet cheeks." Relief lightened the tightness in his chest. He pulled her into his arms. "There's no risk of pregnancy with me, remember?"

A sweet sadness filled her eyes. "I'm sorry," she said, touching his face. "You would make a great father. You handled the kids so well on the field trip. They really look up to you."

Volunteering did fill a space in his life, but he'd never considered parenting. Until now.

Too easily, he could imagine Nel pregnant with his child. If he'd bitten her during sex, they could well be on the path to parenthood.

His throat tightened with emotion. He really was falling in love.

Nel kissed him sweetly and he found it more touching, more stimulating, than any kiss he'd ever received.

An easygoing give-and-take had developed between them. He found comfort in simply being with her and he cared, actually cared about what mattered to her. And whatever he asked of Nel, she was at least willing to try.

If he could ensure their affinity for each other wouldn't change, he would dive headfirst into a mateship with her. No holding back.

"Hungry?"

She nodded, her smile dampened with concern.

"Nel," he said warmly. "Don't worry. Everything will be fine."

He led her carefully from his little piece of paradise.

Something settled in his spirit, knowing he'd always sense her here, and he was grateful for it.

The midafternoon sun dappled their picnic area. Nel sat on the blanket and unpacked the lunch basket. Tristan reclined beside her, appreciating every moment. He'd never felt so content just basking in a woman's presence. They ate in comfortable silence, even stealing pieces of each other's food. He delighted in the shared playfulness.

"Any more fishing?" There was a hesitant hopefulness in her voice.

"Not today," he answered regretfully.

They packed away the food containers. Reluctance slowed his actions. He was having a harder and harder time parting from Nel. The thought of dropping her off and going home alone sent a pang of unbearable regret through him.

A familiar scent wafted in the air and his hackles rose. "Stay here," he warned.

Tristan only took a few steps before a large tawny wolf appeared.

"Wow, he looks a lot like your wolf." Nel said as she came up behind him. "But yours has cuter ears."

A bad feeling curdled the food in Tristan's stomach. Without taking his eyes off the wolf, he leaned toward Nel and whispered. "Go back to our place behind the waterfall. Wait for me there—"

Without warning, Jaxen shifted into his human form. "Dammit, Tristan. I'm not going to hurt her."

Nel's horrified gasp sounded like a trumpet in Tristan's ear. The color drained from her face, making her eyes look too large for their sockets. She stumbled backward, trembling hand to her lips. "This can't be real."

"Oops." Jaxen shrugged without apology. "Guess she didn't know."

"Have you lost your damn mind? What were you thinking?" Tristan had no way to keep them both in view. If he turned to check on Nel, Jaxen would be on his blind side, yet it was killing him not being able to sight Nel.

But he could hear her, retching behind him.

"You shacked up with her. I figured she knew." Jaxen stood before Tristan. "You're in the sanctuary, man. This is your fuckup, not mine."

"Get the hell away from us." Something dark and primal stirred in Tristan's consciousness.

"If I don't—" Jaxen laughed "—are you gonna take me down?"

Tristan's fist flew straight and true, slamming dead center into Jaxen's face. There was a crack, followed by the scent of blood.

Jaxen staggered backward cupping his hands over his nose. "Goddammit!"

"Stay away from her, Jaxen."

"I told you, I would never hurt a woman," Jaxen snarled.

"Do you think she's *not* hurt by what she saw you do?" Tristan pointed at Nel, on her knees, her stomach violently expelling the lunch they'd shared. "You had no right!"

Tristan should've been the one to reveal the truth to her, should've been the first to share his wolf. Because he hadn't, Jaxen had violated Nel's sense of reality, shredded her trust.

"Get out of here before I kick your ass out of the territory. Again."

Jaxen's features darkened. Icy eyes fixed on Tristan, he squatted and shifted.

The wolf launched. Tristan blocked the attack with his arm and Jaxen's teeth sank into Tristan's flesh. "Damnit, Jaxen!"

He punched the wolf's ribs and slung his arm. The wolf thudded to the ground and darted away.

"You better run!"

Nel's soft whimpers tempered Tristan's anger. He ran to where she had huddled, hugging herself.

"Nel?" He touched her shoulder and her startled cry broke his heart.

"Nel, please." His voice cracked from the burn rising in his throat. "I won't hurt you."

He slowly reached for her again. She shuddered, but didn't cry out.

"You've had a terrible shock, but I need you to trust me."

She stared at him with wide, uncertain eyes.

"What you saw really happened. It wasn't a trick. Jaxen is Wahya, a wolf shifter. And so am I."

Nel clamped her hand over her mouth. Already pale, her skin went ghostly white.

"This isn't how I wanted you to find out about us," he said.

"You were telling the truth," she finally said. "The day we met, you really were in the woods as a wolf, weren't you?"

"Yes, and you know my wolf, Nel. Whenever you saw him from your kitchen window, you were actually watching me. There's no need to be afraid of me or him."

"How is this possible?" Although a measure of distrust wavered in her gaze, her nerves seemed steadier and she no longer looked on the verge of fainting.

"Evolution. Our species developed alongside humans. We've always been around, and in the far distant past humans knew us. But somewhere along the line, humans began to fear us. Then hunt us. We went into hiding in plain sight as a matter of survival."

"Is it just your family or are there others?"

"We're all over the world."

"Oh, boy!" Nel rubbed her temple.

"We live in packs. My pack is here at Walker's Run."

"The Co-op?"

"Yes, and what I said is true. We're about family, Nel. That is what's most important to us. We would never hurt you. I would never hurt you."

"Would you have ever told me?"

"I don't know." He squeezed her hand. "I don't want you to see me differently. And I didn't want to burden you unnecessarily."

"People have a right to know your species exists. You shouldn't have to live in secrecy."

"No one has a right to know anything, and it's our choice to live as we do. Our lives are good and of our own choosing. We don't want or need human bureaucracies managing our lives, especially when they have no experience to do so."

"So you have no rules, no governance? What's to stop one of your Wahyas from killing someone?"

"We aren't lawless. Each pack has an Alpha who manages the welfare and well-being of the pack. All packs submit to the Woelfesenat, our overseeing wolf council. Our two most stringent laws are to never harm a human and never expose our species to humanity. Violation of either is a death sentence."

"That's why you won't hurt me."

"I won't hurt you because—" *I love you.* Damn, how had he allowed himself to get so wrapped up in this human female that he'd fallen in love? And when Gavin found out what happened today, this whole mess would get a lot more convoluted. "Because you're a friend and care about you."

"A friend?" She rolled her tongue against the inside of her cheek.

"More than a friend, actually," he said. "I don't know if there's a word to describe what you are to me."

Mine!

Tristan pressed his fingers against his temple. Apparently, Gavin's interference wasn't required to complicate the situation. Tristan and his inner wolf were doing a fine job all on their own.

Chapter 29

The awkward silence nearly drove Nel insane on the drive back to the cabin.

And she could've choked on the tension.

Still, when Tristan backed out of the driveway, she broke into tears.

Cassie ran out of the cabin and put her arms around Nel.

Before they left the sanctuary, Tristan had told Nel that Cassie and Grace were humans married to Wahyas. Then he'd called Cassie from the truck and asked her to meet them.

Cassie steered her inside. "I know you've had an awful shock." She sat on the couch next to Nel. "But it's survivable."

Grace came into the living room carrying a tray with three mugs. "Here you go." She handed Nel a steaming cup of coffee. "It's double leaded."

"Thanks."

Cassie took the cup of tea and Grace claimed the second coffee mug as she sat in the sofa chair.

"How did the two of you handle it when your husbands came out with their wolves?"

"Compartmentalized," Cassie and Grace said in unison.

"At least until our perception of reality adjusted." Cassie patted Nel's leg. "It will take time, but remember that Tristan is still the same person you fell in love with."

"I never said I fell in love." But she had. Heart and soul.

"He loves you, if he showed you his wolf." Grace smiled over the rim of her mug.

"He didn't. We were on a picnic and a wolf showed up. Tristan tried to send me away. The next thing I knew, Jaxen was crouched naked where the wolf had been."

"Oh, for Pete's sake." Grace gulped her drink.

"This doesn't mean Jaxen is in love with me, does it?" Nausea rocked Nel again. After what he'd done to Tristan, she would never get involved with Jaxen.

"Jaxen probably thought Tristan had already revealed his wolf." Cassie tucked a curl behind her ear. "When Tristan is with you, he acts like a wolfan in love. His posturing, the way he watches you, how he's attentive to your every need and want. Everyone can see it."

"Tristan doesn't do relationships."

"I didn't, either," Grace said. "Now, I'm happily married with twins."

Oh, no. "Brenna and the twins? Will they be like their fathers?"

"Yes." Cassie seemed to have no worry about raising a wolf child. "Wahya genes are dominant, to ensure the survival of their species. A child born of a Wahya–human mating will always be Wahya."

Nel's heart beat faster with every breath. "Tristan said he couldn't get me pregnant, but that's not true, is it?"

"If he hasn't claimed you, then no. You won't get pregnant." Grace sipped her coffee.

"What do you mean by claimed?"

"Tristan should be the one to have this conversation with you," Cassie said.

"He's the one who called you, dropped me off on the doorstep and left, so, apparently, he's not interested in having this talk with me." Nel held her fingers to her lips and swallowed her rising emotions. "Sorry. But I deserve to know about the conspiracy I'm involved in."

"A mate-claim happens when a wolfan male bites a woman during sex. It binds them together and triggers a biological response that allows him to father children with her."

Whatever else Cassie may have said was lost in the clamoring panic that drowned out all sound.

It had only been a nip, not really a bite.

And they weren't actually doing *it* when it happened. Yeah, they were fooling around and getting hot and bothered, but Tristan wasn't inside her when he bit her.

"Nel, are you okay?" Grace asked. "You look pale."

"I'm overwhelmed." Nel rubbed her stomach, trying not to imagine a wolf baby growing inside her. "I've been sleeping with a man who isn't human."

"Have you ever dated someone of another race or culture?" Grace offered her a smile.

"Yes."

"This is no different, Nel," Cassie said.

"Of course it is. Those men were human. Tristan is part animal."

"Wahyas retain their human consciousness in their wolf forms. They feel love, sadness, fear, loss, just like we do," Cassie said.

"When I was trapped in a room with no way out and the building was burning down around me—" Grace placed her cup on the coffee table "—my husband was on the other side of the door. He could've gotten out of harm's way, but he refused to leave. He was willing to die with me rather than live without me." Tears shimmered in Grace's eyes. "That, Nel, is how deeply a Wahya male loves. I know of no other animal that would've done what Rafe did."

"Both of you are forgetting that Tristan doesn't love me. It's a summer fling. Nothing more."

"Who are you trying to convince?" Grace asked. "Us? Or yourself?"

"I'm trying to get a handle on the fact that werewolves exist."

"Wahyas," Cassie corrected. "The term werewolf is offensive to them."

"My brain feels turned inside out." Without having sipped the coffee, Nel set her mug next to Grace's on the table.

"It will for a while." Grace pulled the band out of her hair, then retied her ponytail. "But this can become your new norm, Nel."

"Since coming to Walker's Run, you've blossomed from a shy wallflower into a strong, confident woman." Cassie toed off her shoes and tucked her tiny feet beneath her legs.

"If, as you say, you and Tristan are nothing more than a summer fling—" Grace's blond eyebrow lifted in a delicate curve "—there are plenty of other wolfan males available."

The problem was that, despite everything, Tristan was the one Nel wanted.

"What happened to your arm?" Brice stood in the doorway of Tristan's apartment, Rafe slightly behind him.

"Jaxen bit me. I'm fine, go away." Tristan swung the door but Brice caught it before it closed. Neither he nor

Rafe cared that they had not been invited in. They simply waltzed inside and made themselves at home.

Other than Nel, Tristan hadn't had his friends in his apartment, though he had stopped by their homes for short visits. From the looks on Brice's and Rafe's faces, this would be a rather long one.

"I feel like shit, so whatever you want to say, make it quick." Tristan plopped onto the couch and stretched out.

"We've been where you are." Brice smacked Tristan's bare feet and waved for him to move over.

Tristan replied with an irritable growl but complied.

Silently, Rafe sat in the armchair. He wasn't much of a talker, which was okay because Brice, the pack lawyer, could talk enough for three people.

"Do you love her?"

"I haven't claimed her nor do I intend to." Tristan's gut seized.

"Not the same thing," Brice said.

"I don't know what I feel." Tristan scratched the day's growth of beard beneath his chin. "I think about Nel a lot. I like being with her, but I don't imagine us spending the rest of our lives together," he lied. No need to confess something when there was no hope for it.

He'd been a fool to take Nel to his favorite place *inside the sanctuary.*

He'd bang his head if it didn't already hurt so damn bad. Nearly as bad as his heart.

"What does your wolf tell you?" Rafe asked quietly. Near feral when adopted into the Walker's Run pack, Rafe had always been more in tune with his wolf instinct.

"He's in hibernation," Tristan lied. "Haven't heard a peep."

"We're wolves, not bears." Rafe cut his eyes at him. "Try again."

"Nel is sweet and gentle and trusting, so my wolf and I feel protective of her. Dammit, I'm a sentinel and a sheriff's deputy. It's how I'm wired."

"Hmm." Brice whipped out his phone.

"Who are you calling?"

"Shane. He's a sentinel and studying criminal justice and wants a career in law enforcement. I'm checking to see if he feels the same about Nel."

Tristan's inner wolf snarled, ferocious and irritated. "Hang up." Tristan smacked Brice with a couch pillow.

Brice chuckled and shoved the phone back into his pocket.

"Nel and I aren't going any further than we've gone," Tristan said. "I want her to be happy. And you know I can't be."

"Tristan," Brice began.

"End of discussion." Tristan put up his hand.

Rafe's gaze narrowed. Though he said nothing, his jaw worked behind sealed lips.

"Unless there's something else, I need to catch a couple of hours' sleep." Although, Tristan didn't expect he would sleep, since every time he closed his eyes he saw Nel crying on the front porch and Cassie whisking her inside the cabin. Away from him. "I go on duty at the sheriff's office at midnight."

"Dad wants to see you tomorrow. He's called a meeting with Jaxen and your dad."

Tristan thumped his head against the couch headrest. A family meeting with the Alpha, fucking great.

Chapter 30

"Are you feeling better?" Sitting in the resort dining room, Cassie stabbed a piece of lettuce in her Caesar salad.

Not really, Nel thought. She hadn't slept a wink and her heart hurt.

Tristan had neither called nor texted and she'd really wanted him to. Even knowing that he wasn't human, she hadn't been able to convince her heart that not hearing from him was for the best.

"I'm just tired," Nel finally answered.

"Oh, Nel. Please don't worry yourself sick over what happened yesterday. Everything will be fine. I promise."

"On my first day, you warned me not to get involved with Tristan." Nel had no one to blame for her heartbreak except herself. "I should've listened."

"You fell in love," Cassie said. "It happens to the best of us."

"But not to Tristan."

"I think you're wrong about him." Cassie pushed her salad plate aside and folded her arms on the table. "I've never seen Tristan engage with someone the way he does with you."

"That doesn't really matter now."

A server walked past carrying a food tray loaded with a large bowl of shrimp and grits, a steakhouse burger platter and a broiled mountain trout still with its head attached.

Nel placed her hand on her belly to settle her stomach, queasy since yesterday's fiasco.

"Give yourself time to adjust and remember, he's adjusting, too."

Nel sipped a chilled glass of water.

"Will you be all right to drive back to Atlanta today?"

"I'll be fine." Nel had dinner plans with Tristan's mother and *the* Gilbert Michaud of the Michaud Galleria d'Art to discuss her portfolio.

Nel wasn't looking forward to attending this meeting without Tristan. After all, he was the whole reason there was a meeting to attend. If Suzannah hadn't seen Nel's artwork while visiting Tristan, Nel would never have caught the attention of one of Atlanta's leading art brokers.

"I hope you don't let Suzannah sweep you off your feet," Cassie said.

"What do you mean?"

"When you get to know her, Suzannah is a nice lady, but she likes ritzy parties and flashy friends. Her life in Atlanta is a whirlwind. It's easy to get caught up in the frenzy."

"I prefer to keep things simple."

Cassie smiled. "We keep things simple in Walker's Run. Well, as simple as we can. We have a place for you here, Nel."

"I'm still processing what happened yesterday. I can't think about a new job or moving or anything else right now."

"No pressure," Cassie said. "It's simply an option to consider when you're ready."

Nel glanced at her watch. "I should get on the road."

"Let me know when you get there and what happens tonight. And when you start back." Cassie's genuine concern brought tears to Nel's eyes.

Over the last few weeks, she had forged personal connections with people that she hadn't been able to make with coworkers and neighbors she'd known for years.

"Hey." Cassie scurried around the table to give Nel a hug. "You're not alone, okay?"

Nel dabbed her eyes and offered Cassie a grateful smile as they got up to leave.

Jimmy, at the valet stand, brought the car to her. "You look lovely today," he said, holding open the car door. "I mean, you're always beautiful. But today, you have a glow."

"That's sweet, Jimmy. Thanks." Nel sat in the driver's seat. "Tonight could launch my career as a *real* artist."

"Wow. I'll be able to say I know someone famous." Jimmy grinned. "Drive safe."

He closed the door and Nel clicked her seat belt. Before putting the car in gear, she saw Tristan, in uniform, exiting his truck, which was parked in the spot for resort security. Before he entered the resort, he turned and his gaze locked onto her.

Nel gripped the steering wheel.

Conflicting emotions flickered across his face, yet he made no move to approach. Because of the man Tristan was, Nel would have to be the one to reach out to him. Until that moment, she hadn't known if he wanted her to try.

Unfortunately, the timing was off. He was probably headed to another meeting with Gavin and she had to get to Atlanta. While she might have reservations about spending time with Tristan's mother, a Wahyan she-wolf, Nel might never get another chance to meet with Gilbert Michaud.

She peeled her fingers off the steering wheel and gave Tristan a finger wave. He responded with a slight nod and an infinitesimal smile she didn't know how to interpret.

She cranked the car and drove off. The weighted feeling of his gaze followed until she was long gone.

"About time you got here," Gavin snapped.

Tristan squared his hunched shoulders and took a deep breath. Seeing Nel had taken more out of him than he'd anticipated. Now his mind raced, his restlessness hit an all-time high and his hands shook from the restraint it had taken not to rush to her car, pull her out and kiss her until she was breathless.

He quietly closed the door to the Alpha's office.

The only other person in the room was Brice.

"I told you I'd be late. I was on an accident call." Tristan sat in the leather captain's chair next to Brice. "Where's my dad and Jaxen?"

"I've already met with them." Gavin's grim face turned grimmer.

"About what happened yesterday…" Tristan leaned forward. "I take responsibility for that incident. I brought an unauthorized human into the sanctuary. Considering my behavior with Nel, Jaxen didn't know I hadn't revealed my wolf to her."

"I think he did." Gavin's dark brows drew together. "You might believe that I dismissed your concerns about Jaxen and the incident with Cybil. I assure you, I didn't."

Tristan glanced at Brice, who said, "He had Reed shadow Jaxen."

"You knew?" *And didn't tell me?*

"Not until this morning."

"Only Cooter and Reed were involved," Gavin assured Tristan. "I wanted to minimize your involvement."

"You didn't trust me not to tell Jaxen?"

"No. You have too much on your plate and didn't need something else to contend with."

Gavin's explanation made sense but failed to make Tristan feel better. He was a lead sentinel. He had a right to know if the Alpha had concerns about a pack member's behavior, even if suspicions involved blood-kin.

"What did Reed find out that makes you think Jaxen knew I hadn't revealed my wolf to Nel?"

"Because he's been stalking you."

Tristan's heart froze midstrike. His blood instantly chilled and his gut wrung itself into a double knot. "Why would he stalk me?"

"We were hoping you would know," Brice said. "Jaxen denies it, of course. Said he was always trying to catch up with you to hang out. But Reed's accounts show that Jaxen had plenty of opportunities to approach you and rarely did."

Images of the past few weeks flooded Tristan's mind. His heart started beating again, but instead of starting off slow, it raced like a rabbit being hunted by a wolf.

"Nel?" Most of his off-duty time had been spent with her. "Are you sure Jaxen wasn't stalking her?"

"Reed was sure he wasn't," Gavin said. "Jaxen always stayed on your trail. Human or wolf, he was never too far behind."

"It doesn't make sense for him to stalk me."

"Your father and Jaxen said the same." Brice nodded at his father.

"I've ordered Jaxen to stay away from you."

"He's moving in with your dad," Brice said cautiously. "Since you seem to be the only one looking after Ruby, we didn't want any conflicts with Jaxen to arise when you visit her."

Tristan shrugged. He rarely saw his father anyway, and even though Ruby didn't appreciate his help, she needed him. Especially now that she'd come down with the wolfan flu. "Does she know?"

"I had Nate call her from here, using the speakerphone so I could monitor what he said."

"He didn't mention the stalking, right?"

"No." Brice shook his head. "Nate told her the move would make it easier for him to take Jaxen to work sites."

"Is he actually going to do that?"

"Yes." The stony look on Gavin's face was probably the same one he'd shown Nate when giving the order. "I have serious concerns regarding Jaxen's behavior since his return. I clearly expressed to him that I will not tolerate any further offenses."

"How did he take it?"

"Very courteously." Gavin's steepled fingers tapped against each other.

That didn't sound like Jaxen. With the Durrance temper, Tristan would have expected his cousin to explode at the threat of being turned out of the pack a second time.

Brice shrugged. "Jaxen said he intends to rectify past mistakes and move forward with his life."

The night Jaxen came home, he'd said the same to Tristan. Yet here Tristan sat, trying to recover from another one of Jaxen's careless mishaps.

An awkward silence fell.

"If there's nothing else, I need to check on Ruby and catch a few hours' sleep before sentinel duty with Cooter tonight."

"Have you given any thought to my dad's suggestion of scaling back on some of your responsibilities?" Brice asked diplomatically.

"I'm managing."

"I don't want my pack members to *manage*," Gavin growled softly. "I want them to be happy."

"Never said I wasn't." Although, at the moment, he was pretty damn unhappy. His head hurt. He felt restless, irritable. He wasn't hungry when he woke up this morning and he never missed a meal.

"Life is more than work," Brice said quietly.

Not for Tristan. What else did he have?

"Tristan, as Alpha it's my responsibility to care for and direct the pack for maximum benefit. One day, it will be Brice's responsibility."

"I've never disputed that, so what are you getting at?"

"Right now, your priorities are divided. You have too much for one man to do. You're going to make a mistake and I don't want it to be at the pack's expense."

Tristan's gut twisted, his chest tightened and bile from his empty stomach rose in his throat. "Are you firing me from sentinel duty?"

"Don't be ridiculous." Gavin's icy-blue gaze pinned Tristan to the chair he was rising from. "I want you to quit the sheriff's office. And, claim Nel as your mate."

Chapter 31

"What is this crap?" Ruby's raspy voice grated on Tristan's raw nerves.

After Gavin's bombshell, Tristan was surprised he was able to drive safely to her house. The Alpha sincerely believed that his orders were in Tristan's best interests as well as the pack's. Tristan, however, refused to be forced into either action.

"Chicken and rice soup." He adjusted the pillow behind Ruby's back so she could sit up better to eat.

"I prefer dumplings." She stirred a spoon through the bowl on the lap tray and squinted at him.

"Maybe next time." Tristan wasn't in the mood to roll out dough for fresh dumplings. He'd barely managed to cut up the chicken, an onion, some celery and a carrot.

"Jaxen moved out." Ruby's fevered gaze latched onto Tristan.

"Where did he go?" Feigning innocence, Tristan returned to the kitchen.

"Nate took him in. Said Jaxen was doing so good at the business, he needed him close by to help with more stuff."

Tristan took a breath. "Are you okay with him leaving?"

"I can look after myself."

Tristan doled out soup portions in single-serve containers, placing them in the refrigerator for her to heat up later. He left one serving warming in the pot. Before he left, she would want another bowlful.

Even though she complained terribly about his cooking, she always ate whatever he prepared.

He cleaned the kitchen, tuning out her running commentary on the afternoon soaps. He refilled Ruby's iced tea and served her the second bowl of soup.

"Gonna rush off like you always do?"

The ever-present weight on his shoulders got heavier. "I can stay awhile." He collected the tray of dishes and returned to the kitchen to rinse, dry and put them away.

"I don't need you. Just saying that you never stay long."

Always rushing between work, sentinel duty and the youth center, he rarely stayed long anywhere.

Except when he spent time with Nel.

He handed Ruby a cup of hot tea then sat in the overstuffed chair next to the couch, trying to relax his mind.

Something jabbed his leg. He opened his eyes, eyes that he hadn't realized had closed.

"You work too much." Ruby poked him again with her cane. "How are you going to find a mate when all you do is work, work, work? I ain't gonna be around forever to take care of you."

Tristan bit his tongue. "I don't want a mate."

"Something wrong with ya?" She prodded for the third time.

"No," he said, a little too defensively.

"You afraid?"

Hell, yeah, he was afraid.

"Mateships are doomed in our family," he said quietly.

Ruby fell silent, her gaze focused on the large flat-screen TV Tristan had given her. He couldn't tell by her tired, fixed expression if she'd taken offense at his remark or simply lost interest.

Tristan stood and stretched. "I have to go," he said, leaning down to collect her empty dishes.

"Always thought you were the smart one in the family. Too smart for your breeches sometimes." She pulled the afghan from the back of the couch and spread it across her thin legs. "Don't be stupid and screw up your life."

"I'm trying hard not to, Ruby."

"Are you? Cuz the way I see it, you're determined to be miserable. It's like you ain't learnt nothing from us."

Oh, he'd learned plenty. That was the problem.

For the hundredth time, Tristan rubbed his runny, stuffy nose.

The wolfan flu sucked! It came with high fever, chills, body aches and a killer headache.

He hadn't had it since he was a kid. As a healthy male in his prime, to be waylaid by it now was humiliating.

He opened the refrigerator door. The shelves were stocked with fruit, lunch meat, a couple of beers and leftover pizza.

Blech!

He wished he had some of the soup he'd made Ruby. Wishing didn't make any materialize, so he slammed the door and shuffled to the sink. He filled a glass with water and downed the contents before returning to his fortress of blankets on the couch.

His phone rang and his shoulders sank at the ringtone.

If he had any sense, he'd send the caller to voice mail then delete the message.

"You still living?" Ruby's critical voice sounded over the speakerphone.

"I'm breathing." Wouldn't necessarily call that living.

"I won't be for long." She coughed. "My inhaler is almost empty."

"Did you call in the prescription?"

"Wouldn't do no good to call you if I didn't."

"Ask Jaxen to pick it up."

"Why can't you bring it?"

"I'm sick, Ruby." As if on cue, he began coughing like he was hacking up a lung.

"You gotta get well. There's a lightbulb in the kitchen that needs changing."

"Jaxen can take care of it."

"He's busy. You always do it for me."

"Anything else you need fixed?"

"I ain't a house inspector."

Tristan blew a long breath. "I'll come by when I feel better."

Disconnecting the call, he rolled off the couch, his joints achy and his muscles sore. His left leg trembled in a light spasm. "Man, this sucks."

Sucked worse to be sick and alone.

He hobbled into the bathroom, shucked off his sweatpants and stepped into the shower, hoping to cool the raging fever. Unfortunately, the cold water triggered hard, rocking chills. He towel-dried as quickly as possible and staggered into the bedroom for a clean sweatshirt, sweatpants and socks. He even pulled on a wool skullcap. Too exhausted to make it back to the living room, he collapsed onto the bed.

Hours later, the pounding in his head jarred him awake. Groggy, he sat up.

The pounding continued, but it wasn't just inside his head.

He struggled to his feet. With great effort, he made it

as far as the bedroom doorway. The door frame provided the support he needed to catch his breath and garner the strength to make it into the living room.

"Tristan!" Nel shouted. "Open the door. Your truck is in the parking lot, so I know you're home."

A strange current fired down his spine and spread into his limbs, causing incoordination in his steps, but he made it to the front door.

"What are you doing here?"

Her lips were pressed into a tight, thin line. Her face was pale and uncertain.

A fiery heat flushed Tristan's skin and he broke into a sweat. "What's wrong?"

He saw her mouth move but coherent words failed to reach his ears. His head felt swarmy, his body felt much too heavy, and then a violent surge shook him head to foot. His shoulder and hip absorbed the impact of the fall.

Tremor after tremor rolled through his body. His muscles hardened and seized until it felt like the fibers would rip from the tendons.

Discordant facial spasms caused his teeth to chomp his tongue until his jaw locked. He tasted blood. His eyes shuttered like a slideshow stuck in fast advance mode.

He wasn't quite sure he was breathing or if he was simply shaking so hard that the outside air was forced into his nostrils and down into his lungs.

Darkness advanced from the outer edge of his vision. His thoughts began to splinter.

He was a fool for not telling Nel he loved her. And now she'd never know.

Chapter 32

Nel sank beside Tristan convulsing on the floor. Her rational brain knew this had nothing to do with the news she'd delivered; still, the insecure part of her brain latched onto the fear that he was absolutely and utterly horrified, so much so that it induced a stroke.

A door down the outdoor walkway opened and a familiar-looking woman wearing a Taylor's T-shirt peeked out. "I heard a scream. Is everything okay?" Her gaze registered the scene. "Shit!"

She dashed to another apartment and pounded on the door until it opened. Shane stepped outside.

"It's Tristan," the woman said. "He passed out in his doorway."

Tristan's tremors eased and Nel touched his sweat-streaked face. "He's burning up."

"What happened?" Shane knelt beside Nel.

"He had a seizure," Nel said, thankful she wasn't alone in the crisis.

"Angeline, grab his feet. I'll get his shoulders." Shane stepped over Tristan to get into position. "If he has another seizure, he might shift. We have to get him out of the doorway."

Nel glanced from Shane to Angeline. Cassie and Grace had mentioned a correlation between the pack and the Co-op, but Nel hadn't made any associations yet.

"It's okay, Nel. We know that you know about Wahyas." Angeline wrapped her hands around Tristan's ankles. "We're a tight community."

"That's code for gossip mill." Shane hooked his arms under Tristan's shoulders.

"You're the blabbermouth who told me."

Shane rolled his eyes. "On three."

He and Angeline lifted and carried Tristan to the couch.

"He probably has the wolfan flu," Angeline said, stepping into the kitchen to wet a cloth. "It's running through the entire pack. I had it last week, but not this bad."

"I'm calling Doc." Phone in hand, Shane stepped away.

Angeline handed Nel the damp cloth.

"Thanks." Nel placed the cool rag against Tristan's forehead. He moaned and moved restlessly but didn't open his eyes. Nel perched next to him, running her hand along his arm.

"Your scent might calm him," Angeline said. "Place your hand to his face."

Nel cupped his whiskered cheek and he turned, pressing his nose into her palm.

He inhaled deeply, a weak smile trembled his lips and he sighed her name.

"Oh, Tristan." There were dark shadows beneath his closed eyes. His face was thin and had several days' worth of beard growth. His dry lips were cracked almost to the point of bleeding.

"Doc is sending an ambulance." Shane sat in the sofa chair.

"Did anyone know Tristan was sick?" Nel asked.

"About the only time I see him is when he comes into Taylor's," Angeline said.

"He's missed some sentinel duties, but I heard he was taking time off." Worry creased Shane's brow. He glanced at Nel. "I figured with all the stuff going on, he needed some space."

Nel had thought the same when she called after returning from Atlanta on Sunday afternoon. Tristan had been on duty but said they would talk later. She called again Monday and Tuesday, leaving messages both times.

Even if he considered their affair over, it was out of character for him to ignore a call. Which was why she'd showed up at his door.

The front door opened.

"How's he doing?" A woman, with the name Anderson stamped above the medical insignia on the upper left side of her dark blue T-shirt, came in.

"Still out," Shane said. "Is that normal?"

"Depends on what's wrong with him." Anderson took Nel's seat. "Did he hit his head when he fell?"

"No," Nel answered, easing onto a counter bar stool to stay out of the way.

Anderson flashed a penlight into Tristan's eyes, listened to his heart with the stethoscope, took his pulse and blood pressure, and ran a device over his forehead. "His vitals are good and strong, but he has a high temperature."

Two men appeared at the door with a gurney. A flurry of activity surrounded the couch.

Flashbacks of being pulled from the wreckage after the car accident that killed her parents rushed through

Nel's mind. Her throat closed and she choked on the breath stuck in her windpipe.

"He'll be okay," Angeline assured. "Doc is the best there is."

Shane came over. "They want something with your scent to keep Tristan calm on the ride to the hospital."

"I don't understand."

"Give him something you've worn close to the skin," Angeline said. "It will have your scent on it."

Nel removed the short-sleeved summer sweater she wore over her sundress and gave it to Shane. He handed it off to Anderson, who placed the garment on Tristan's chest before the other paramedics wheeled him out of the apartment.

"I know where Tristan keeps his spare key. I'll lock up, so you go ahead to the hospital," Angeline said.

"Thanks." Nel's hands shook taking her keys out of her dress pocket.

"I can give you a ride, Nel," Shane offered.

"Thanks, but I'd rather take my car." That way, she wouldn't be stuck at the hospital if Tristan didn't want her to stay.

"Then I'll drive you in your car and catch a ride back from someone later."

Gratefully, Nel handed him the keys.

Shane gave her fingers a gentle squeeze. "Tristan's a tough guy. He'll be as good as new in no time."

Nel hoped so. She certainly couldn't face what was coming alone.

Smothered in oppressive darkness, Tristan sensed a gentle, sweet presence nearby. "Nel?"

"I'm here."

His heart received a needed jolt and he struggled to shake off the weighty lethargy.

At the cool touch of soft lips pressed against his brow, he found the strength to open his eyes.

"Hey there," she said, smiling. A halo of soft light surrounded her head and shoulders. God, she was beautiful.

Mine!

Though distant, the declaration continued to drum softly in his mind.

"Where am I?" His sigh took great effort.

"You had a febrile seizure. You're in the emergency clinic."

"What?" He tried to sit up.

"Shhh." She placed her hand against his shoulder. "Save your strength. You aren't going anywhere until you finish getting fluids into your system."

Tristan looked at the tubing stuck in his arm and tethered to an IV bag.

"You're severely dehydrated," Nel said. "But Doctor Habersham said you shouldn't suffer any permanent damage."

Tristan toyed with her fingers. "How did the meeting go with Gilbert?"

Nel's eyes sparkled despite the worry lines crinkling the corners. "He selected a few of my pieces for his local artists display and he's invited me to participate in his annual Extravagance d'Art d'Automne charity gala."

"Fantastic."

"Yeah." A shy smile plumped her pink cheeks. "It's kind of a big deal."

"I know." Tristan resisted the urge to kiss her knuckles. Kiss her cheek.

Kiss her mouth, hard and deep, branding her with his tongue. "I've attended a few with my mother."

Nel smoothed back his hair. "How are you feeling?"

"Thirsty," he said with a slight cough. "My throat is dry and scratchy. I feel like I swallowed a sandbag."

Nel lifted the plastic pitcher from the bedside tray, poured water into a small paper cup and held it to his mouth. Tristan molded his lips around the straw and sucked down the entire contents. The coolness eased the burn in his throat. "Thanks."

She started to pour another cup but he waved her to stop.

"I'm glad you came by the apartment on your way back from Atlanta. I've been wondering how the meeting went."

"Tristan, it's Wednesday evening."

"What?"

"I called you Sunday afternoon, but you were on duty and couldn't talk. Do you remember?"

Tristan focused his achy brain. Somewhere in the grogginess, he vaguely recalled speaking with Nel.

"I phoned again on Monday and Tuesday because you never called back."

"I must've been out it." Tristan shook his head. "I wouldn't intentionally ignore you."

A shadow of doubt crossed her features. "Do you remember what I said when you opened the door?"

"No." All he remembered was the rush of happiness when he saw her face, even though her brow had been wrinkled with worry and her eyes filled with uncertainty. Had she been afraid of how he'd receive her?

His fault, really. He hadn't reached out to her since the unfortunate incident with Jaxen at the sanctuary.

"I'm pregnant." Nel's words exploded in his ears and the repercussive force deafened him to her voice.

Disbelief. Betrayal. Jealousy. Outrage.

He didn't know what to feel first.

They'd never discussed exclusivity, he'd just assumed.

If Nel was pregnant, she had to be sleeping with someone else. Tristan couldn't be the child's father because he'd never claimed Nel as his mate.

"I know what you're thinking." Angry, she jabbed a pointed index finger at him. "I have never cheated on anyone in my life, so don't say that I did."

Tristan inhaled sharply and locked his emotions inside his chest. "I haven't claimed you, Nel. Pregnancy can't occur unless—"

"—you bite me during sex," she interrupted. "I know. Cassie and Grace told me."

"Then you should understand it's not possible for me to be the baby's father."

"Our first time, during the storm. Remember how the thunder startled me and I bumped you in the nose? You nipped me, right here." Nel swept her hair off one shoulder and tapped the spot where her neck and shoulder joined.

Tristan stilled. "It would have to break the skin."

"It did," she said, her gaze unflinching. "After the condom broke and I went into the bathroom, I noticed a small abrasion and cleaned it with a damp cloth. It was only a tiny amount, but there was blood."

"It doesn't work like that."

"Apparently it does." Nel perched on the side of the bed. "I was so nauseous when your mom came by my apartment on Saturday that she took me to her doctor thinking I had a virus. I asked him for a pregnancy test. It was positive."

"This can't be happening." Tristan's stomach churned. Now he was the one who felt nauseous. He sat up, swinging his legs over the opposite side of the bed from where Nel sat.

"Counting back, this happened the night you bit me and the condom broke."

"Unbelievable!"

"I expected you might be upset." She blew out a disappointed breath. "I'm prepared to do this on my own, if necessary."

"Nel." Tristan reached for her hand. "I haven't fully processed the news that I'm going to be a dad. What kills me is that I forced a mate-claim on you."

"You didn't force anything. The bite might've been an accident, but can you honestly tell me that everything that followed wasn't the real us?"

No, he couldn't. Tristan had been more real, more himself with Nel than with anyone.

"Your mom told me about your home life as a child. I get that your parents weren't the best role models, but neither were my aunt and uncle."

"Did you tell her that you are pregnant?"

"No." Nel shook her head. "I haven't said a word to anyone."

Nel's tentative smiled reeled him in. "We can do better than your parents and my guardians did, Tristan. At the very least, we have to try."

"You're not having a heart attack." Arms crossed over his chest, Rafe leaned against the counter in the hospital room.

"Just because your father is a doctor—" Tristan paused, gasping for air "—doesn't make you one."

"You're having a panic attack."

"How do you know?"

"Chest hurt? Light-headed? Can't breathe?"

Tristan nodded.

"Feel like you're dying?"

"More like a black hole swallowed me and I can't get out."

"Panic attack," Rafe said confidently. "I used to get them after Lexi died."

"What do I do?"

"Stop panting. Hold your breath if you have to, but slow down your breathing or you'll hyperventilate."

Tristan held his breath for a ten count and slowly let it out. After several repetitions, the tightness in his chest began to ease.

"What was the trigger?" Rafe poured Tristan a cup of water.

"I might have accidentally claimed Nel." Tristan downed the entire contents in one gulp.

"Ah, hell." Rafe scratched his short beard. "Define *might have.*"

"It was just a nip, barely broke the skin." Tristan pointed to the spot on his neck that corresponded to where Nel's mark would've been. "But she's pregnant."

"That's a mate-claim." Rafe stared at him, eyes pinning Tristan without a flicker of doubt. "There's not a *might have* in that scenario."

"This is a goddamn nightmare." Tristan rubbed the back of his head, his hair damp along the hairline.

Nel's pregnancy wasn't the issue; what he couldn't accept was claiming Nel without her consent. Instinct be damned, he would never force her to remain in a mate-ship with him.

Tristan swung his legs over the side of the hospital bed. "I can't, I won't do this to her. There must be a way out."

"What does Nel want?"

"She wants to try to make things work, for the baby's sake."

"If she's not unwilling, then do it."

Tristan shook his head. His fever was gone and the virus had likely run its course, but his muscles were sore and he felt tired. "Look at my family history. Not one happy mateship for as far back as anyone remembers."

Nel would grow to resent him, it was inevitable. Tristan would be in a state of constant expectation, waiting for the day it happened.

He loved Nel. Loved her enough to want her happiness more than his own. And, he would do everything in his power to ensure she would be.

"Do me a favor," Tristan said. "Don't tell anyone about the pregnancy, not even Grace."

"I don't keep secrets from her, Tristan. She'll sense something is off."

"You know how news travels. I just don't want Gavin to get further involved. His initial disapproval nearly caused Brice to lose Cassie, and Grace left you after Gavin's convoluted plan to manipulate her blew up in both of your faces."

"We came through it," Rafe said quietly.

"Because of the mate-bond?" Tristan studied his friend, mulling over his thoughts. No need to hurry him along. Rafe always took his time and never spoke his mind until good and ready.

"I don't think you should worry," Rafe finally said. "There is a biological component to a mate-claim, but the real issue is a mate-bond."

Tristan's anxiety shot through the roof.

"No one in my family has ever experienced a mate-bond. I don't think it's possible for it to happen to me."

"Just follow your instinct. If it leads you to her, well, there's your answer. If it doesn't, that's an answer, too."

Chapter 33

Tristan in the kitchen in the mornings was just as sexy as in bed at night.

Fully recovered, he bebopped around the breakfast bar, clearing dishes while Nel finished her coffee.

"I've decided to break the apartment lease. Three flights of stairs are a lot for you to handle."

"What's that supposed to mean?" She put down her mug.

"When you're nine months pregnant, do you really want to go up and down that many stairs?" Tristan looked over his shoulder. "How about when toting the baby, a diaper bag, a stroller?"

Good point.

Tristan flashed her a smile, but ever since he'd learned of their predicament, his eyes didn't warm her quite as much.

He returned to the dishes. The subtle tension in his body becoming more pronounced. "I checked the online listings and found a few houses in Maico that look nice. Or the Co-op has a great lot between the resort and the sanctuary where we could build. My dad's crew is fast and good. We could move in before the baby comes. What do you think?"

Nel sat down her cup. Tristan had been at the cabin for a week, and they hadn't discussed anything further into the future than supper.

"I think you're making plans without involving me in the process."

"Isn't that what I'm doing now?"

"You've asked me to choose from your preferences here. I don't remember you asking me where I want to live."

"Are you saying you don't want to live in Walker's Run?" He turned, drying his hands on a dish towel.

"Maybe." She wasn't sure and definitely didn't want to make any snap decisions, especially since a major one had already been decided by circumstance.

"Nel, my pack is here, my job is here. I have responsibilities, commitments. My entire life is in Walker's Run."

"And mine is in Atlanta." Nel's stomach churned, but it wasn't from morning sickness. "I teach in a small private school. They're expecting me to come back in two weeks. Plus, I have the charity gala with Gilbert. Would you seriously ask me to give up my first showing or the opportunities that may come with it?"

He answered with a slight shake of his head, his eyes dark and turbulent.

Nel's watch beeped. "Time to go." She slid off the bar stool. "Can we talk more about this later?"

"Absolutely." He wrapped her in a warm, comforting hug. Then he tipped her chin and kissed her madly. Deeply. Possessively.

"Any more of that and I'll be late."

Tristan walked her to the car. "I'm working noon to

midnight. I can put a roast in the Crock-Pot for your supper."

Nel held her hand to her mouth. Lately, the only meat she could stomach was chicken. "Take it to your aunt on the way to work. I'll pick up a rotisserie from the market."

Tristan kissed her again, lightly and full of longing. "Have a good day."

"Be safe."

"Always."

"Come with me, right now." Jaxen's icy fingers wrapped around Nel's wrist. He grabbed the basket in her hand and dropped it on the floor inside Anne's Market.

"Let me go." Nel yanked but his grip held firm.

"We don't have much time." He began walking at a fast clip, pulling her alongside him. "We have to hurry."

She dug in her heels. "If you don't tell me what's going on, I'm going to scream until the cops come."

"We're wasting time." Jaxen's blue eyes were nearly colorless and his face had gone pale. "He's hurt, Nel. Hurt bad."

"Tristan?" A soul-piercing cold swept through Nel.

Jaxen nodded. "I'll take you to him." He resumed a brisk walk with Nel in tow.

A sliver of caution ran through her mind.

"Why you?" she panted over staccato breaths. "Why did you come and not someone else?"

"I saw you come in here when I stopped at the pharmacy to pick up my mom's medication." Jaxen pushed open the glass doors. "Got the call from Nate while waiting in line. Figured you would want to know sooner rather than later."

Nel's heart couldn't decide if it wanted to claw out

of her chest or up her throat. All it knew was that she needed to get to Tristan.

The light rain that had been falling when she'd arrived now came down in earnest. Soaked the moment she stepped off the walkway, Nel darted behind Jaxen to his car. He didn't wait for her to fasten the seat belt before squealing out of the parking lot.

Nel prayed. Prayed for a lot of things. Mostly, she prayed their child would not grow up fatherless.

"You passed by the hospital." Nel's anxiety grew.

"He isn't there. It wasn't safe to move him."

"Where are we going?"

"Meadowbrooke. He was on a domestic violence call there when it happened. Those family squabbles can turn deadly." Jaxen kept his eyes focused ahead, his fingers locked around the steering wheel like steel bands.

Something didn't seem quite right. Slowly, she reached for her purse. Before her fingers wrapped around the cell phone inside, Jaxen snatched the purse and tossed it in the back seat. "There's no one to call. Everyone is on their way."

Lightning flashed in the sky and her soul rumbled with the thunder above them. A cold sweat swept her skin and Nel doubted very much that anyone was headed to wherever Jaxen was taking her.

Chapter 34

"Tristan." Locke's dark eyes flashed and his craggy face looked more annoyed than usual. "Have you heard anything I've said?"

No, not really, because he was a bit frazzled. He'd stopped by Ruby's on the way in. She was sick, so instead of the roast he'd planned to put in the Crock-Pot, Tristan had decided to defrost and cut up a chicken for soup. He'd accidentally let it slip that Nel was pregnant. Ruby would tell his dad; his dad would tell his mom.

Everything would spiral down from there.

"Are you getting sick again?"

"No, I'm just tired." A lot had happened over the summer and he didn't have his bearings yet.

The sheriff returned to his monologue, but Tristan's thoughts drifted again, his senses homing in on something he couldn't quite register until it erupted from deep within and manifested as a cold, primal fear.

Nel!

Tristan flew to his feet, his chair sprawled on the floor. Locke's face registered annoyance.

His heart beating harder, faster, Tristan pulled out his

cell phone. "Pick up, pick up, pick up," he chanted but the line kept ringing.

"What's going on?" Locked demanded.

"Something's happened to Nel." Tristan rubbed his temples, trying to think.

For god's sake, he was the one people called when in trouble. Why was he having a brain freeze?

He paced. The dizzying rush he felt was definitely from fear not entirely his own.

"Sheriff, I have to go." Tristan didn't wait for authorization to leave. He bolted out of the station, dashed through rain and climbed into his truck.

Nel, where are you?

At the cabin? The resort? The market? Stranded on the highway?

He had no idea where to start looking for her.

Dammit. He should've asked Rafe about how to use the mate-bond rather than trying to figure out how to block it.

He closed his eyes. If he could feel Nel's panic, she could likely sense his.

Calming his mind, Tristan followed his instincts and reached out telepathically.

"Nel, sweetheart. What's wrong?"

Her frantic voice kept running through his mind, calling his name.

"Nel!" He forced his thoughts to be stern. *"Calm down."*

If she couldn't calm herself, he'd never sense what he needed through the static.

"Tristan!"

"I'm here, baby. What's wrong?" He opened his eyes, cranked the engine and tore out of the parking lot with his lights flashing and the siren wailing.

"Jaxen. He's taken me..."

"Where, Nel? Where has he taken you?" Tristan couldn't explain why, but he headed toward the market where Nel should've been.

"Are you all right? He said you were hurt."

"I'm fine, sweetheart. Tell me where to find you." Tristan slowed for the lights, but when the traffic stopped in all directions, he shot through the intersection.

"We're in a house."

Well that didn't narrow the possibilities much. *"It's new. No furniture."*

"Do you know where?"

"Meadow something."

Now he knew he was headed in the right direction. Meadowbrooke was just east of town.

"Tristan? Are you okay?"

"I'm fine. Are you safe?"

"For now. But Jaxen is still here. I hear him walking around the house."

Tristan exhaled a tight breath. *"Hold on, sweetheart. I'm coming."*

Chapter 35

"Where is she?" Drenched, Tristan stood in the doorway of an unsold home in Meadowbrooke, a new housing community his father's construction company helped build.

Jaxen's humorless grin distorted his mouth. "I knew if I rattled her, you would come."

"I'm not going to ask again." Teeth gritted, Tristan stepped inside the house as thunder exploded in the sky. "Where is my mate?"

"I told you, cuz. I don't hurt women. You, however…" Hatred glittered in Jaxen's eyes. "I will take great pleasure in hurting you."

"What's this about?" Tristan stepped left, countering Jaxen's every move. Nel was somewhere in the house, and until he figured out where and how to get her out, Tristan needed to keep Jaxen talking and distracted. "Still blaming me for your banishment?"

"This goes back much further," Jaxen snorted.

"To the day you pushed me off the rock?"

Their steps fell in rhythm so that they were circling each other in the barren room.

"All this time, I thought you were mad at me for leaving your scrawny ass—" Jaxen made air quotes "—to get help. Damn, cuz, I never thought you actually remembered."

"Why did you do it?"

"Don't remember that part, huh?"

Tristan shook his head. The entire day was a blank.

"You're the reason I grew up without a father, Tristan."

"He died in a car accident. How is that my fault?"

"It wasn't a fucking car accident, you bastard!" Jaxen swiped the spittle from his mouth. "Suzannah's brothers dragged my father out of our house in the middle of the night and ripped out his goddamn throat because of you!"

As a law enforcement officer, Tristan had stared unfazed into the eyes of madmen. What he saw in the depths of Jaxen's gaze chilled him to the core of his being.

"Let Nel go, Jax. She's innocent in all this. Once she is safe, you and I can settle this however you like."

"She is safe. I'm not going to hurt her, though I am going to kill you." Jaxen's cold laughter slithered down Tristan's spine. "It's perfect, don't you think? I grew up without my father, your child will grow up without you. Like Nate stepped in, I'll be there for your kid. I'll even go a step further and claim Nel as my mate."

"Over my dead body."

"That's the plan." Jaxen advanced, shifting midstride, and launched.

Tristan blocked the large wolf's strike, but the momentum threw him backward and his head cracked against the drywall. He slung the wolf to the floor.

The animal swung around, eyes focused on Tristan like icy daggers; ribbons of spittle dripped from his snarling mouth.

"Jaxen! Don't. This won't end well for you."

The wolf hesitated for a mere second. Tristan caught the animal midleap. They tumbled to the ground.

Large, sharp teeth snapped at Tristan's face. He shoved the animal away, but before Tristan got to his feet, the wolf whipped around and clamped his jaws around Tristan's calf. The wolf's teeth tore through his khaki pants, sank deep into his muscle and ripped away the flesh.

Tristan ignored the pain throbbing through his leg. He had to stay focused on the task of subduing Jaxen. The slightest distraction could result in devastating consequences.

Even with his size, Tristan couldn't successfully fight the wolf in his human form. He had to even the odds.

Using his uninjured leg, he kicked out, striking the wolf's ribs with enough force to send him flying across the room. Tristan shifted, everything in his body disintegrating from the eruption of energy responsible for the transformation.

Jaxen's paws scratched the wood floor as he barreled toward him. Tristan, touching only his three good legs to the ground, charged head-on. The collision nearly knocked him senseless. Jaxen dropped, looking as stunned as Tristan felt.

They shook off the disorientation and circled each other. Since they were equal in mass and strength, it was going to be a helluva battle.

Jaxen attacked. His nails sliced down Tristan's shoulder. Tristan responded with a defensive bite.

They wrestled throughout the living room, smashing the front window as they fought for dominance. Tristan had a hard time guarding his left side. Jaxen knew his weakness and sought every opportunity to work his way into Tristan's blind spot.

Blue lights flashed outside. Help had arrived, but Jaxen remained a viable threat to Nel and the baby.

Tristan doubled his efforts, but so did Jaxen. They rolled beneath the broken window. Rain had slicked the floor. Tristan tried to gain footing but slipped. It was all the advantage Jaxen needed.

Sharp teeth sank into the vulnerable spot at the back of Tristan's neck. Jaxen taunted him, bearing down and easing up. Tristan heard heavy footsteps run up the porch.

The door flew wide, shattering the frame.

Jaxen released Tristan and launched at the armed man in the doorway. The gun fired, deafening.

Yelping, Jaxen fell to the floor.

"Durrance? Ms. Buchanan?" Locke stepped around the injured wolf, gun drawn on Tristan still in his wolf form. "Anyone here?"

Exhausted and hurting like hell, Tristan pushed himself up. He wasn't keen on shifting in front of Locke, especially when the sheriff had a weapon trained on him.

"You stay put," Locke said. "I'll shoot you, if I have to."

Tristan believed him.

"Durrance? Where are you?" Locke took a step, his head tilted, listening for a response.

Tristan sensed, rather than saw the movement to his left. Barking, he sprung into the air, knocking Locke out of the way. Coming up beneath Jaxen while he was in midjump, Tristan clamped his jaws around the wolf's throat and jerked.

Both wolves thudded to the floor.

Jaxen's lifeless body returned to his human form.

"Holy shit!" Locke stumbled backward.

Tristan rolled to his paws and shifted. He stared up at his boss. "Don't shoot. It's me."

Darkness shrank his field of vision.

"Durrance?"

How did the sheriff get so far away?

"Don't you die on me, Durrance! You hear?"

Tristan's tongue felt too thick for his mouth. "Find Nel." He hoped the sheriff wasn't too far away to hear.

The pounding in Tristan's head would drive him feral if it didn't stop. His entire body felt weighted with lead and he'd spent an eternity trying to raise his eyelids. He sensed a presence close by, but it wasn't Nel. He tried turning his thoughts inward to search for her but there was too much static in his mind.

The antiseptic smell told him he was in the hospital. He had no recollection of how he got there or how long he'd been unconscious. Or what to expect when he opened his eyes.

He marshaled his strength, forcing open his eyelids. A dim halogen light above the sink cast the room in a soft glow, easier on a wolfan's eyes than bright, harsh fluorescence.

"Welcome back to the land of the living." Carl Locke folded the paper in his hands then lifted his booted feet off the upright bed rail.

"Nel?"

"Safe and resting," the sheriff assured him. "Pyke had her tied up and gagged in the master bathroom."

"What are you doing here?" Tristan's parched throat made his voice raspy.

"You're my deputy," Locke said. "Injured in the line of duty. Where else would I be?"

"Sheriff, I—" Words jumbled in Tristan's mouth.

How many times had he asked Gavin to confide in

Locke? Now the secret was irretrievably out, Tristan would never have the sheriff's trust or confidence again.

"I've seen a lot of shit in my time." Locke leaned forward in his chair. "I have to say, what I saw this afternoon was one hell of a doozie. I appreciate what you did to save my life."

"How did you know where to find me?"

"I called for a radio check. You never answered, so I had Carla ping the GPS on your truck," Locke said. "A lot of the Co-op incidents are making sense now. One thing I realized is that you can't keep doing everything on your own."

"Gavin said the same."

"I plan to have a sit-down with you and Gavin when you get out of here."

"Have you talked with Gavin?"

"Hell, no." Locke *hmmphed.* "I told Walker I'd get around to him after I talked to you."

Silence enveloped the room.

Tristan was used to having his finger on the pulse of everything that was going on. Right now, he felt utterly useless.

"He should've let me in on the Co-op's little secret. It's my job to protect all the citizens of Maico. Not just the human ones." Locke sighed. "I'm a fair man, Tristan."

"I know, sir." Locke was hard, but fair. "I told Gavin you were."

"Before or after I shot Rafe Wyatt's wolf? Looking back, I guess it was really Rafe." Locke scratched his cheek. "Feel damn bad about that now."

"It was only a tranq and Rafe doesn't harbor any bad feelings toward you." Of course, had Grace been hurt in the unfortunate incident, not even the Woelfesenat would've been able to stop Rafe's retaliatory rage.

Locke hit the call button.

"Yes, Sheriff?" came an immediate response.

"Tell Doc that Tristan is awake."

"Yes, sir."

"Has my family been notified about Jaxen?"

"Gavin handled it."

There was a knock and Doc entered the room.

"Take good care of my deputy."

"I always do." Mouth in a grim line, Doc tipped his head as Locke left.

"How's Nel?"

"She's finally resting. Cassie and Grace are with her, so she isn't alone."

"I want to see her." Tristan threw off the hospital sheet.

"Your ass will stay in that bed. You lost a lot of blood and I won't have you passing out and frightening Nel all over again."

Tristan ceased struggling to get out of the bed and Doc made sure none of the IV lines had kinked or pulled loose.

"Reach out to her through the mate-bond," Doc said. "It will soothe you both."

Tristan closed his eyes, willing his mind to settle and his being to connect with Nel. In a moment, a familiar essence ebbed into him like a gentle tide.

Nel.

Despite the easygoing manner he projected, Tristan's world had been harsh, cold and barren until she came into his life.

He craved her softness. Her warmth. Her tender resilience.

She was spring to his winter.

But in the end, winter eventually destroyed the beauty of spring. It was the nature of things.

No matter how civilized they pretended to be, Wahyas were wolves in human skin. For them, the brutality of what happened was merely the inevitable outcome. It could not have ended any other way. Once Jaxen threatened Nel, Tristan had to put him down. It was simply the wolfan circle of life.

Humans, on the other hand, had a need to reconcile, restore, even to redeem.

And, Nel was such a gentle soul. A childhood trauma gave her a creative outlet, he didn't want one to take it all away. Eventually, it would.

He'd claimed Nel without her permission, gotten her pregnant. Because of him, Jaxen kidnapped her. How much more could she endure before the resentment germinated and blossomed into hatred?

Then and there, he knew.

No matter the cost to him, Tristan had to be the better man. He had to make a different choice.

He had to let Nel go.

"A mistake?" A sharp pain pierced Nel's heart. And it wasn't from the exertion of helping Tristan up three flights of stairs. She should've known something was wrong when he insisted on coming to the apartment instead of returning to the cabin.

"You think our being together is a mistake?" Nel tucked her fisted hands beneath her arms. "That our baby is a mistake?"

"No, I would never say our child is a mistake." Tristan rubbed his temple. "I will do everything I can to provide for you and the baby. But us, as a couple..." He shook his head. "I can't do it right now. It's best that you go back to Atlanta. My mother's birth pack will take you in. They'll help you when I can't."

"I don't understand. You claimed me. I thought that was a permanent deal."

"We'll always be connected, especially since we've created a child. Consider the separation like a divorce."

"I don't want a divorce, Tristan. I want always and forever. I love you."

"Think of all that's happened, Nel. Your emotions have been in a heightened state. When everything settles down, you might feel completely different."

"I won't." Nel sat beside him on the couch. "I don't want you because you bit me or because I got pregnant. I want you because you make me laugh, you encourage me to try new things and you hold my hand when I do. You're the first person I want to talk to when I have good news, bad news or no news at all." She didn't want to do this without him.

Tristan's gaze searched her face. "I've never felt what I feel for you but you don't understand the odds we're facing."

"Why can't the odds be for us?"

"Because they aren't." Tristan cradled her face, his thumb softly strumming her cheek.

Nel stood. "I care for you more than I've cared for anyone since my parents died, but I won't beg to be part of your life. If you don't want me, so be it. I spent my entire life in a holding pattern until you helped me find my momentum. I have to keep moving forward."

If she didn't, she'd end up right where she started. Nowhere. She had to keep going, even if it meant leaving Tristan behind.

Heart breaking, she kissed his forehead. Emotion swirled in his gaze as a tear leaked from his eye.

"Goodbye, Tristan."

Chapter 36

The sealed silver urn grew heavy between Tristan's jaws as he trotted carefully through the forest.

Nearly a week had passed since the fight that killed Jaxen, and every muscle in Tristan's body still ached. Especially his heart.

While Ruby and his parents attended the small memorial at the Co-op's cemetery, Tristan carefully carried his cousin's remains to his actual final resting place.

Wolfans chose cremation over burial, believing the spreading of ashes in a favored spot was more natural than being trapped in a box six feet under for all eternity.

The memorial at the cemetery was merely a tradition adopted from humans, giving families a place to mourn their loss.

Stunned beyond words didn't come close to how Tristan felt when Ruby had told him he was to take Jaxen to his final resting place—a small cave they'd called their fort when they played as kids. They'd spent many happy afternoons there, playing, wrestling, being the best of friends.

Before the accident.

The accident that had nearly blinded him and opened his eyes to the type of person his cousin really was.

Tristan's nails dug into the soft, damp ground. The musky scent of moss and earth twitched his nose. Tall, thin pines stretched high into the sky, blocking all but a faint splattering of sunshine. The air was still, but not stagnant, and slightly cooler than the open areas warmed by the summer sun.

He loped down the incline into a small ravine and jumped the rotted logs scattered around the clearing where Jaxen used to chase him, building Tristan's speed and agility.

Jaxen had also taught him to track and hunt. Harming any creature inside the sanctuary was strictly forbidden. Jax had never cared for rules and killed his prey for the sport, but Tristan never had the heart to do the same.

He hadn't returned to the fort since the accident. Still, he knew exactly where to step, where to turn and which veil of vines to nudge aside to find the secret opening.

The ground inside the small cave had been recently disturbed. Large paw prints marred the soft dirt, as did human feet.

Emotion burning his throat, Tristan wondered if Jaxen had come here to reminisce, to remember when they weren't enemies—or if that time only existed in Tristan's mind.

He carefully set the urn on the ground and flopped beside it. The cold hard ground against his belly and chest was a welcome relief from the heat clinging to his fur. He panted in the cool, dank air, his body temperature dropping.

I never wanted things to end like this.

He stared at the silver urn.

Both of them unable to get past their anger, unable to forgive, they failed each other.

Dammit, Jaxen! We could've done better than this. I should've done better.

Tristan pushed to his paws and dug furiously until his shoulder muscles ached from fatigue. He shifted into his human form. Hands black, dirt jammed deep beneath his nails, he reverently picked up the silver urn and removed the lid. Wordlessly, he emptied Jaxen's ashes into the deep hole.

Tristan stared at the thick gray dust until his eyes were dry and itchy, the salty moisture on his face had dried and the filtered light outside the cave grew dim. He removed the old photo taped to the bottom of the urn. Lightly, Tristan traced his finger over the two tawny-headed boys, smiling big for the camera.

Acid scalded a throat already raw with too much emotion.

He dropped the photo onto the ashes and shoved the dirt back into the hole.

Obligation fulfilled, he shifted into his wolf and padded slowly to the mouth of the cave, then paused.

After several long moments, he looked over his shoulder at the makeshift grave.

Rest in peace, Jaxen.

Tristan nudged aside the hanging vines and started the long, lonely walk to an empty home.

Chapter 37

"Don't give up." Cassie sat on the bed while Nel packed. "Tristan will figure everything out, and when he does, nothing will keep him away from you."

"We had fun for a while, but maybe that's all it should be."

No matter how much Nel believed their relationship had meaning, if Tristan didn't, it was a moot point.

"It was more than fun and games for Tristan. I've never seen him be with someone the way he was with you."

"He shut me out, Cassie. I know he's hurting, but if he wanted something real, something lasting, he would let me be there for him."

"Don't give up, Nel. More than anything, he needs your faith."

"Where is his faith in me?"

Cassie rolled her lips together before answering. "He doesn't know how, Nel. He's never been able to rely on his family. His best friend was murdered, and Jaxen used to be like a brother to Tristan. I think Jaxen's death put Tristan in a tailspin. He's pushing you away to protec you." Cassie tucked a red curl behind her ear. "Give him just enough space to catch his breath, but not enough to lose sight of you."

"How?"

"You're pregnant, so there's no doubt about the mate-claim. Even though Tristan is pretending it isn't bonding you, I think it is." Cassie patted the mattress for Nel to sit. "Have you ever sensed Tristan's presence or heard his voice in your head when he wasn't around?"

"Yes, and I know Tristan sensed me. That's how he found me when Jaxen took me."

"Perfect."

"Does it have something to do with the mate-claim?"

"Nope." Cassie grinned. "What you and he experienced is a mate-bond, and it only develops between true mates. When Wahyas fall truly in love, a special connection forms between the wolfan and the person they love. It's a psychic connection on every possible level. It's why you can hear him, feel him."

"Tristan has never told me that he loves me."

"Maybe not in words, but Nel, Tristan looks at you the same way Brice looks at me and Rafe looks at Grace."

"Really?"

Cassie nodded. "That man loves you to the moon and back. He's involved you in very personal parts of his life. Parts he hasn't allowed anyone else into."

"A lot of good that did me. I still ended up dumped."

"Nel, nothing I say will convince you of anything. Trust your instincts and have faith in Tristan. Use the mate-bond to tell him every day how much you love him and miss him. If you don't, you'll be turning your back on something really wonderful."

It sounded kinda out there to Nel, but then again, so was the existence of werewolves.

What could it hurt to try? She'd already lost one family due to tragic circumstances. She didn't want to lose another.

Something poked Tristan's ribs.

"Tristan. You hear me?" Ruby's stern voice ricocheted inside his head.

His gut clenched, along with his jaw.

"Yeah, you hear me," she said.

At least she finally stopped poking him.

He scooted up in the chair, where he'd fallen asleep.

"Don't forget, my toilet is running again. You need to fix it."

"I can't do it today." Tristan dragged his gaze over to his aunt finishing the lunch he'd made for her.

They had yet to talk about the circumstances of Jaxen's death and it had been nearly a month.

"That water's gonna keep on running," she huffed. "Can't sleep with all that racket."

"I can't sleep, either, Ruby. I haven't for weeks." Since Nel had returned to Atlanta, Tristan only seemed to sleep in snatches. She filled his dreams, his waking thoughts. He couldn't get the damn woman off his mind.

"Nightmares?"

"No, why?"

"You had them for a while when you were a kid, and again after you fell off that boulder."

Tristan wiped his palm over his khaki-clad thigh. "I didn't fall, Ruby. Jaxen pushed me. He said I was the reason his father was dead. It's why he took Nel and why I had to do what I did to protect her."

"Neither of you boys were ever supposed to know what happened." Ruby squinted at him. "Orwell's death was his own fault. Not yours, Tristan. He was a hard man to love, even harder to live with.

"He hit me and Jaxen more times than I could count. But when he hit you…and sent you to the hospital…" Ruby shook her head. "Your mama might look all high-falutin, but she is a force to be reckoned with. So are her brothers."

"I don't remember any of it."

"You were only four. So cute and happy all the god-damn time. It got really annoying." Ruby sipped her tea. "After Orwell hurt you, well, you were never quite as happy, or trusting. But you did love Jaxen. Until that day on the rock."

Pregnant silence filled the room.

"Jaxen had too much of his father's venom in his blood. No one was ever gonna save him, Tristan. Don't blame yourself for not trying."

"Honestly, Ruby. I don't."

"Well, what the hell is wrong with ya? You've been moping around for weeks." She patted the lunch tray.

"I don't want to talk about it." Tristan lumbered out of the chair to take her dishes to the kitchen.

"Why did you send your mate back to Atlanta?"

"Not your business." Tristan washed up the few lunch dishes.

"It is when you're feeling so sorry for yourself that I can't get my toilet fixed."

Tristan dried his hands.

"Is she your true mate?"

"Durrances don't find true mates."

"Are you daft or something? Of course, we do. But we got a stubborn streak as wide as the Tennessee River. When you butt heads often enough with neither willing to budge, things get cracked."

Tristan's already knotted gut tightened, as did the band around his chest.

"If she is your true mate, you better make up with her, fast. Or you'll end up miserable, just like the rest of us."

Chapter 38

Soft instrumental music played through the overhead speakers throughout the art gallery. For all its lack of soothing effects, it could've been an off-key brass band.

Nel massaged her temples, but the achy headache wouldn't relent. Neither would the nauseous churn in her stomach. Morning sickness was a lie, hers lasted all day.

She shook off the discomfort. Tonight marked a momentous event. Either a turning point or breaking point. Whichever it turned out to be, she was ready.

The gala was by invitation only. To move forward with her future, without blight, Nel had had an invitation sent to her estranged aunt and uncle. They had not contacted her in reply, nor did she expect them to attend, but at least the effort cleared her conscience.

Tristan had also received an invitation, along with everyone she knew in Walker's Run, and it made Nel's heart flutter to hear Brenna's high-pitched squeal above the muted chatter. "Pen-pe!"

The little girl wiggled valiantly against her mother's tight hold.

"Be still, Brenna," Cassie warned in a motherly tone. "Remember, it isn't polite to cause a ruckus in public."

Brenna's pigtails bobbed with a nod of her head.

Grace accompanied them, holding one of the twins against her chest, dressed adorably in an infant-sized tuxedo.

Nel's heart soared to see friendly, familiar faces.

She walked confidently toward them, noticing several gentlemen's admiring gazes.

A few months ago, Nel wouldn't have dared to wear a clingy black evening dress or strappy silver heels. Nor would she have thought to be turning heads when she did.

One of the many turns her life had taken since meeting Tristan. Nel smoothed her hand over her stomach. Before long, her pregnancy would show.

"Pen-pe!" Brenna practically launched from her mother into Nel's arms.

"I missed you, too, sweetie." She hugged the child for as long as Brenna allowed, which was about ten seconds before she reared back.

"Good grief." Cassie held out her hands for Brenna to return.

"Where's Reina?" Nel asked.

"With Rafe. She's a terror when she's not with her daddy."

"Rafe stayed with Brice. He's got—" Cassie dropped her voice "—a man cold. Thinks he's dying."

"He's all right, isn't he?"

"Oh, yeah. Stuffy nose, sore throat. That's all. Trust me, it's just a cold. Nothing like the virus that went through the pack during the summer."

Suzannah Durrance waltzed over. "Penelope. You must mingle. Patrons love meeting the artists."

"Please excuse me." She squeezed Grace's and Cassie's

hands. "Don't feel obligated to bid on anything. I'm just happy you're both here."

"Of course they're obligated," Suzannah said sharply. "That's why we have showings, dear. To sell, sell, sell."

Nel was fast learning to not like that part of the business. "But this is for charity, right?"

"Of course, dear. Come, come."

Cassie gave her a thumbs-up. "We'll find you later. Enjoy yourself."

Suzannah spun Nel toward patron after patron. Names and faces became a blur, and as the evening whirred along, Nel's anxiety heightened.

She constantly surveyed the crowd for Tristan's broad shoulders and tawny head. Each time her search came up empty, the knots in her stomach tightened.

Since returning home, the only times Nel had seen Tristan was when he came to Atlanta for her prenatal appointments with a wolfan doctor.

The Walker's Run pack in Maico, she'd learned, wasn't the only pocket of Wahyas in the world. Atlanta had its own—the Peachtree pack, of which Suzannah was a member by birth. Tristan, by right of his mother's bloodline, was also considered a member. So would Nel's child. Of course, the same could be said of the Walker's Run pack because of the blood ties to Tristan's father.

Just like Walker's Run, the members of the Peachtree pack were welcoming and kind. Nel appreciated the support of Tristan's maternal pack, but she missed her Walker's Run friends terribly; they'd become family. Most, including Gavin and Abigail Walker, had come tonight. The show of support from everyone was nearly overwhelming. Still, the one she searched for, the one she needed to see, was glaringly absent.

Tristan's gala invitation was not meant as an ultimatum, yet in her spirit Nel knew if he missed this, it meant he didn't care to be part of her life. When they'd met last week at the doctor's office, he didn't say anything about tonight's event. But he usually didn't say much anyway.

She used to be able to read his moods, hear his thoughts. Not so much anymore.

Sometimes, at night, she'd awake with a sense of him holding her and that feeling was what had kept loneliness at bay.

Until now.

Stress and disappointment turned her stomach. She excused herself from the elderly couple Suzannah had engaged and hurried to the restroom. Thankfully, the stalls were deserted. Afterward, she dampened a paper towel and patted her face. The queasiness had eased but the tightness in her stomach moved into her chest.

Though Nel's heart hurt tremendously, Tristan had taught her that she was braver than she'd ever realized. She could go on. She would go on. And she would be happy.

He gave her that gift. For it, she would always love him.

Tucking away her melancholy, Nel rejoined the celebration.

"There you are." Suzannah linked her arm with Nel's. "Come with me. Gilbert is introducing the artists." She escorted Nel through the crowd and stopped near a small podium engulfed in the spray of a spotlight.

Nel clapped for each artist introduced, relieved they only spoke a few words in greeting. Someone tapped her shoulder, but when she turned no one was close enough to have touched her. She caught a glimpse of a man in the shadows beyond where most people had gathered.

Her heart skipped, hoping just maybe…

She turned for a better look. *Tristan?*

If someone had been there, they had walked away.

"Nel." Suzannah shook Nel's arm. "You're on."

The thunder of clapping filled the space and clanged in her head.

Gilbert took Nel's hand and helped her up to the podium.

Cassie and Grace maneuvered to the front of the crowd and gave her encouraging smiles.

"I'm deeply grateful to everyone who came out tonight. And to Gilbert Michaud for including me in tonight's gala. I never considered myself an artist. As a child, I painted to cope with the loss of my parents. As I grew older, I used painting as a way to endure life. But I recently met a man who taught me life isn't meant to be endured. Life is about embracing every single moment with love and wonder. And it doesn't matter if how we live is exciting and dangerous, or quiet and safe, or somewhere in between. All that matters is that we live."

The strappy silver heels Nel had adored at the beginning of the night were now the object of her curses. Her arches burned, her toes showed signs of blisters, even her calves had cramped. She gave serious consideration to ripping them off and turning the bubbling water fountain into the world's largest footbath.

"Nel?"

"Um." She jerked her hand out of the water. "Gilbert, hi."

"My dear, you are an absolute success tonight. All of your paintings had top bids."

"That's fantastic, Gilbert." Forgetting her sore feet, Nel jumped up from her perch and gave the short, balding man a giant hug. "Thank you for all you've done."

"It is your talent that made the sales, Nel. I simply

provided the forum." He hesitated. "There is one painting that you did not wish to sell."

Some of the elation leaked from her spirit. "Yes. I'll take it with me tonight."

Gilbert pressed his fingertips together. "You see, there is a very interested buyer."

"Absolutely not." Nel had poured her heart and soul into that painting. She could never part with it.

"I tried to explain this, but the buyer insists and is offering an amount equal to all your bids tonight."

"Seriously?" Nel sat hard on the tiled edge of the waterfall.

"A cashier's check can be issued tonight, payable to you or tonight's charity."

"Wow." That would be a substantial sum for the charity. She wouldn't feel right about taking the money for herself.

"Shall I tell the buyer we have a sale?"

"I'm sorry, Gilbert." The offer was tempting, but Nel's heart simply would not allow her to part with it. "I can't."

"In the event you chose not to sell, the buyer asked simply to meet you."

"No. I don't want to be pressured to sell. My mind is set."

"I believe the buyer is simply enamored, my dear." Gilbert lifted her hand. "Surely you wouldn't mind giving a quick and gracious greeting?"

"Only if I can take my shoes off. I doubt I could take one more step in them."

"Of course."

Nel slipped off the accursed, but beautiful, heels. Gilbert escorted her up the sprawling, spiral staircase and down the open corridor. He ushered her into his dimly lit, but spacious office with a gorgeous view of downtown.

"Please make yourself comfortable. The buyer will be with you shortly." Gilbert was gone before Nel had a chance to ask him to stay.

She dropped her shoes on the settee and made her way to the painting Gilbert had taken from the gallery and placed on the lighted easel in his office.

The canvas of the man fly-fishing in the river with a wolf watching from the shadows of the forest was breathtakingly beautiful and even she believed it deserved to hang in a gallery.

Her fingers caressed the brushstrokes as lovingly as she had the man.

"Why can't you sell it, Nel?" Tristan breathed against her hair.

She held her fist against her mouth to keep from crying out. Her heart, hurting for so long, felt as if it would break.

"Nel." Her name was a ragged moan. "Tell me."

"Because it's you." Nel resisted the urge to turn around. Afraid of what she might see in his gaze. "While I painted it, I thought of every single thing that I love about you. Your kindness. Steadfastness. Your strength, your agility. Your ability to make me laugh, how you helped me find courage. Your companionship. Your confidence. Your dedication."

"Nel, please stop." His hands settled gently on her hips. "I'm a coward."

"Only in your eyes, Tristan. Never in mine." Nel faced him.

Dressed in a tux and cleanly shaved, he took her breath away.

"I love you so much, Nel. It scares the shit out of me. But what scares me more is losing you." He cupped her face, his thumbs caressing the apples of her cheeks. "I shouldn't have pushed you away. So much happened in a short amount of time, I couldn't accept that your feelings or mine were real. Especially after I learned I had forced a mate-claim on you. I'm so sorry, Nel, for taking away your choice."

"You accidentally bit me, but everything that followed was my choice and with my full consent. And I loved every minute of it." Sliding her arms beneath his jacket, she stepped into his warmth.

A ragged breath broke in his chest and he folded around her. "I've missed you."

"Why didn't you tell me how you felt when we were at any of the doctor appointments?"

"I was giving us time. If what we had wasn't real, the distance would've lessened the pull between us. But I can't bear it anymore, Nel." He squeezed her ribs and buried his face in the curve of her neck. "I want you. I need you more than I have ever needed anyone. I love you and I'm never going to stop loving you."

Her body sighed against his. "I've been waiting to hear you say those words."

Tristan took a step back and knelt. "You wouldn't consider my offer for the painting." He withdrew a small blue-velvet case from his pocket. "Would you accept this, instead?" He opened the box. Inside was a large marquise diamond set in platinum.

"Tristan, it's beautiful."

"Penelope Nel sweet cheeks Buchanan, will you please be my mate for now and always?"

"Yes! Oh, yes!"

Tristan slipped the ring on her finger, kissed her knuckles and stood. Tears blurring her vision, Nel wrapped her arms around his neck and buried her face in his shoulder. "I love you so much."

"I love you, too," he whispered against her hair.

Tristan gently rocked Nel until she was all cried out. He handed her the handkerchief from his pocket.

"What's that?" She dabbed her eyes, looking at the white envelope sticking out of his pants pocket.

"My secret weapon. If my straight-out, on-the-knee proposal didn't work, I planned to bribe you with tickets to Paris."

Nel snatched the envelope. "These are for the honeymoon?"

"Unless you have another destination in mind."

"Nope. This will do."

"God, I've missed you." Tristan's mouth crushed her lips, possessively branding her with his taste until, breathless, he broke the kiss. "We need to get out of here, unless you want me to claim you again, right here in Gilbert's office."

"Let's go home." Nel hooked her arm around his.

Tristan brushed aside a long ribbon of hair that had fallen across her face. "I am home whenever I am with you."

Smiling, Nel leaned into his warmth. Tristan had opened her to whole new world and she couldn't wait to explore it, with him.

* * * * *

Can't get enough of
CHARMED BY THE WOLF?
Check out Kristal Hollis's previous werewolf books:
AWAKENED BY THE WOLF
RESCUED BY THE WOLF

Available now from Mills & Boon Nocturne!

MILLS & BOON®

Why shop at millsandboon.co.uk?

Each year, thousands of romance readers find their perfect read at millsandboon.co.uk. That's because we're passionate about bringing you the very best romantic fiction. Here are some of the advantages of shopping at www.millsandboon.co.uk:

* **Get new books first**—you'll be able to buy your favourite books one month before they hit the shops

* **Get exclusive discounts**—you'll also be able to buy our specially created monthly collections, with up to 50% off the RRP

* **Find your favourite authors**—latest news, interviews and new releases for all your favourite authors and series on our website, plus ideas for what to try next

* **Join in**—once you've bought your favourite books, don't forget to register with us to rate, review and join in the discussions

Visit **www.millsandboon.co.uk** for all this and more today!